Outside the moon was complete............ by ......
flakes drifting earthward. They were huge—like tissue-paper cutouts, floating on the still air.

Sara's face was lifted to the night sky.

He watched as wet flakes kissed her cheeks, her hair, her eyelashes. When she looked back at him, she was smiling. Not the self-mocking smile he'd seen earlier, but a soft, slow, real smile.

The wall he'd put up, the barrier he'd worked so hard and so diligently to build, crumbled.

Ever since that night on the beach, he'd known that he had to have her, possess her. But now everything had suddenly turned around.

Now he wanted more. . . .

LONG NIGHT MOON

LONG NIGHT MOON

THERESA WEIR

NEW YORK TORONTO LONDON SYDNEY AUCKLAND

LONG NIGHT MOON

A Bantam Fanfare Book/April 1995

ISBN 0-553-56379-3

Published simultaneously in the United States and Canada

Bantam Books are published by Bantam Books, a division of Bantam Doubleday Dell Publishing Group, Inc. Its trademark, consisting of the words "Bantam Books" and the portrayal of a rooster, is Registered in U.S. Patent and Trademark Office and in other countries. Marca Registrada. Bantam Books, 1540 Broadway, New York, New York 10036.

PRINTED IN THE UNITED STATES OF AMERICA

RAD   0   9   8   7   6   5   4   3   2   1

To used bookstores—thanks for keeping those out-of-print books in circulation.

To the Chicago gals, especially Kathy Chwedyk and Jennifer Coleman—thanks for the help and support.

To Jackie Schauer—did you notice how those '94 Stanley Cup winners had so many ex-Blackhawks on their team? Including the coach? Hmmm . . .

It happens in December
when the moon's path is low on the horizon . . .
closer to the earth than any other time of the year—
the long night moon

Prologue

Springfield, Illinois
1982

A man waited outside the courthouse, behind the security tape. Reporters bumped him; he didn't notice. His eyes were intent upon the closed doors. Doors that would soon open. How long he'd waited on the marble steps, he couldn't say. Time had no meaning.

The doors opened.

The man on the steps moved carefully. Slowly, deliberately, so as not to draw attention to himself. When the time was right, he slid a revolver from inside his coat. He aimed. He squeezed the trigger. The recoil from the blast shuddered up his arm. People shouted. Women screamed.

He put down the gun and waited to be arrested.

Stateville Penitentiary, Joliet, Illinois

He began by marking off the days in a notebook. But he soon came to learn that the counting, the keeping track of the passage of time, was another sort of prison. On the fifth day of his sentence, he threw away the notebook.

Remember, son, many a good story has been ruined by oververification.
—James Gorden Bennett

Chapter One

Chicago
1995

Bald tires squealed across cement, the sound echoing off the walls of the downtown Chicago parking garage. Nash Audubon drove up the ramp and shot into the first empty space he saw. He threw the gearshift lever into park, turned off the ignition, and shouldered open the door of his '76 Ford Fairlane.

Hinges creaked. Belongings tumbled out.

A shirt. A pair of jeans. A sneaker. Big Mac wrapper. Plastic Hardee's collector cup.

He gathered up everything and shoved it back inside—behind the front seat this time—grabbed his camera from the dashboard, then quickly slammed the door before anything else could fall out.

It probably wasn't what the ads meant when they bragged about experiencing the world in a whole new way. But living in your car sure made it easy when you decided to move on. What other guy could just settle down in his living room, stick the key in the ignition, and take his home for a spin?

With the smell of burning oil reminding him that he'd better put in another quart before leaving the parking garage, he slung his camera around his neck and shrugged into his leather jacket.

Wind, coming in off the lake, lifted his hair and whipped it about his head.

For a fraction of a second he felt a flicker of what he'd always thought of as life. It came from somewhere deep inside him. Then, as fast as it came, it was gone. Like a comet. Like a falling star. Leaving behind nothing but a vague, nagging memory, something too transient to fully recall.

A crossed signal, he told himself. Those kinds of feelings weren't a part of his life. Hadn't been for a long, long time. Never would be again.

He moved through the orange glow of the setting sun, past graffiti-covered walls and pillars, down two flights of stairs. When he reached Michigan Avenue, a gust of wind hit him full in the face. Cool air. Sweet air.

There it was again.

That bittersweet echo of yesterday.

He shook it off and moved along the street in the direction of the Renaissance Hotel.

Rush hour. People hurrying. Clutching their jackets closed against the fall chill. In the distance, an elevated train rattled along the track, carrying people home. Occasionally someone would look in his direction, but for the most part, people minded their own business. That was one of the things he liked about the city. Anonymity. A person could be invisible in the city. A person could disappear in the city.

Under the red canopy leading to the Renaissance's revolving doors, a caped doorman eyed him suspiciously, but didn't try to stop him.

Nash pushed a hand against the sluggish door. Rubber seals beat against metal framework as it turned. Inside, across the polished lobby, the elevator was about to close.

"Hold the door!" Nash shouted, running.

Someone slammed the open button and the doors silently reversed.

He squeezed in, faded jeans and brown leather rubbing sequined gowns and black tuxedos. An expensive mix of perfume stung his nostrils.

He caught a glimpse of his reflection in the mirrored wall.

Probably should have taken a little more time with his grooming, he thought, running his fingers through dark hair—hair that had needed a good trim two months ago. Maybe when they got upstairs he'd find the men's rest room.

People stared.

"Press," he said, by way of explaining his casual attire.

"What paper?" The question came from a woman in a low-cut, black sequined gown.

He patted the pocket of his shirt, then pulled out one of his phony business cards and handed it to her. *"Chicago Journal."*

If he'd told her he worked for *Shoot the Moon*, they'd have stopped the elevator and dumped him out on his ass before you could say, in-your-face tabloid.

He remembered his fake badge, pulled it out of his jacket pocket, and clipped it to his shirt.

WALTER DEVLIN
CHICAGO JOURNAL

The badge wasn't really fake. He'd found it in a rest room in the John Hancock Building and had kept it as a souvenir. It had come in quite handy on more than one occasion.

"I'm doing an interview with Sara Ivy," he said.

The woman smiled. White teeth. Sexy mouth. Hair that was a rich burgundy. Short, swept up.

"If her husband will let her out of his sight long enough," the woman said. "They're terribly devoted to each other. Honestly, they're like a couple of newlyweds." She made a face that said she'd been there and it wasn't what it was cracked up to be.

"How sweet," he said dryly. He'd been there too.

She laughed, and he laughed.

The interview wasn't important. He could make that up. What he really needed was a photo of Sara Ivy for the paper's Local Yokel column. Rumor had it that the devoted wife was having an affair with Russell Cray, one of her husband's business associates. And when the husband in question was running for city alderman, an affair on either side was news. Nash's job was to try to get a photo of Sara Ivy and Cray together.

The elevator stopped at the fiftieth floor—the penthouse. Everyone got off.

Nash didn't waste any time locating the can. The place was carpeted, with wall sconces and plush finger towels, deodorant, cologne, razors . . .

A transient's delight.

He stripped down to his jeans. Bare-chested, he leaned over the oval sink, soaped his face, and quickly shaved away two days' worth of stubble. Then he brushed his teeth with the toothbrush he always carried and followed it by washing and drying his armpits with a monogrammed towel. He tossed down the towel, gave himself two squirts of deodorant—stuff didn't smell too bad—dampened his hands, and slicked back his hair.

He check out his reflection. Not ready for *GQ*, but he'd get by.

He was buttoning his shirt when a tuxedoed gentleman walked in. Nash calmly tucked in his tails, shrugged back into his leather jacket, picked up his camera, and made his way to the party.

The first thing he noticed was that it had gotten dark while he'd been attending to his toilette. He strolled over to the wall of glass and checked out the view.

Nothing like Chicago at night. There was the Wrigley Building. Across from it, the Gothic architecture of the *Chicago Tribune*.

His gaze panned east, past Lake Shore Drive to Navy Pier. Boat lights dotted the lake. The majesty of the view made him think of great, highly motivated people and their grand aspirations. People who had struggled against insurmountable odds and won. People like Frank Lloyd Wright and William LeBaron Jenney. People who had made an impact on the world.

Nash didn't have any grand illusions or delusions running around in his head—thank God.

He'd leave greatness to somebody else.

People called him a cynic, but it wasn't true. To be a cynic, you had to hate with a passionate hate. He didn't have that kind of emotion left in him. No, he'd come to that bridge, he'd lived on that bridge, under that bridge.

At one time, hatred had burned in him with a flame so hot and so consuming that it had destroyed him. Now there was nothing left. He existed, nothing more, living out each day just like the previous one. Moving through the days. Yesterday. Today. Tomorrow. All the same. He needed that constancy. Couldn't survive without that constancy.

"You don't look like a Walter."

Nash pulled his gaze from the lights below to focus on an even better view. The woman from the elevator. She tapped his identification card with a lacquered nail.

"No?"

She shook her head.

"What's a Walter supposed to look like?"

"Oh . . . I picture him in a three-piece suit. Striped tie."

Nash glanced down at his jacket and jeans, then back at her.

"Short. Light sandy hair. About forty."

She knew Walter Devlin. Damn.

He smiled.

She smiled back.

She was sharp. And beautiful. Someone who wasn't looking for something long-term. Someone who would be satisfied with a one-nighter. Who might be *looking* for a one-nighter.

"Notice how there are more and more guys with one name?" he asked. "It used to be mainly women, but not anymore."

Not missing a beat, she jumped in. "Men's lib is responsible, I believe."

He laughed. "I know a guy on the South Side who'll get you a legal name change for two hundred dollars."

"So you could go there and get your name legally changed to Walter Devlin?"

"Now that's an idea."

Her gaze swept across the room. "There's Sara Ivy. You might want to get your interview while you can." She lifted her chin, indicating a cluster of people. "She's wearing the white gown. You can't miss her. She's the one who looks like a princess or an angel or something."

The woman from the elevator handed him the phony business card he'd given her earlier.

"My real name and number are on the back," she said. Then she smiled and walked away.

He turned the card.

Mary Jane Francis.

He slipped the card into the breast pocket of his shirt, and for a moment he thought about forgetting the Ivy business. He was tempted to follow the sway of those sequined hips.

But then he looked across the room again. The crowd had shifted, and this time he was afforded an un-hindered view of Sara Ivy.

She wasn't at all what he'd expected the wife of a sleaze like Donovan Ivy to look like. She was beautiful. Not Marilyn Monroe, sex-goddess beautiful, but Audrey Hepburn, Joan of Arc, ethereal beautiful.

Waiflike, she wore a wispy white gown that covered her from the tip of her chin to her delicate wrists and ankles. Her hair was dark, almost black. It hung straight and shiny to her shoulders. A clump of short, straight bangs gave her an even more fragile appearance.

Nash found himself cutting through the crowd un-til he stood next to her. "Ms. Ivy," he said, trying to get her attention. "I'm here for our interview."

Her eyes, when she turned in his direction, were huge, too big for her face, and of the strangest color. A sort of misty gray.

The floor beneath his feet seemed to shift a little.

"Interview?" she asked, her brow creasing.

"We talked on the phone last week," he said, feel-ing a brief pang of some unfamiliar emotion. Guilt? Something close to it, anyway.

It had always been his boss's idea to mix styles. The literate and biting shared paper and ink with the ab-surd. Interspersed with alien stories were articles and pictures about people who needed to be exposed. Who needed to be . . . well, hurt a little. He said it gave the tabloid purpose. A sort of honor. Validity.

Nash didn't give a shit about validity, or honor, or

purpose. He didn't give a shit about anything. When his boss asked for an article, he did it. That was that.

The only other thing he was certain of was that this woman, with her pale skin and dark circles under her eyes, didn't look capable of withstanding a five-mile-an-hour wind.

"I'm with the *Chicago Journal*. I'm covering the literacy auction you're having this weekend."

"Oh," she said vaguely.

He could tell she was still trying to recall a conversation that had never taken place—and he felt another pang of guilt. He pushed it to the back of his mind.

What the hell was wrong with him? Over the last two years, he'd done hundreds of stories, pasted hundreds of pictures, and so far he'd never regretted any of them.

This women was married to one of the most corrupt men in Chicago, he reminded himself. She couldn't possibly be as innocent as she looked.

"Of course. The interview."

She lifted a delicate, fine-boned hand. Her draped sleeve slid to her elbow, revealing a few inches of pale skin.

The room was a little on the warm side, but she looked as if she would be cold to the touch, porcelain cold. He had the craziest notion—he wanted to wrap a thick blanket around her and take her someplace else, someplace safe.

"Perhaps we could—" she began, but before she could finish, a tuxedoed man appeared at her elbow.

Donovan Ivy.

Nash couldn't figure out what women saw in the guy. Sure, he was big and muscular, but the muscles weren't natural. He'd reshaped his body into something that bordered on freakish. And along with all that mus-

cle was an air of debauchery that made him almost
spooky, made him like the kind of thing you wanted to
pick up with a stick.

"Come, darling," Ivy said to his wife. "I have someone I'd like you to meet."

Sara Ivy's expression became blank. One moment
Nash was there, talking to her, the next, he didn't even
exist. Typical rich bitch.

"Ms. Ivy?" Nash said, trying to draw her attention
back to him.

She had to have heard, and yet she ignored him.
More than ignored. She looked past him. Through him.
He didn't exist. He wasn't even worthy of an acknowl-
edgment. Not so much as an 'I'm sorry but I can't talk
now.'

Years ago, such a blatant snub would have pissed
him off. Now he just shrugged, lifed his camera, and
looked through the viewfinder, framing the Ivys. His
boss wanted a story; he'd give him one.

He was using 400-speed film. Push that to 1600
and he could get a halfway decent picture without
drawing attention to himself with a flash. And anyway,
a clear shot wasn't always the best. A little fuzz around
the edges didn't hurt a thing in his business.

He pushed the shutter release. The camera whirred.
Good. He had a photo of Sara Ivy. Now to find Cray in
the crowd.

*He had been kicked in the head by a mule when young
and believed everything he read in the Sunday papers.*
—George Ade

Chapter Two

Sara Ivy lifted the coffee cup to her lips just as
Donovan slammed down the newspaper on the
breakfast table.

She jumped, scalding herself.

"What the hell's this?"

Shaking hot liquid from her hand, she looked at the
paper. *Shoot the Moon.* A local tabloid. A paper that was
considered a joke, even among other tabloids. On the
front page was a photo of her in the gown she'd worn
to the champagne reception last night. Standing next to
her, a possessive hand on her elbow, wasn't Donovan,
but Cray. Below the picture was the caption: WIFE OF
BUSINESSMAN-TURNED-POLITICIAN REFUSES INTERVIEW.
DOES SHE HAVE SOMETHING TO HIDE?

"What were you doing with Cray last night?" Donovan's voice was level and controlled, but Sara knew
how deceiving that could be.

"I never even saw him," Sara said, trying to keep
her own voice steady. "The picture has been fabricated
somehow."

"Look. Inside."

She refused to touch it, refused to be baited. "You
can't believe what you read in a trashy paper like that."

Donovan picked up the paper, riffled through the

pages, folded it open, and slapped it down in front of her.

Inside was another photo, this one of two people locked in a passionate embrace. Their faces were hidden. They could have been anybody. Below the photo was a poem.

> *Roses are red,*
> *Violets are blue,*
> *While hubby's out running for office,*
> *What's a bored socialite to do?*

There were no names mentioned, but the implication was obvious.

Why?

She recalled the man who had approached her at the reception. The man who claimed to have talked to her on the phone and scheduled an interview. A phone conversation she couldn't recall. A lie, she now realized.

She should be used to lies by now, used to cruelty, but it still hurt, still took her by surprise, especially the cruelty of a complete stranger.

He had been fairly tall, broad-shouldered. She had noticed him before he noticed her. Partly because he hadn't been dressed like anyone else, partly because . . . because . . . she didn't know. She had quickly looked away, not wanting to catch his eye, and then he had walked over to her. Talked to her. He'd been polite. His bearing had been just what it should be, and yet—

Those direct blue eyes, with no hint of obeisance, feigned or otherwise. She had found him attractive in a scary, dangerous sort of way, which had instantly put her on guard. There had been a time when she'd found Donovan attractive, too.

She recalled the man's reaction when she snubbed him, recalled the brief flash in his eyes of something close to anger. Then, in a fraction of a second, it had vanished, replaced by bland boredom, or acceptance.

By refusing the interview, she'd done him a favor. Donovan didn't like her talking with other men.

"Are you having an affair with Cray?" Donovan asked.

That he believed the paper didn't surprise her. She was used to his suspicion, his paranoia.

She played for time, hoping to think of something, anything that would placate him. "Am I what?"

"You know *what*. Having sex with Russell."

His voice was deeper, more strained. His face grew red as he leaned forward, his hands braced on the table, waiting for her reply.

He was wearing one of his tailored suits, his black hair wet from his shower and slicked back. She could smell his expensive after-shave. It almost made her gag.

Such a gentleman, she often heard women say. *You're so lucky.* Then there were the slyer comments: *I'll bet he's something in bed.*

He was something all right.

Her mind jumped from one thing to another. She should have gotten dressed. Why hadn't she gotten dressed? She was especially vulnerable in her gown and robe.

She thought of a thousand things she might say in her own defense.

How could I have an affair? I'm almost never alone. Or, *I wouldn't want a physical relationship with anybody. After you, the thought of sex repulses me.*

"Are you?" he roared, his anger breaking loose.

"No!"

It was coming. She could see it in his eyes.

Her heart beat frantically. Her breathing was short and shallow. She got to her feet. She took a step.

She used to have a voice in her head that cheered her on, that talked her through, that kept her going, that told her to hang on, that one day her life would be different.

She rarely heard that voice anymore. Over the years, she'd learned not to think. At all. About anything.

His hand came up and he hit her against the side of her head. She stumbled backward and struck her arm against the counter. She cried out—another weakness—hating herself for vocalizing her pain, her fear. But then, she'd never had much practice dealing with pain, or fear.

As a child, she'd never been able to tolerate pain. It had always been a joke in her family. The smallest thing—a stubbed toe, a splinter—reduced her to a blubbering idiot. She hated herself for that. She hated herself for a lot of things.

Until Donovan, no one had ever laid a hand on her. Until Donovan, she'd never known *real* pain. What a sissy she'd been all those years. Crying over stubbed toes and splinters.

"Don't break your arm again," Donovan warned.

With her ears still ringing from his blow, she straightened, pressed her lips together, and nodded. She wouldn't. Last time she'd broken it, he hadn't allowed her to go to the doctor for three days. It hadn't healed right, and now, when the weather was damp, her bones ached.

"You know what people will think when they see this, don't you?" He picked up the paper and began folding it over and over, until it was as small as something someone might use to strike a dog.

Or a person.

"They'll think I'm not satisfying you, that you had to go somewhere else because I can't keep a woman in my bed.'" He smacked the paper against the edge of the table.

Crack.

Sara flinched.

He hit the table again, and again.

Crack, crack.

Each time she flinched.

"That's not true, is it?" he asked.

She shook her head, hating herself for not standing up to him. But she'd stood up to him before, and she knew what would happen.

She turned. And even though she knew better, she ran.

Ten steps away, he caught her, knocking her to the floor.

"Never run from me."

His voice was low, his teeth gritted in rage. He hit her on the mouth, not as hard as he could have—maybe because of the upcoming auction they were expected to host together. It wouldn't do to show up with a battered wife.

He took off his jacket and tossed it behind him. Then he unzipped his pants and sprawled on top of her. He outweighed her by over a hundred pounds. She was no match for him. She had never been any match for him. Once, years ago, she had scratched his face. She'd never done it again.

A few seconds later, he was forcing himself inside her.

Pain.

Grunting, he pounded into her while she took herself someplace else, someplace far away.

Her father's farm. How she had hated it there. How she would love to be there again . . .

When Donovan was finished, he grabbed a handful

of her hair and tugged, holding her face just inches from his, making her look into his eyes. "Are you having an affair?" he asked again, while still inside her.

She couldn't answer. She was too terrified, too humiliated.

He tugged harder. Tears filled her eyes. "No!"

"If you are, and I find out, I'll kill you both."

She believed him.

"Hear me?"

She nodded. Yes, she heard him. Yes, she believed him.

After he was gone, she stood in the shower for a long time, but she couldn't remove the taint of Donovan's touch from her bruised body.

As the warm water ran over her, she tried not to think about what had happened, about how many *times* it had happened, about how many times it would happen again, but that was impossible. Her entire existence was her fear of her husband. There was room for nothing else.

Looking in from the outside, a person might wonder how a woman could have gotten herself into such a situation, such a mess. And why she didn't get herself out. But it wasn't that simple.

As a child, living in the rural community of Sigourney, Wisconsin, she had been extremely shy. Shyness was a curse. Shyness had a way of blinding people to the world around them. Shy people looked inward, not outward. They were so caught up in their own misery that they very often missed the messages being sent by the people around them.

She had missed Donovan's messages.

Her parents had never understood where her shyness had come from. No one else in her family was so afflicted. While her father wasn't loud, he didn't hesitate to speak his mind. And her mother and sister loved being around people. They thrived on it.

No, Sara was the odd one, an oddity who had been a constant embarrassment to her mother.

Sara's looks had been a problem too. Where she grew up, pretty girls were soft and blond, with dark tans. Girls with figures. Girls who, as some of the boys her age liked to put it, were "more likely to provide heat in the winter and shade in the summer."

Sometimes Sara overheard women commenting on her homeliness, on the paleness of her skin, skin that was so light, so transparent, that there were always purple smudges beneath her too big, too deep-set eyes. At school, in Ms. Austin's sixth grade, Sara used to sit and stare at the picture of Anne Frank on the bulletin board. And she would think, That's me. Those are my eyes.

No, Sara had struck out all the way around, having neither looks nor charm. But her father didn't seem to mind, although he would sometimes laugh and call her 'duckling.' Sara would add the 'ugly.' When other girls were shopping and going to school dances, Franklin Hart welcomed Sara's company. He would ruffle his youngest daughter's stringy hair and tell her he needed help with chores.

Instead of dating, Sara found comfort in art. She spent hours and hours bent over a sketch pad. Later, she grew to love the softness of watercolor, the starkness of pen and ink. With watercolors, she painted landscapes, rolling fields of grain under blue skies. With pen and ink, she drew people.

Those were good times. Happy times. Halcyon days.

But all good things must end. Her mother died.

Sara graduated from high school and went away. Not far. A hundred miles to a liberal arts college.

It was there she met Donovan. . . .

She found herself grudgingly attending a party put on by some of her sorority sisters.

She noticed him right away. His startling good looks would have gotten anyone's attention, but he also had a presence that couldn't be ignored.

She caught him looking in her direction a couple of times. She quickly glanced away, afraid he would think her bold if she met his gaze. She was *unworthy* of his gaze.

The next thing she knew, he was standing beside her, talking—to her? Surely not. His voice was a deep bass rumble in his chest. His words, to her flustered mind, were nothing she was in any state to comprehend.

She turned and looked behind her. Nobody. She looked back.

His lips moved. He smiled down at her.

Her heart began to hammer louder than the band's drumbeat. Her palms began to sweat.

She looked toward the door. She glanced frantically around the room. She looked back at him.

He was still smiling at her, but there was a question in his smile, as if he'd asked her something and was waiting for a reply. Maybe he wanted to know where the bathroom was. Maybe he wanted to use the phone. Maybe he was looking for someone. Someone tan and blond and filled out.

She stared, hoping for a clue to his question. She stared, her gaze moving over his perfect face, his perfect brows, his perfect nose. His perfect mouth.

Heat blossomed in her cheeks. He was truly the most beautiful man she'd ever seen in her life.

The perfect lips moved. "Dance?"

"Dance?" she asked, dumbly. What about a dance?

"Dance," he repeated. "Would you"—he pointed to her—"like to dance"—he pointed to himself—"with me?"

He wanted to dance? With *her*?

He was asking her if she wanted to walk out there in the middle of the floor and start flinging herself around? With *him*?

She didn't dance.

It was one of the many publicly humiliating things she made it a point to never engage in. She didn't ski, either. She didn't skate, she didn't speak to a group larger than two, and she didn't sing. In church, she mouthed the words.

She didn't dance.

He took her by the hand. The pads of his fingers were smooth and warm, every bit as intriguing as the rest of him.

He pulled her through the crowd, until they were on the dance floor, until they were facing each other.

"I-I don't dance," she said in a shaky voice, hoping he would be able to hear her over the music. Surprisingly enough, she wasn't embarrassed. She was too dazed, too confounded to be.

He took both of her hands and pulled her closer. And once again she was aware of the smoothness of his skin, of how different his hands were from her father's cracked and callused palms.

"Put your feet on top of mine," he instructed.

She looked down at his brown suede shoes with their thin laces. One of his hands moved to the small of her back, urging her closer.

In life, there were those who led, and those who followed. And there were those, like Sara, who watched others lead and follow. But now Sara found herself becoming an active participant. Now she found herself doing as he bid.

She put first one sandaled foot atop his, then the other.

The music wasn't fast, and it wasn't slow. It was pulsing. *She* was pulsing. With her legs spread against his, she could feel the tautness of his thighs. She could feel the hardness of his chest, feel the strength of his arms.

"What's your name?" he whispered.

"Sara."

She answered hypnotically, distantly wondering what this beautiful man was doing with her. She must prepare herself for the moment when the dance would end, when he would walk away and she would never see him again. She wasn't sure if she could live through it.

"Will you go out with me, Sara? Tomorrow."

He wouldn't come. She told herself he wouldn't come, but she got ready anyway. Just in case.

She started hours early, changing several times. She'd never given clothes much thought, always gravitating toward what was comfortable rather than fashionable. Now nothing she owned suited her. Nothing was right for Donovan Ivy.

He came.

He was right on time with his flashy car and impeccable clothes that made her feel all the more dowdy, all the more gauche.

He took her to a fancy restaurant where an imposing man seated them. It was a place with a wine list and candles and cloth napkins.

Her nerves were frayed. Her stomach was in knots.

She didn't know how she could possibly eat anything, let alone keep it down.

Maybe a drink of water would help.

She lifted the glass to her lips and it rattled against her teeth. She put down the glass.

He ordered wine.

She didn't drink, but as soon as the wine was poured, she attacked hers. She gulped one glass, then another.

She began to relax.

Donovan talked about himself, and she wanted to hear everything he had to say. He lived in a suburb of Chicago, but was thinking of moving downtown, maybe getting a house in the Gold Coast section of the city. He was in Wisconsin for a relative's wedding.

She learned that he came from a wealthy background—no surprise. His parents had insisted he go to college, but school bored him. It wasn't enough of a challenge. So he quit.

He leaned closer. "I was out of school four years when I made my first million."

Sara had never cared about money, but the fact that he had done so much in so little time, and without a college education, was amazing. She told him so, giving him what he needed. Adoration.

In her shyness, in her blind infatuation, she missed the warning signs. They were there. She just didn't see them. Maybe she didn't want to see them.

Sara was a dreamer. A romantic. An idealist. Much of her time was spent alone reading books that ended in true love, in happily ever after. She had expected nothing less . . .

A month later, Donovan asked her to marry him.

"You can't mean you're leaving," her father said

when she told him of Donovan's proposal. "You don't know anything about the man."

"Yes, I do!"

"He's not like us."

"I know!"

She looked at her father in his bib overalls and flannel shirt, ashamed that Donovan had seen him dressed that way. "I *know*!"

She would have told her father that she loved Donovan, and that he loved her, but her family didn't speak of things like love.

Franklin Hart's jaw went rigid. "You can't marry him. I forbid it."

Forbid it? Were they living in the Dark Ages? She was twenty-two years old!

Sara's father had always assumed she would marry a local boy and together they would take over the farm. It had never even been discussed. No one had ever asked *her* what *she* wanted.

"This may come as a surprise to you," she told him, "but the purpose of my existence isn't to fulfill your dreams, to live your life." He was trying to take away her only chance at happiness. And she knew if she didn't leave now, she might never get away.

"Have you ever considered what *I* want?" she asked, a hand to her chest. "Well, I can tell you what I *don't* want. I don't want to spend my life scraping a living from the dirt, in a place where every single day is the same as the day before, where every *year* is the same as the year before, where nothing changes, because *nothing ever happens*. I don't want to marry a farmer and grow old before my time!"

Her father's face paled. "Don't talk to me like that."

"I'm telling you how I feel! Is there something so terribly wrong with that?"

From her father's closed expression, she could see it was no use. He was so caught up in the land and tradition that he would never try to see things through her eyes. He *refused* to even consider her viewpoint. For him, there was only one answer, one solution, one way to live, and it was his way.

She had once asked why he stacked hay bales in a certain order when putting them in the barn. He had simply answered that his father and grandfather had done it that way, so that was the way it was done. End of conversation.

How could a person fight something like that?

"I'm going to marry Donovan," she told him.

Her father pointed a shaking hand to the door.

Fear for him jumped in her chest. *He's getting old. When did that happen? Why didn't I notice before?*

"Go marry your rich boyfriend. Go live in the city. But once you walk out that door, *don't come back.*"

She didn't even pack a suitcase. She left with just the clothes on her back. Left to start a new life as the wife of Donovan Ivy.

Ten years. She'd been with him ten years.

Long enough to look at her situation analytically. Long enough to know she was the typical abused wife, having been through all the stages numerous times. She'd even gone to a safe house, but there was no escaping him. He always found her. And when he did, there were the thinly veiled threats to her father, her sister, her sister's children.

She had soon found it was safer to live with him, to obey him, than to look over her shoulder in fear, constantly wondering where the enemy was.

In truth, she'd lost the will to fight. In truth, she

blamed her situation on herself, on her stupidity, her blind trust.

She didn't deserve any other life.

Don't come back.

Deep down, she had always thought her father would bend, would come around, but he didn't. A month after he'd disowned her, she received a box with no return address. Upon opening it, she found it packed with some of her childhood treasures, plus all of the things she'd made for her father from as far back as she could remember.

She had pulled out her stuffed animal—a gray cat with all the fur rubbed off and the eyes gone. It had been with her through chicken pox and pneumonia and scarlet fever. She had hugged its flat, hard body to her and cried. Cried for herself, and for her father, and for the innocence she'd lost.

What purpose does a tabloid serve?
—Irate reader
Sir, of what purpose is a pimple?
—Harley Gillette
    Editor, *Shoot the Moon*

Chapter Three

Harley Gillette made his way through the hallowed halls of *Shoot the Moon*, the hem of his grunge shorts falling below his knees, the worn soles of his leather sandals slapping against the cement floor, his long brown hair hot against his back and neck. For the second time that day he wondered if he shouldn't get his hair cut. After all, it had been two years since scissors had touched it. Maybe he should try to look a little more like a businessman.

Nah.

Plenty of time for that when he grew up.

As he walked, he thought of how the *Trib* had some of its famous headlines reproduced in brass plates. The *Trib* had Gothic architecture tastefully complemented by a lighted fountain.

The front pages of *Shoot the Moon* were taped to chipped cement block walls. *Shoot the Moon* was located in a four-story brick warehouse with a bad roof and a third floor that had been converted into office space. Its fountain was a rust-stained porcelain sink and a toilet with a handle that had to be jiggled.

No, you wouldn't find *Shoot the Moon* on any of the

Chicago architectural tours, Harley decided as he absentmindedly scanned some of the headlines.

FROG WITH HUMAN FACE. *"He's cute,"* scientists say, *"and smart as a whip."*

HUMAN BABY SIRED BY ALIEN. *Except for her uncanny ability to read minds, little Audrey is normal in every way.*

LOST STEER FINDS ITS WAY HOME. *"We can't send him to market now,"* says farm wife. *"He's like one of the family."*

Harley found Nash in the sterile, somewhat cluttered copy room, a room that had originally been Harley's office until *Shoot the Moon* expanded to take up half the third floor. Nash was leaning over the copy machine, genius at work. In one corner, a computer hummed.

Harley preferred to use something that didn't emit a green glow—like his manual Royal. Of course, Nash wasn't the type to worry about a little thing like radiation.

But Harley did.

He was only twenty-seven and he already thought like an old man. He worried about the ozone—who didn't?—but he also worried about things that weren't so tangible, like the dehumanization of America.

And change. Things changed too fast. Some smart person had once said, Hang on to your colloquialisms. Harley agreed. And hang on to the old ways.

His livelihood depended on the computer world, and yet Harley longed for the good old days he'd never lived through. When people took time to sit in the shade and talk. He worried that America had lost its youth.

Afternoon sunlight cut through the slanted blinds. Harley crossed the room and tried to shut them. Metal clanged against metal. Dust floated in the bright light, activating Harley's asthma. He started getting that tight feeling in his chest.

"The only people who can work those things are women," Nash said over his shoulder.

"No shit." Harley couldn't get the blinds closed, so he gave up and whipped out his inhaler. "Why is that?" *Puff, puff.* "Are we just too stupid?" he asked on a held breath.

"Something in the genes, I think."

Nash pushed the button on the copier. The machine whirred. Beneath the lid, the light flashed. For once, the paper didn't get hung up somewhere along the way.

Nash lifted the photocopy. "Instant gratification," he announced, handing the picture to Harley. "What do you think?"

Harley pocketed his inhaler and looked at the picture—a classic Nash Audubon cut-and-paste of at least two photos, to go along with their feature cover story about a boy with a birthmark shaped like the map of Africa.

The picture was of a kid about ten years old, holding up his shirt. On his protruding stomach was the map of Africa, not only complete with the Nile, but also labeled with towns and seaports.

Harley burst out laughing. He laughed until tears ran down his cheeks, until he began to wheeze. When he'd finally gotten control of himself, he handed the picture back to Nash.

"Great," Harley said, rubbing at his irritated chest. "One of your best."

"Just what I was thinking."

Some papers, such as *World News*, were into morphing using all the advanced computer technology they could get their hands on. If they kept it up, cutting and pasting would be a lost art. And *Shoot the Moon* was dedicated to keeping art alive. *World News* just didn't get it. Part of the fun was making pictures that were *obviously* fake. That was the whole idea. The beauty of it. The fun.

Whenever someone asked why he'd started a tabloid, Harley always told them that he saw *Shoot the Moon* as a relief valve for society. Most of the feature stories were absurd to the point of total ludicrousness. If anybody believed them, then that person belonged in the nuthouse. *Shoot the Moon* was a parody of other tabloids, and most readers were savvy enough to understand it, to get the joke. It wasn't meant to be taken seriously. By anybody.

But at the same time, he usually ran an article or two that dealt with a local issue, or a local politician or big shot. Maybe an issue that needed to be aired, maybe something the other papers—the *real* papers—wouldn't touch.

That was Nash's department. It was called the Local Yokel, but Harley often thought of it as the voice of the invisible. Nash was a master at catching people in not so much compromising positions as foolish ones. Like the mayor's wife stepping out of the rest room with five yards of toilet paper stuck to her heel.

The main thing that made the column so entertaining was Nash's total lack of fear. The guy wasn't afraid of anything. Harley found it bewildering to think about what a person might have to go through, live through, to achieve that kind of mind-set.

Nash had once put together a revealing little piece about a crooked Chicago businessman. The next day he'd gotten an anonymous phone call, a threat to burn down his house.

Nash had laughed into the receiver and said something about taking his wife and kids hostage, too.

You couldn't take what a person didn't have.

Harley looked at Nash. He was bent over the copy machine again, readjusting a picture.

Hard living. That's what he made Harley think of. Not old. Late thirties, maybe. But hard. Hard as nails. Lean, without an ounce of fat. He rarely smiled, not even when he said something so outrageously funny that people were rolling on the floor, trying not to wet their pants.

When he wasn't sacked out on the shredded orange couch in his office, he lived in his car.

Coming from an upper-class home, Harley had never known anybody who lived in his car.

It hardly seemed possible considering his present situation, but Nash had come pretty far in the last two years. He'd been living on the streets when Harley had first met him.

It had been late winter. Cold as hell. And there was no cold like Chicago's, when the wind blew across a frozen Lake Michigan. Close to zero, with the wind-chill factor making it more like forty below. Nash had been half sick, sitting in a doorway. Harley had stuffed a couple of bucks in the pocket of his flannel jacket and told him to get a hot meal. But before Harley took ten steps, Nash was roaring after him, shoving the money back in his face.

"I don't want your damn money!"

Harley looked at him and wondered if, in the same dire circumstances, he'd have had the guts, the pride, to refuse. No, he'd have taken the money and run.

"Then how about a job?" Harley asked.

He didn't even *know* the guy. He could be a drug dealer, a pimp. Hell, he could have murdered somebody. He could have *done* time. And Harley didn't have any damn money to pay a secretary, let alone a . . . a . . . whatever the guy would be.

"Job?" Nash asked suspiciously, his upper lip curling. "Doing what? I don't front dope. And I don't pimp."

That was a relief to hear. But was it the truth?

"Working for me." Harley put a splayed hand to his chest. "I'm a young entrepreneur."

Nash threw back his head and laughed until Harley felt his face and ears turn red. *Young entrepreneur.* What a stupid thing to say. What an *asinine* thing to say. What an arrogant, pompous thing to say.

With an elegant flourish, Nash swept off his filthy wool stocking cap. Bending at the waist, right leg extended, he made a graceful bow. "Ah, *bonjour,* Mr. Manure."

Then he laughed again.

The guy was certifiable, Harley decided as he turned and walked away, as the sound of the man's laughter echoed after him.

But that night Harley couldn't get the street person out of his head; he couldn't quit thinking that it could have been him. Under the dirt and beard, the guy probably wasn't more than ten years his senior. Homeless. Without a job. Yet too proud to take money from a stranger. Harley found himself reluctantly admiring him.

The next day Harley went back to the same spot, but this time he found an old lady with an overflowing shopping cart. He asked if she'd seen the man he was looking for. She shook her head and muttered to herself. Harley pulled a five-dollar bill from his pocket—five dollars he couldn't afford to part with—and gave it to the woman. She snatched it from his fingers, looked over both shoulders, then tucked it somewhere deep within the recesses of her jacket, a place Harley didn't even want to think about.

Harley went back two more times. The third time was indeed the charm, because he spotted the man he'd spoken to before.

"Mr. Manure!"

This time the title came without the flourish. And this time Nash looked in worse shape than ever. Harley guessed he had pneumonia.

"Thought anymore about that job I offered you?"

Nash coughed and coughed, then finally got out the words, "Don't want charity."

"Do you know how to read?"

That seemed to get his attention. Pique his interest just a little. He didn't answer, but at least he was listening.

"Can you spell?" Harley asked.

"Does a rabbit's tail come off if you grab it? Does an unopened can of diet pop float?"

"Spell souvenir."

Nash spelled it. But was it right? Did souvenir have two Es? Harley wasn't sure. Spelling was one of his weak points. Spelling and women.

"I could really use a proofreader," he said.

One of Nash's brows lifted. His eyes glinted with interest. Or fever. Or madness.

Harley plunged on. "Ever heard of the publication *Shoot the Moon?*"

"I've heard of shooting the moon, but it didn't have anything to do with publishing."

"It's a weekly paper. We're just getting off the ground, but pretty soon everybody will have heard of us."

"What kind of paper? Not some cult thing, is it?"

"Of course not."

"Not some liberal save-the-whales thing, is it? I hate causes."

For someone who didn't have a bed to sleep in, or a dime to buy a cup of coffee, he sure was picky. "A tabloid. *Shoot the Moon* is a tabloid."

Harley braced himself for the typical reaction, the one similar to his mother's, which involved a lot of wailing and arm tossing.

"A tabloid?"

After a pause, the man's face broke into a slow smile.

And he took the job.

Harley discovered that Nash could proofread. With the aid of a dictionary, he could spell. And later Harley found out he could write halfway decent copy. Not great, but okay. He could even take pictures. But better than that, he could cut up those pictures and make totally new ones.

A gold mine.

Harley had found a gold mine sitting in the doorway of an abandoned tenement at Eighty-eighth and Vine.

It wasn't long before they were out of the red and into the black. Nash bought a used car, but he refused to find a place to live. Said it felt too permanent. So he slept in the office. Showered in the bathroom down the hall. Harley knew that one day Nash would move on, most likely without even telling him. But until then, he was there.

What was weird was the fact that Harley didn't know anymore about him now than he had that first day. He'd once made the mistake of asking him if he had any relatives. Nash had gotten a strange look on his face, the kind he got when confronted with too much reality, and told him no. His eyes said, don't ask me again. Ever.

Harley never asked again.

And even though Nash could be funny, even though he was probably the funniest guy Harley had ever known, Harley always got the feeling that the humor didn't quite reach him, that he was somehow distanced from it all, on the outside looking in.

"How about a beer at Harpo's?" Harley asked, knowing he was probably wasting his breath, still hoping Nash would come.

Nash checked the wall clock. Past midnight. "I don't know," he said. "I better proof this stuff one more time."

"Don't be so dedicated," Harley said. "Tootie can proof it in the morning. Get her away from that damn crocheting."

"You go on. I might stop by later."

"I'll be waiting," Harley said.

He took off for Harpo's and Nash proofed the map-of-Africa story. When he was done, he put it on Tootie's desk, next to her pile of crocheted squares and overflowing ashtray, left her a note, then remembered Harley's invitation.

Harley wouldn't be lacking company. He might be skinny, and he might be grungy, but he drew women like a newborn baby. Tootie claimed it was because of his big, dark, soulful eyes. Nash thought it might just be because he was nice. Too nice. Nash knew from experience that nice didn't get you anywhere.

Nash usually didn't go to taverns, but for the last several days, ever since he'd done the Ivy story, he'd felt a little bummed. For the first time since he'd started working for Harley, he found himself experiencing an unpleasant nagging.

He'd been on deadline and the story had been printed before he'd had the chance to give it much thought.

Like a letter dropped in a mailbox. As soon as you hear it hit bottom, you want it back, you have second thoughts. But by then it's too late.

Maybe a drink or two was what he needed, he thought, turning out the lights. He locked the door, took the two flights of stairs down to street level, then headed in the direction of the bar.

Too quiet.

His head was too quiet.

The trick was to keep up the flow of monologue. Not let it stop. Once it stopped, he started thinking. He became reflective.

Words.

He filled up his head with words so there was no room for anything else. No thought. No memories.

But they were knocking. They were there. Just on the other side. Daring him. Taunting him. Wanting in.

The night air felt good. Cool. Reviving.

Think about the air.

Fall was coming. October rain. Cold November wind. Cold December snow.

Maybe it was time to move on. Go someplace warmer.

He pulled air deep into his lungs, then, hands in his pockets, he headed down the dimly lit street.

Truth was—and he *did* recognize it as truth, regardless of how many things he hid from himself—the last thing he wanted was a home. The last thing he wanted was a friend. And Harley wanted to be his friend.

He'd had that kind of life once—where people lived in houses and had wives and kids and friends. Didn't it lurk in the back of his mind every day? Didn't he dream about it every night?

In the dream, he would get home from work. He would pull into the garage in the back, get out of his car. Go up the walk. Except the walk was hardly wide enough for his feet. It was more like a tightrope.

When he finally reached the back door, a key would appear in his hand, the extra key he'd never given the realtor when the house had been sold. He would stick it in the lock and turn it just right, lifting and pulling on the door to get things lined up.

The door would swing open. A bunch of strangers would be sitting at the dinner table. *His* dinner table. A family. Kids. Macaroni and cheese. Peanut butter sandwiches. Glasses of milk. A high chair.

They would look at him in horror, and he would suddenly remember that he didn't live there anymore. That the house had been sold. Not last week, but years and years ago. He would stammer an apology. Sometimes he would insist that he'd left something there. He would run through the house, trying to find that something, charging from room to room, his dreamer's viewpoint suddenly erratic, like a hand-held camera. Looking. Looking. Have to find . . . Have to get . . .

What? What was he looking for?

And then he would begin to notice the changes the new residents had made. On his way through the house that was no longer his, he would see evidence of the new occupants. Different furniture. New carpet. Toys, lots of toys, scattered on the floor.

Sometimes he would push the toys aside, searching, searching . . .

The dreams always ended the same. He would suddenly become aware of the people behind him, watching him in baffled, yet unthreatening silence. And he would realize the enormity of what he'd done, realize how crazy it was to charge through their lives as if the house were no more than a movie set. A dream set.

At that point, he would run. Back through the dining room, past the family, through the back door. When he made it outside, it was always dark. He would dive off the porch into that darkness, practically swimming through it, moving away. Away. When he looked back over his shoulder, he would see them all standing on the porch, under the glow of the yellow light. The man always looked like him. And the woman always looked like his ex-wife.

"You! Hey! You!"

Voices. Bringing him back to the present. To Chicago and the dark neon night.

Confused, thinking it might be Harley, he stopped. He turned.

"You Nash Audubon?"

Three men were walking toward him. Three *big* men. Not a good sign. Not a good sign at all.

Nash began inching backward a half step at a time. "Never heard of him."

He spun around and tried to run.

Nash had always thought of himself as a fairly decent runner. Hadn't he placed second in the hundred-yard dash back in grade school? Didn't he jog two miles almost every day? But tonight things weren't going in his favor.

One of the guys tackled him, knocking him to the ground. The air left his lungs in a loud *whoof*, like a dog with kennel cough. Before he had time to pull in a new breath, a hard-toed shoe connected with his rib cage. Were those bones he heard cracking?

When he was jerked to his feet, he got in a couple of good hits, enough to hurt his hand. The pain in his side shot bright sparks across the blackness in front of his eyes.

A thousand fists pummeled his face and stomach.

What did they want? Money? Or was this their evening's entertainment? It was a sick world.

"Watch—"

Smack.

"—who—"

Smack.

"—you—"

Smack.

"—write—"

Smack.

"—about."

Smack, smack.

They let him go. He melted to the ground.

Thank you.

The entire episode had taken no longer than a minute. Blood streamed from his face onto his shirt, and—*damn!*—his leather jacket. Blood ran in his eyes. He wiped at it with his fingers, trying to clear his vision.

They didn't search for his wallet, didn't stick a knife in him—even though he felt as if they had. Every shallow breath was agony. "C-could you tell me why you j-ust—" He tasted blood. He spit. "—beat the crap out of me?"

The biggest guy spoke. "Mrs. Ivy didn't appreciate the story you did on her. From now on, leave her alone."

Sara Ivy? That's what this was all about? She'd sent some of her husband's thugs to work him over because of the story he'd done? She'd certainly had him fooled. She was just as ruthless as her husband.

What she didn't know was that Nash wasn't the kind of guy who stuck his head in the sand. Now he was pissed. Now he was *really* pissed.

In some distant part of his mind he noted that in the space of a few days Sara Ivy had somehow managed to dredge emotions he hadn't felt in years. First guilt, now anger.

Somebody kicked him in the side. "Leave her alone. You hear?"

"Okay, okay."

Like hell.

He'd been through the worst that could possibly happen to a person. He'd come through it shattered and scarred and unrecognizable. What was there to be afraid of after that? What was there to lose?

Keep a camera loaded and on hand at all times.
—Photography 101

Chapter Four

Curled up on his side, knees to stomach, Nash gave himself five minutes to die. That's all it took with a busted spleen, or so he'd been told.

Five minutes later he was still breathing. Still conscious.

He was going to have to get up.

Without allowing himself time to think about how much it was going to hurt, he rolled to his knees and elbows.

Pain.

Red-hot.

Ripping.

He froze, neither inhaling or exhaling.

Gotta quit breathing, he told himself as he waited for the pain to subside.

To make things even more pleasant, it had started to rain. Flashing neon made shifting patterns on anything that reflected light: wet dumpsters, broken glass, motor oil.

Blood.

It dripped from his face, splashing on the bricked alley. He lifted one hand and gingerly examined his face. Along one cheekbone was a cut. A deep cut.

For two years he'd lived on some of the roughest streets in the city, and in all that time nobody had ever laid a hand on him. And in the two years he'd worked for Harley, nobody had ever touched him. Sure, he'd had the usual amount of nasty letters, rude phone calls, and death threats. But no one had worked him over.

Not until Sara Ivy.

He slowly exhaled.

He slowly inhaled.

As he did, he was careful not to pull in a deep breath. Then he shoved himself to his feet.

Upright, the blood from his face ran down his neck. It soaked into the collar of his T-shirt. Soaked into his jacket.

With a hand pressed to his side, he walked. Like an injured dog returning home, he made his way back to *Shoot the Moon.*

Once there, he headed down the hall of yellowed *Shoot the Moon* cover stories, slipping out of his jacket, dropping it on the floor as he went. In the bathroom, he eased out of his T-shirt, then used the shirt to wipe off some of the blood.

In the glare of the light bulb dangling from the ceiling, he saw that his left side, in the area around his ribs, was already turning black and blue. He checked his reflection in the medicine cabinet mirror. His right eye was swollen, his bottom lip puffy. And the cut on his cheekbone was bleeding like hell—quickly giving the place all the characteristics of a grisly murder scene. Blood on the floor, bloody handprints on the sink. He should have jumped into the shower.

He turned on the faucet, cold being his only choice. Water splashed in the rust-stained sink. Elbows resting on icy porcelain, he bent and cupped water to his face until the water ran pink.

A sound.

He paused.

Like a key in a lock.

Like a door being opened.

Nash shut off the water and listened, all of his attention focused on his hearing.

The Ivy goon squad?

There had been a few times when he'd almost bought a gun. He'd even gone so far as to fork over the cash, but when it had come time to actually pick up the weapon, to *hold* it, he couldn't make himself do it.

Guns were made for just such moments. A little cold steel would be very reassuring right about now.

Someone shouted his name.

Harley.

Nash let out his breath and looked around the corner to see Harley running down the hall toward him, following a trail of blood.

"Holy shit!" Harley gasped when he was close enough to see Nash's face. He skidded to a stop. He waved both hands. "Did you call nine-one-one?" He took a step toward his office. He took a step back. "Do you need a tourniquet?"

Nash let out a choked laugh that cut off in midgasp when pain ripped through his side. "Yeah, around my neck," he said when he could finally speak. "It's superficial," he added, trying to remain calm in the face of Harley's panic.

"Like hell. I'd say you hit the mother lode."

Nash swung back into the bathroom.

Harley followed. "What the hell happened?"

Nash tilted his face toward the light and examined his reflection in the smudged mirror. "What you see before you is courtesy of Sara Ivy."

"Ivy? No shit?"

Nash grabbed a handful of brown paper towels.

"Wait," Harley said. "Hold it right there."

Harley dashed out of the bathroom. From the vicinity of his office came the sound of his inhaler—two good tokes. He returned a few seconds later, camera in hand. "We might be able to use this in the *Moon*," he explained as he lifted the camera.

His earlier concern had vanished when confronted with the possibility of a solid cover story. "Too bad we can't afford color. Color would be much more effective."

Harley moved from side to side, testing the light, lining up the shot. "Try to look a little more miserable."

"I *am* miserable."

"You're not evoking sympathy. Your expression is more threatening than anything else."

Nash scowled. "I'm no actor."

"Pretend you have a really bad cold and can't breathe out of either nostril."

"Like this?"

"That's better, but not quite right. Maybe it's the angle. Sit down there on the floor."

Back to the wall, Nash slid to the floor, one hand dangling over bent knee.

"That's it. That's it. Now we're cooking. Oh, yeah."

One roll of film later, Harley was done with the impromptu shoot and Nash was looking in the mirror again, this time with a handful of stiff, wadded-up paper towels pressed to his face. He tried lifting them away. Blood pooled and ran down his face.

"Stitches," Harley said.

"Think so?"

"Oh, yeah. Definitely."

"Maybe if I pull it together like this . . ."

"Won't stay."

"It might."

"See. What'd I tell you."

"Guess so."

"I'll give you a lift to the emergency room."

They were almost to the door when they stopped and looked at each other, then spoke in unison.

"Camera."

Nash waited, leaning against the wall, paper towels pressed to his face, while Harley dashed back to get the camera.

Three hours, five stitches, and some bruised internal organs later, Nash was back in the office of *Shoot the Moon*. Harley had tried to talk him into coming home with him, but Nash had work to do.

Now, lying on the fold-out couch, phone resting on his thigh, he jabbed a series of buttons, then waited.

Six rings later, a groggy voice answered.

"Mason. Hey, buddy," Nash said. "I need some information."

"Audubon? 'Sthat you?" Mason asked, a little more alert now.

In the background, a woman's sleepy voice said, "Who is it, honey? Is something wrong?"

In his mind, Nash pictured the typical cozy TV couple, burrowed deep in their double bed.

Without lowering his voice or taking his mouth from the receiver, Mason answered his wife. "It's just that crazy Audubon. Go back to sleep."

Missed you, too.

"Don't you ever look at a clock before you call somebody?" Mason asked. "Maybe you don't have any kind of structure to your life, but I do. I get up in the morning. I go to bed at night. That's how most people do it."

"You're not a banker, you're a private investigator,"

Nash reminded him. "Late-night calls go with the territory."

"I have a life."

"I need some information," Nash told him again, undaunted by the lecture. They'd been over the same ground before.

Mason let out a resigned sigh. "It'll cost you."

"I gave you four Blackhawks tickets last time. I have credit coming."

"Obstructed view," Mason said. "The tickets were *obstructed view*."

"You're kidding."

Nash had forgotten about the poor quality of the seats, otherwise he wouldn't have brought it up.

"Don't bullshit me. You probably got the tickets for nothing. Try taking two kids to an obstructed-view, standing-room-only hockey game."

"Okay, okay. I'll make it up to you."

"That's what you said last time."

"This time I mean it."

"What do you need?"

"All the dirt you can find on Sara Ivy."

"Ivy? Donovan Ivy's wife?"

"That's the one."

"Kind of out of your league, ain't she?"

"Aren't they all?"

"You got that right."

Two days later Nash was feeling well enough to visit the library. He headed directly to the microfilm section, found the listing he wanted, and got his roll. All the machines were in use, so he hung around the doorway, waiting for someone to leave. The first person to look up—a middle-aged guy in a suit—did a double take, then quickly gathered his rolls of film and slunk away.

Nash sat down in front of the screen, loaded the film, and turned the knob. He found the article in the Chicago Living section of the *Trib*. A feature on the Ivy house, complete with photographs.

Quite a joint. Ostentatious was the first word that came to mind. Ostentatious was the second word that came to mind.

The picture taken from the main entrance looking up the front drive made him think alarm systems, diamond necklaces, and Doberman pinschers. Butlers. Minks. Rolls-Royces.

The article and photos took the reader inside the mansion—where there was a sweeping *Gone With the Wind* staircase, complete with requisite chandeliers. In the master bedroom was a massive four-poster, a replica of a bed that had, at one time, supposedly cradled the body of some king. Off the bedroom were two baths, both with bidet, plus dressing rooms and a powder room.

Grand.

On to the kitchen. It was something a French chef would feel right at home in, complete with a walk-in refrigerator and wine cellar. Off the kitchen was a solarium with a Jacuzzi big enough for a dozen people. Outside were waterfalls and all sorts of flowering plants. A landscaped garden. A damn tennis court. A guest house. A pool shaped like an amoeba. The pool photo had been taken at night in order to make use of the spectacular underwater lighting.

Quite a joint.

Maybe he could get a picture of Sara Ivy and Cray, then superimpose them on a photo of the pool. Title it *Skinny Dipping in the Ce-ment Pond* or something.

He made a copy of the pool picture. Then he turned the microfilm dial, cranking back to the photo taken looking through the wrought-iron gates, up the sweeping drive to the entryway. He made a copy of that, too.

Before returning to *Shoot the Moon*, he swung by Costumes Galore to rent a cheap tux. Nothing was too good for Sara Ivy.

Silverware clattered against banquet hall china as waiters hurried to clear tables. The two-hundred-dollar-a-plate dinner was winding down. Women excused themselves to reapply lipstick. People converged in the lobby for a smoke before the auction.

Sara Ivy remained seated at the table she and Donovan were sharing with Adrian Woodhouse, president of the Literacy Foundation, along with Woodhouse's wife, Margaret. Across from Sara, at the same table, was Russell Cray. It had been Donovan's idea to seat him and his wife at their table, hoping to put an end to any gossip instigated by the tabloid article. Sara didn't know about putting an end to the gossip, but it certainly created an uncomfortable situation for everyone at the table, with the exception of Donovan. She couldn't tell by his expression, but Sara was sure he was experiencing perverse pleasure from everyone else's unease. He got off on that kind of thing.

Elegantly dressed people made their way back to their seats, stopping occasionally to talk with this person or that one. And then it was time for the Ivys to introduce Adrian Woodhouse, their joint delivery another idea of Donovan's.

Like the doting husband he publicly pretended to be, Donovan helped her from her chair. Together they walked to the podium, with Donovan taking his place beside her. He gave her a confident, loving smile.

He looked good and he knew it. Together, *they* looked good. He was wearing a black tux, she the black organdy gown he'd picked out. On her arms she wore long black gloves. Around her neck, lying above the square neckline, against her white, white skin, was a necklace of diamonds.

A show.

Nothing but a show.

She resented the fact that Donovan was there at all. The Literacy Foundation had been her project, something she'd truly believed in, something she felt would give purpose to her life. But then Donovan had stepped in and turned it into a circus, turned it into a media blitz for his own benefit.

He spoke into the microphone. "You look beautiful tonight, darling," he said in the low voice that used to send shivers of excitement down her spine. Now it just sent shivers.

"Thank you," she said woodenly, causing a furrow of displeasure to briefly mar his brow. They were supposed to be partaking in light, entertaining banter.

She looked out over the crowd of elegant people, most wearing polite, expectant faces. It was then that she realized the majority of diners were women. Thanks to Donovan and his influence, two thousand tickets had been sold. Mr. Woodhouse was very pleased.

Over the past year, Sara had become increasingly aware of just how Donovan's popularity had grown. He had somehow gained almost celebrity status in the city.

Had any of the people in the audience come out of concern for literacy? Or had they come to see Donovan?

"You've made a most generous contribution to Chicago's Literacy Foundation," Sara said to the crowd.

They clapped politely.

"As you will see in your program, we have received

wonderful donations for our auction, seventy-two items in all. But before the auction begins——" Her gaze swept over the crowd. "I would like to introduce someone instrumental in putting together tonight's event——"

Donovan's hand was holding hers. Squeezing her knuckles together.

Warning her.

Make me look good.

This could be her moment, she realized. Her opportunity to bring him crashing down in front of everyone.

My husband hits me.

My husband rapes me.

They were waiting. Waiting.

She was afraid.

She was ashamed.

She opened her mouth. She closed her mouth and looked at Donovan. She swallowed, fear making her heart beat frantically in her chest. She quickly looked away, back to the expectant people.

"I . . . ah . . ."

I am a coward. A terrible, terrible coward.

"My darling, are you daydreaming?" Donovan said in a deep, teasing voice.

Sara could feel the sweat gathering under her armpits. Her elegant organdy gown was sticking to her. "Uh, yes . . ."

Donovan leaned forward, closer to the microphone. White teeth flashed. "She's thinking about last night."

A titter moved through the crowd. Women laughed in delight, as if he were flirting with them. There were smiles of sly approval from the men.

When the laughter died down, Sara took a deep breath. "It gives me great pleasure——"

"I told you she was thinking about last night," Donovan drawled.

More laughter.

Couldn't they see how phony he was? Couldn't they see his pasted-on smile? His insincerity? How could they be taken in by him? But then she reminded herself that she, too, had once been taken in.

"I would like to introduce the President of the Literacy Foundation, Adrian Woodhouse."

Coward. Coward.

Adrian appeared at her elbow. "Thank you, my dear."

She was ushered from the podium, Donovan's hand on her arm.

Coward. Coward.

When they reached the table, she didn't sit down. Instead, she picked up her handbag.

"Where are you going?" Donovan asked.

Was she the only one who could detect a threat in his voice?

"To the rest room. I'll be right back."

Coward. Coward.

He let her pass. But even though his hand released her, his eyes gave her a subtle warning.

The ladies' room was empty.

She peeled off her gloves, turned on the tap, and pressed the cool water to her burning cheeks.

Her hands shook. She clenched them into tight fists, willing them to stop.

She was a coward.

She deserved Donovan.

She wiped her hands on her gown, then opened her clutch and searched through it, past lipstick and tissues and mints until her fingers made contact with the prescription bottle she always carried. With hands that still trembled, she tossed two tablets in her mouth and washed them down with a handful of cold water.

Then she capped the bottle and dropped it back in her purse. Hands braced on the sink, she closed her eyes. *I don't want to go back out there. Don't want—*

"Private party?"

Her eyes flew open. Her stomach dropped.

Reflected in the mirror was her own bloodless face. Behind it, just over her shoulder, was the man from the Renaissance. His name? Nash. Nash Audubon.

With heart racing, she slowly turned around.

His face. Oh, God.

She must have winced, because he said, "Not a pretty sight, is it?" He stepped closer, then pulled the prescription bottle from her open purse and looked at it. "Darvon." There was no surprise in his voice.

He wore a black tuxedo jacket, complete with tails. But instead of slacks, he had on a pair of extremely faded jeans. Instead of dress shoes, grubby white high-tops.

He turned the bottle in his hand until he came to the orange warning label. He read it to himself. "This along with a couple of glasses of stiff booze, and you'll be ready to operate some pretty heavy-duty machinery."

She snatched the bottle from his hand, dropped it back in her purse, and tried to push past him.

He blocked.

She stepped to her left.

So did he.

She stepped to her right.

So did he.

She knew she should be afraid, but she wasn't. After Donovan, what was there to fear? "What do you want?" she asked.

"To show you this." He pointed to his swollen eyelid. "And this." He pointed to his cheekbone. "Five stitches."

What did it have to do with her?

"You sit in your ivory tower and give orders without ever having to deal with the consequences." He pulled the tail of his white dress shirt from his jeans, then quickly unbuttoned the shirt, exposing an expanse of black-and-blue flesh. "These are the consequences." He put a splayed hand to his bare chest. "*I* am the consequences."

And then it came to her.

Donovan.

Donovan had done this to him.

Her throat tightened. There was nothing she could say. She had already missed her chance.

Coward. Coward.

Tears threatened. She tried to shoulder past him. Once again, he blocked her path, this time forcing her against the wall. With his body, his hands, he held her there. She could feel the pulse beating in her neck. And now she *was* afraid.

She turned her face to the side and squeezed her eyes shut, waiting to feel the blow of his hand across her face.

"Look at me." He shook her. "Take a good look at me."

She could feel the heat of his naked, bruised stomach pressed to her, she could feel the heat of his chest, his hands on her arms.

Then she felt his fingers on her chin, her throat where her pulse was beating wildly. He turned her face to his. "Look at me, damn you!" he whispered loudly.

She opened her eyes. His face was just inches from hers. She could see the lined pattern in his irises. His eyes were a deeper blue than she remembered.

"I bleed just like you," he said. "I feel pain just like you."

He thought *she* was behind his beating, thought *she* had ordered it. What a ludicrous idea. As if she had that kind of power. As if she would do such a thing. Men were so blind.

He let go of her chin. She recoiled, again closing her eyes, again bracing herself for a blow.

It never came. Instead, he put his hand back to her arm. Not a painful hold, just steady pressure. "You've made an enemy," he told her in a smooth voice. "Wherever you go, whatever you do, I'll be watching."

She opened her eyes and lifted her chin—a trick she'd learned in order to keep her mouth from trembling. "There's an anti-stalking law."

He laughed, humorlessly. "There's a law against beating the shit out of people, too."

He was going to blunder around and get himself killed. She had to warn him. "My husband is powerful," she said. "I'd be careful if I were you."

"Is that a threat?"

"I'm just telling you that Donovan doesn't play games."

"And you? What about you?"

"I don't, either."

He jerked his head in the direction of the banquet hall. Dark hair tumbled over his forehead. "That show out there doesn't fool me. You people with your causes. You don't give a damn about fighting illiteracy."

He was looking at her again, his eyes bold and angry and unwavering. "In my book, there are two kinds of people who take up causes. The ones who do it because their lives are empty and a cause gives them a feeling of purpose—"

Maybe he wasn't so blind after all.

"And the others, who are strictly in it for publicity. To get votes."

"Doesn't anybody do it simply to help?"

"Not people like you."

He wasn't holding her as tightly. And it seemed he'd used up most of his anger. His eyes, slightly curious now, examined her face. There were lines of puzzlement between his dark brows.

"I don't get you," he said. "Is it worth it? Sleeping with someone like Donovan Ivy in return for a cushy life? For a Jacuzzi and a Rolls?" He touched the diamonds around her neck. "For a bunch of rocks?"

That hurt. Even from him—a stranger. Even from someone she didn't care for at all. The injustice of it mocked her.

The voice she hadn't heard from in years and years stirred.

Why was she taking this from him? What did she care what he thought? A tabloid reporter. A man who made a living telling lies.

Hurting people.

From somewhere deep within her, anger smoldered, burned, exploded.

"Oh, it's worth it," she said.

She could have told him the truth, but he wouldn't have believed her. Instead, she did it his way in order to get back at him as best she could. "You want to know something else?" she asked.

His eyebrows lifted.

"I told them to kill you."

He grew very still. She could see that he was digesting what she'd said. And for a moment she thought he might bring his hands to her throat and squeeze the life out of her.

And she realized she didn't really care.

When he didn't try to strangle her, she lifted her chin a little higher. "Let go of me."

He did.

As if her skin had burned his palms. As if she were something soiled. Contaminated.

And she was. Oh, she was.

He backed away.

And then he was gone.

Sara let out her breath, leaned her head against the wall, and closed her eyes.

She was still shaking inside when she heard a movement at the door, followed by the simultaneous flash and whir of a camera.

The bastard. The sneaking bastard.

Is there a photograph in existence that isn't a manipulation of light and shadow?
—Nash Audubon

Chapter Five

In the darkroom, the metallic smell of developing solution filled the small, confined area.

Nash used a squeegee to scrape the excess water from a negative, then clipped up the strip to dry.

"These are great," Harley said, attaching a weight to the bottom of the strip and examining the processed negatives. "This one on the bathroom floor . . . It evokes such . . . such . . . Help me out here."

"Pathos?"

"Yeah. Pathos. And these two, when you got the steel brush and stitches. I love the agony you were able to express. It even shows up in the negative."

"I was *in* agony," Nash reminded him dryly.

Conversation lulled. They stared at hanging strips. Finally Harley said, "You know we can't run these."

Nash braced his hands on his hips. He wasn't a coward, but he wasn't a total idiot either. He couldn't bring the Ivys down if he was dead. "You're right," he reluctantly admitted. "We can't run them—not now, anyway."

Harley made a sound of affirmation. Then, "What about this one?"

He was indicating a negative that was by itself on a strip of black, blank frames.

Sara Ivy. Leaning against a wall, her eyes closed. Her head tilted back in a pose that made her look maddeningly vulnerable. Maddeningly innocent.

I told them to kill you.

At the time, Nash had fallen for it. But later, after his anger had cooled, he'd found the line a little tough to swallow. No matter how hard he tried, he just couldn't make himself believe she was that ruthless.

What did that say about him? That he was a fool. That he was getting soft, losing his edge.

He was still staring at the negative. Everything dark was light. Her hair. Her dress. Her eyes. Her lips. He felt a strange need to see the developed photo. As soon as the negative was dry, he would make a print. "Keep it," Nash said. "It might come in handy, too."

Three days later, Nash sat slouched in front of the computer, feet propped on the desk, keyboard across his lap, entering the information Mason had dug up on Sara Ivy as it came across the phone line. They'd been at it a couple of minutes, and so far the private investigator hadn't come up with anything useful. Didn't the woman have a life? Or was Mason losing his touch?

"Used to wear a size eight, now wears a size four."

"What the hell does that mean?" Nash asked, not bothering to type it in. He used the hunt-and-peck method, and he wasn't typing in any more worthless information.

"You asked me to find out what I could about Sara Ivy. I'm telling it like it is."

"Okay, okay." Nash didn't want to piss off one of his best sources.

"Used to buy a lot of chocolate ice cream. Now she seems to have a particular fondness for hard liquor."

Nash groaned. "Tell me something I don't know."

"Rents movies. Old stuff. Things like musicals. Nothing worse than a damn musical, is there?"

Nash laughed and agreed.

"What else have you got?"

"Birthday's January ninth. She's thirty-two."

"This is *nothing*. You're telling me nothing."

"Give me a chance. She has four dental fillings. Does most of her shopping by catalog."

Nash let out an exasperated sigh.

"Back in '85 she had a miscarriage."

Nash straightened. "Now we're getting somewhere." With receiver braced between his head and shoulder, he typed.

"After that, she made several trips to the doctor and is still being prescribed some pretty heavy-duty tranquilizers and painkillers."

Nash's hands paused over the keyboard. "And . . . ?"

"She seems to be somewhat accident-prone. Had a broken arm a few years back. Another time, a concussion."

Nash typed.

"She grew up on a little two-hundred-acre farm in Wisconsin. Youngest of two girls. Hardly a pot to piss in."

"That would explain some of Donovan's appeal," Nash said as he typed.

"She has no contact with her family."

"Too good for them now," Nash said, remembering how easily she'd snubbed him.

"Maybe." Pause. "No friends. Nothing."

"What else?"

"That's it."

"That's it?"

"Sorry I couldn't do better."

"You're supposed to be a private investigator."

"Which means that, unlike you, I don't make stuff up. Now how about some decent Blackhawks tickets?"

"You don't deserve any damn tickets."

"You don't deserve a friend like me. Remember who gave you the lead on the phony minister who was fleecing old ladies? And what about that bridge bomb scare?"

"You break my heart."

"Don't you wish you had one."

"Go to hell."

"Remember, I knew you when you were a bum."

"I'm still a bum. When I was little and my mother asked me what I wanted to be when I grew up, I said, a bum."

Mason let out a snort, then a couple of loud belly laughs. "You're nuts."

"Take it easy."

"Yeah. You, too."

Nash hung up and made a note to pick up four Blackhawks tickets. Then he leaned back in the swivel chair, hands locked behind his head, and stared up at the design stamped in the tin ceiling.

What he needed was a real photo. And a real story.

What he needed was to go on a stakeout.

Nash had never been on a stakeout. It turned out to be everything he'd expected—boring as all hell.

He'd parked his Fairlane about a block up the street from the Ivy estate, hoping his car wouldn't attract too much attention. Not many people along the Gold Coast drove a beauty like his.

The house and surrounding property looked quite a bit like the photos he'd come across in the library. But as far as he could tell, there weren't any Dobermans.

Animals were messy. People like the Ivys wouldn't want any animals around, not even a guard dog. But the dog didn't matter. Nash didn't want *in* the place. The last thing he needed was to get arrested for breaking and entering. No, he was waiting for someone to come out, but it seemed tonight was going to be another bust, just like the night before. And the night before that.

It was past midnight. Earlier, he'd watched the devoted couple leave together, and he'd watched them come home together. Right now they were probably upstairs doing it. For some reason, the thought of her in Donovan Ivy's bed disturbed him in a way he didn't want to analyze.

What was his problem? It was nothing to him.

He pushed back the car seat to make more room for his legs. He crossed his arms at his waist, leaned back his head and closed his eyes.

Sara Ivy sat on the bathroom floor, eyes closed, head against the wall, a nearly empty bottle of twelve-year-old Scotch resting against her thigh. She was still wearing the white evening gown with beaded and sequined trim, still wearing the teardrop diamond earrings and matching necklace.

From the adjoining bedroom came the sound of Donovan's even breathing. Asleep. He always fell into a deep sleep after staking his claim on her.

She should shower. Wash him away. Have to wash him away. But it never did any good.

Don't you feel sorry for yourself. Don't you dare feel sorry for yourself.

But she did. Sorry as hell.

I'm sorry. You're sorry. We're all sorry.

She ran her tongue across her lips. She tasted salt. And Donovan. She could smell his after-shave. His sweat.

Slut. She felt like a slut.

She sat there for a few more minutes. Then, with carefully orchestrated movements, she shoved herself upright, the tile floor cold under her bare feet. No pantyhose on. No underwear. Donovan had taken care of that.

Is it worth it? Sleeping with someone like Donovan Ivy in return for a cushy life?

No. No, it wasn't.

Two thoughts took up residence in her brain.

She hated herself.

She had to get out.

She lifted the bottle to her lips, finished off the contents, then carefully placed the empty on the countertop. She looked at her reflection in the mirror. At the smeared lipstick. The circles under her eyes.

I hate you.

She leaned forward too far and lost her balance. She grabbed at the marble countertop, catching herself, knocking over a glass decanter of perfume.

It didn't break. She didn't understand why it didn't break. It should have shattered into a million tiny pieces.

Donovan.

She listened. Had the noise wakened him?

Breathing.

From the bedroom came the sound of steady, steady breathing.

She let out her own breath, righted the decanter, then made her way out of the bathroom, to where Donovan was sprawled facedown across the bed. Nude.

Donovan was proud of his body. He was *obsessed* with it, working out every day.

He mumbled something, hugged the pillow tighter, and then was quiet.

With arms hanging limply at her sides, she stared at him.

She wished he were dead.

No, she wished *she* were dead.

With the crystalline clarity that sometimes came with too much drink, she understood what she must do.

With a calm, sure serentiy she hadn't felt in years, she slid the diamonds from her ears and let them drop to the carpeted floor where they fell with a soft thump. The necklace followed. Then she turned and left the room. She walked down the stairs. When she reached the first floor, she shut off the alarm system, unlocked the front door, and stepped outside.

Barking.

A dog was barking.

It wasn't an I'll-kill-you bark, but an annoying lets-make-noise-for-the-hell-of-it bark.

Off in the distance, another dog heard it and took up the cry.

Nash came awake in stages, slowly realizing that he wasn't in any of his usual sleeping spots: the battered lawn chair on the roof of *Shoot the Moon*, or inside his car in the parking garage.

Stakeout.

He was on a stakeout. At the Ivy House.

Nash was straightening from his slouched position when someone in white moved through the main gate.

Sara Ivy.

All right. This was it. The moment he'd been waiting for. She was sneaking out in the middle of the night for a secret rendezvous.

Heart pounding, he slumped back down in the seat and watched through the steering wheel, expecting to see someone pick her up.

No one came.

There was no traffic. Every sane person had been asleep for hours.

Without hesitation, she crossed under the yellow glow of the streetlight before being swallowed by the darker shadows as she moved down the sidewalk.

Not wanting to lose sight of her, he waited as long as he dared, then turned the ignition key, the roar of the ordinarily quiet engine seeming as loud as a dragster's.

She didn't notice.

She had two blocks on him, but her white dress was a shifting, shimmering glow in an otherwise dark street.

He inched away from the curb, lights off, letting the car coast, trying to keep to the shadows. But it didn't matter. So intent was she on her liaison that she never looked back.

With a remote part of his consciousness, he dimly understood that he'd wanted her to be more than she appeared. Now he discovered she was everything he'd suspected—and less.

Disappointment dropped like a tiny stone deep in his belly.

Who was she meeting? Cray? Somebody else?

As he rolled along, his eyes on Sara Ivy, he felt on the seat beside him for his camera. He switched on the flash, the charging battery creating a high-pitched whine.

Where the hell was she going? All the way to Lake Michigan?

He watched as she crossed the boulevard.

Deciding to follow the rest of the way on foot, he pulled to the curb and cut the engine. Nash grabbed his camera, shoved open the door, and slid out. Glancing over his shoulder, he eased the door shut, then took off in the direction Sara Ivy had taken, the slap of his sneaker soles sounding like gunshots in the still of the cool September night.

Twin beams from car headlights cut through the darkness. Nash hung back until the car passed, then hurried across the lanes, taking cover behind a stand of tress. Ginkgo trees—the ultimate survivors, he noted with the total irrelevancy that sometimes came to him at odd times.

The beach. She was meeting someone at the beach.

Talk about a windfall, he told himself, trying to drive away his disappointment, trying to dredge up some conviction and enthusiasm for the project at hand. He couldn't have come up with a better setting if he'd done a cut-and-paste.

He glanced around, searching for a car that might belong to her boyfriend, her lover.

Nothing.

It looked as if she may have been stood up.

Even though there was no more than a half-moon, the night wasn't all that dark due to the glow generated by the city. Light pollution. Was there any purity left anywhere? Was there anyplace pristine and untouched?

Off in the distance, beyond Sara Ivy, was the black of the lake, as big and endless as the ocean, with shifting silver reflections.

Sara Ivy walked toward those reflections. She moved with purpose, never hesitating, never looking in any direction but straight ahead.

Toward the water.

What the—?

He could see the white of her dress, moving, moving . . .

What the—?

She walked to the water's edge . . . *and kept on walking.*

She walked until the water met her knees. She walked until the water met her thighs. She walked until the water met her waist.

A midnight swim?

She cut smoothly through the water, stroke after stroke, moving away from shore.

Away, away.

He waited for her to turn and come back.

He waited.

And waited.

There was nothing out there but eighty miles of water.

And then it came to him that she wasn't meeting any lover.

Not unless that lover was death.

Suddenly he was running, his feet flying. Just short of the place where the sand became damp and solid, he dropped his camera. Then, not bothering to untie his shoelaces, he tugged off his sneakers.

His jeans.

Time. Was there time?

He lost sight of her.

There! He spotted a flash of white in the water.

He unbuttoned, unzipped. He shucked denim down his legs and kicked the jeans free. Then he was charging through the water, fighting the drag, feeling as if he were moving in slow motion.

When the water reached his thighs, he made a surface dive.

Cold.

Jesus, it was cold.

The shock took his breath away.

He began the crawl, using long hard strokes, combining the scissor kick with a flutter for added momentum.

Now that he was in the lake, his field of vision had dropped to almost nothing. Through the water that stung his eyes, he tried to spot her, but there was nothing but black water.

Was he moving in the right direction? She could be three feet to his left and he might not know it. He might miss her.

She could be anywhere.

There.

A flash of white. Ahead. To his left.

He stroked harder, his lungs beginning to burn, his shoulder beginning to ache.

He shouted, trying to get her attention, swallowing a mouthful of lake water. He inhaled, choked, and kept moving in the direction of the white flash—which had again disappeared.

Black.

Everything was black.

Son of a bitch.

Son of a—

His fingers brushed something. Cloth? He grabbed again, and this time he made contact with wet, clinging fabric and ice-cold flesh.

He dug his fingers into the fabric and didn't let go.

He yanked.

He felt her weight shifting.

She went under, taking him along.

He was going to die.

They were going to die.

He wasn't afraid of dying. He'd just never thought

it would happen like this. A gunshot wound would have been more his style.

With one hand still buried in the folds of her dress, another gripping her arm, he kicked. His head broke the water's surface and he inhaled, pulling in life-giving air.

She fought, shoving at his chest, trying to struggle free of his grip.

They went under again.

They surfaced.

He could feel her dress, wrapping around his legs, ensnaring him.

"Let me go!" she sobbed, pounding and shoving at his chest while he struggled to keep them both afloat.

He complied.

She immediately sank, then surfaced, gasping for air, yet at the same time moving away from him.

He grabbed her again.

"What are you doing?" she cried.

He thought about all the clichéd things he could say. *You don't want to kill yourself, do you? Nothing's ever as bad as it seems.* "Still looking for that interview," he said.

"Leave . . . me . . . alone—"

He was done talking.

There was a good reason for holding a potential drowning victim by her chin. So you didn't become a victim, too.

He maneuvered her onto her back, cupped a hand beneath her chin, and began swimming toward shore—which suddenly seemed extremely far away.

She didn't fight him long.

As soon as she stopped struggling, he realized how exhausted he was, realized she was probably even more exhausted.

She was small, but her dress was made out of some kind of beaded crap, weighing her down. That made the going tough. Real tough. The lights of the shoreline didn't seem to be getting any closer.

Don't think. Just keep moving.

His lungs burned. His legs and arms screamed. His face, with the stitches that weren't supposed to get wet, felt as if someone had taken a branding iron to it. He began to doubt that he would make it.

Just when he thought he couldn't go another foot, she got a second wind and started fighting him again.

Both of her hands tugged at his forearm, trying to loosen his grip. Her body bucked.

He wasn't going to make it. Wasn't going to—

His knees crashed against the lake bed. He took a few staggering steps, let go of her, and collapsed on his hands and knees. He was pulling air into his burning lungs when he realized she was floundering beside him, coughing and sputtering and breathing in more water than air.

He grabbed her by the back of the dress and dragged her through the water to the packed sand where he let go and fell to his hands and knees.

She coughed and coughed, gagged up water, and coughed some more.

She finally collapsed beside him, her cheek against the sand, hair like seaweed across her face.

It was cold. Cold as hell.

That was his first coherent thought as he struggled to bring his breathing under control.

Beside him, she wasn't making any noise.

He crawled over and rolled her to her back. He brushed the hair from her face, the sand from her icy, alabaster cheek, his fingers lingering . . .

Her eyes opened.

Water clung to her lashes, making them thick and spiked. She stared up at him. And stared. And stared. Hypnotic.

He had the strange sensation of looking in a mirror, of seeing himself reflected again and again and again.

Finally her blue, shaking lips moved. "Why?"

The yellow light cast by the street lamps rendered her dress transparent. He could see that she wasn't wearing anything underneath. *Not a thing.* He could see the dark circles of her nipples. He could see the dark triangle between her thighs.

"Why?" she asked again.

Why he had pulled her from the lake. That's what she wanted to know. "Let's just say—" He paused, fighting for breath. "I don't like to stand by and watch a person kill herself."

"Is that something"—Her chest rose and fell as she, too, struggled to regulate her breathing—"you prefer to . . . take care of . . . personally?"

He could pretend to misunderstand, but he knew she was talking about what he did for a living. But who was she to condemn him?

"You have no qualms . . . about destroying a person's life on paper, so why . . . should you try to save mine now?" She was breathing easier. "To make sure I'm around . . . to give you more ammunition for your . . . tacky articles?"

Killing her with words. Was that what he was doing? Was that how she saw it?

He pulled his gaze from hers long enough to reassure himself that his camera was where he'd dropped it, a few yards away in the sand. Then he looked back at her. Her nipples, her thighs, her face. Her sweet, deceptively innocent face.

He could take a picture of her now, like this.

For a fleeting second, he wanted her to be the innocent, wanted her to be more than she was. And he wanted to be whole, and new, and unbroken. For a fleeting second . . .

He somehow found himself touching her, stroking his fingers down her cheek, her jaw, following the thin column of her throat. His thumb moved across her pulse point.

With one finger, he traced a line from her Adam's apple to the indentation where collarbone met collarbone.

He needed to know what had driven her to go for a stroll in the lake. "What happened?" he asked. He needed to know that he hadn't had anything to do with it.

He thought about her pampered life, about the way she was wasting it with Ivy—a man to whom she was nothing more than a bauble, a possession. Such an existence would be harder to take than living on the street. At least on the street, you were your own person. You didn't have to answer to anyone.

He suddenly found himself feeling a reluctant admiration for her. She was either awfully brave, or awfully foolish. But death . . .

"It's so final," he found himself saying.

Her eyes grew distant as she focused on something in her mind. "Yes."

The single word was spoken with a bleak, wistful longing that sent a shiver up him.

"What made you want to kill yourself?" he whispered.

The unexpected directness of his question seemed to jar her, wake her up, bring her back to reality. And reality was him: Nash Audubon, tabloid journalist.

Her eyes lost their faraway look. Her jaw stiffened.

Her face took on the same resolve he'd seen the night she'd snubbed him at the Renaissance.

She grabbed his hand and shoved it away, then said through gritted teeth, "I broke a nail."

Another way of telling him it was none of his damn business.

He laughed, then moved away to sit with his crossed arms resting on bent knees.

She sat up. The front of her dress molded itself to her. Her nipples were stiff from the cold. She rolled to her knees, her bottom to him. He could see the dark cleft between her buttocks.

He grew hard.

She got to her feet. She took a few steps to stand swaying over him.

He had to tip back his head to look at her. God, she was beautiful.

She glanced in the direction of his camera, then back at him. She walked over, picked up the camera, then strode toward the water.

She was going to throw it in the damn lake.

When she reached the water's edge, she stopped and held it out, above the water, poised to drop it, waiting for his reaction.

All he could do was look at her, dumbfounded.

Like wet tissue. Her dress was wrapped around her like wet tissue.

He ached. He throbbed.

He let out a groan and buried his face against his arms.

A few seconds later, she came to stand beside him. Looking under his arm, he could see her bare feet. He wanted to take one of them in his hand. He wanted to wrap his fingers around her ankle. He wanted to move up her calf, her knee, her thigh . . .

"Take it."

He lifted his head.

She stood over him, legs spread, camera in her hand. "Take it," she repeated.

He would like to take *her*. Right now. On the beach.

Slowly, he reached up and lifted the camera from her hand.

"Take a picture of me."

He stared at her, confused.

"That's what you wanted, wasn't it?"

He nodded.

She took a few steps back. "Then take it."

He looked at the camera. It suddenly seemed alien to him. For some reason, he couldn't remember how to operate it. The hands that were holding it trembled.

He turned it . . . and saw that the light for the flash was still on. It was ready to go.

Without conscious thought, he lifted the camera to his face. He framed her in the viewfinder. He focused, automatically adjusting the aperture. Blurred image became sharp, crystal clear.

The black of the lake behind her. Her white skin. Her dark eyes. Her black hair. Her nipples . . . Her nipples . . . The dark triangle of hair between her thighs . . . Her thighs . . . An erotic angel.

He pressed the shutter release. The flash lit up the night, momentarily blinding him.

When he could see again, she was gone. Vanished.

He turned, half expecting to see her taking to the water, maybe this time as a mermaid. But no, he swung back and spotted her beyond the ginkgo trees. She was moving in the direction of her home, going back to where she'd come from. Back to her mansion and her pool. Back to Donovan Ivy.

Human kind cannot bear very much reality.
—T.S. Eliot

Chapter Six

The frigid water had sobered her, and she was much more cognizant on her way back to the house. During her walk to the lake, she had been unaware of her surroundings. This time she could feel the hard sidewalk beneath her bare feet, the impact jarring her heels. The night breeze, as it moved over damp skin, caused goose bumps to surface. Water from her dress trickled down her legs, and dripped from the ends of her hair, falling on her shoulders.

The changes weren't just physical. Before, she'd walked to the water with no thought, her mind numb, her body moving on autopilot. Now she was thinking.

Suicide.

A good idea.

Who would have thought the reporter from *Shoot the Moon* would suddenly turn into a Boy Scout?

She had been prepared to die. She had *wanted* to die. It seemed she couldn't do even that right.

And yet her thoughts weren't all dark, all negative. There was something deep within her that hadn't been there before. A spark. A little whisper of her old, old self.

When she had handed Nash Audubon the camera and dared him to take her picture, she had felt *alive*.

More alive than she'd felt in a long time. The irony didn't escape her.

From behind came the sound of an approaching car. She didn't turn. She didn't look.

The car slowed until it kept pace with her.

Was it him?

"Ma'am?"

Not him. Not Nash Audubon. She turned her head slightly.

A police car. A policeman.

Her heart rate increased.

"Do you need help?" he asked. The passenger window down, he leaned over the seat, craning his neck to see out.

He was young. A little hesitant. Not quite sure of what to make of her.

"You shouldn't be out here this time of the night, by yourself. Get in and I'll take you home."

She'd heard about men who disguised themselves as police to prey on unsuspecting women. But this car had the emblem on the door, the caged backseat. About as authentic as they came.

She stopped.

The car stopped. He opened the passenger door.

Home.

To Donovan.

Yes. She would go home. But it would be the last time.

She got into the car and closed the door.

The officer put up the automatic window, pulled down on the gearshift lever, and eased away from the curb. "Been swimming?" he asked conversationally.

"Yes."

"The beach closes at nine o'clock." His voice was patient, calming.

"I know."

Maybe he would arrest her. Maybe he'd put her in jail. Maybe she could stay there a long, long time. Locked up. Safe.

"You shouldn't swim alone."

"No."

But she hadn't been alone, not for long anyway. If she'd been alone, she wouldn't be sitting in a police car right now.

"Turn here," she directed.

When they reached the black, wrought-iron gate that marked the southernmost boundary of the Ivy estate, she said, "This is it."

He stopped in front of the gate. "Donovan Ivy's?" he asked incredulously. "You work for him?"

She put her hand on the door handle and looked the policeman in the eye. "I'm married to him." Then she opened the door and stepped out.

"Remember, no swimming after nine o'clock. And . . ." He cleared his throat. "Mrs. Ivy? Next time you go for a swim, don't go alone, and don't forget to bring something to cover up with."

She thought about telling him that she usually didn't run around half naked. That she was a nice girl, modest, conservative. But it was too much of an effort. And he probably wouldn't believe her anyway. No, she had more important things to do than chat with Officer . . . Officer—She squinted at his badge—Officer Sherrard.

He swallowed, and she thought she detected rising color in his face. "I could write you up for indecent exposure, but I won't. Just don't do it again."

She nodded, then walked to the gate and entered the safety code on the electronic keyboard. The gate swung open and she walked up the lane, to the house.

* * *

Donovan woke up cold.

In the darkness, he reached for his wife, his hand coming in contact with nothing but empty bed.

"Sara," he called groggily, pulling the covers over him. "Sara," he said, more impatient, beginning to come more fully awake.

He heard a sound in the hallway.

The bedroom light came on. He blinked and lifted a hand to shield his eyes from the glare.

Standing in the doorway was his wife. Still wearing the dress she'd had on earlier. And it was wet. Her hair was wet. . . .

"Sara?"

She remained in the doorway, her hand on the light switch.

There was something odd about her, something more than just her wet clothes and wet hair.

He looked at her more closely. She didn't seem drunk.

And then it came to him. The fear. The fear he usually saw in her eyes was gone.

"Where have you been?" he asked. "Swimming in the pool with your clothes on?"

As if he'd never spoken, she walked past him to the dresser. She opened a drawer and pulled out a pair of sweatpants. A sweatshirt. Underwear.

When he'd been about ten, he'd owned a dog for a short time. What was its name? He couldn't remember. It didn't matter. What was important was the way it acted around him. He used to call it, and the dog would come to him, crawling on its belly, pissing all over itself. Then, when it reached him, Donovan would kick it.

Something about the dog obeying him even in its

fear had turned him on, had given him an almost sexual satisfaction.

"Sara. Come here."

She straightened and faced him. And again, he could see no sign of fear in her eyes.

"I'm leaving," she said.

A second passed.

Then two.

He threw back his head and laughed. She wouldn't leave him. At least never so blatantly. She didn't have it in her. And anyway, she loved him. She *needed* him.

And he needed her. Upon occasion. He threw back the covers so she could see just how much he needed her. How big and hard he was for her.

Over the last couple of years, she'd quit exciting him. That was, until the business with Cray had started, and now he couldn't get enough of her. "Come here, Sara."

He watched her face, waiting for the fear to jump in her eyes.

She stared at him, her bundle of clothes pressed tightly to her chest. "No."

She sounded tough, but he knew better. Now he could sense her fear. Hell, he could practically smell it. That knowledge excited him even more.

She turned toward the door.

The chase.

He liked her submissive and trembling, liked her scared and dry and crying, but he also liked the chase.

He was fast.

She'd taken but two steps when he lunged and caught her, grabbing her, pulling her around to him, his fingers digging into her arms.

"Never walk away from me!"

He brought up his hand.

She flinched. He experienced a hot flood of pleasure.

"I'm leaving," she repeated, her mouth trembling, her breathing coming fast.

Words. That's all they were. Words. She would never leave him. He'd never let her. She belonged to him.

He grabbed a handful of her hair, burying his fingers deep within the wet strands. He tugged. "You ungrateful bitch," he said through tightly clenched teeth, his voice low. "You were nothing when I met you. I gave you *every*thing! *Everything!*"

He tugged at her hair, bringing tears to her eyes.

She would come around. She always did. In the end, she always obeyed him.

"I'm leaving," she said for the third time, as if trying to convince herself that it was really going to happen.

Damn her! She was pushing him. Couldn't she see how she was pushing him? Didn't she know how many times he'd restrained himself, he'd saved her from being beaten to a pulp?

Saved her.

He stared and stared into her gray eyes, and as he did, he slowly became aware that the fingers ensnared in her hair were making contact with something gritty.

Sand.

In her hair. On her neck.

Sand.

She hadn't been swimming in the pool at all.

She'd been to the beach. With Cray. She'd been to the fucking beach with Cray.

Rage exploded. His vision burned red. Muscles bunched in his neck. His vocal chords stretched taut.

"You bitch!" he shrieked. "You ungrateful, sneaking bitch!"

He hit her.

She fell, striking her head on the door, which crashed against the wall. Almost immediately she was on her feet.

She ran from the room.

Donovan's world was a volcano of rage. With hands in front of him, he charged.

He could hear her pounding down the stairs.

His feet pounded after her. He moved, unaware of the steps beneath him. Through an angry haze, he saw her on the ground floor. Telephone in her hand.

"Help! Help me! Please!"

He ripped the receiver from her hand and slammed it back in the cradle.

Then he hit her. "You won't leave me! You'll *never* leave me!"

He was losing control, and he didn't care. Losing control and he loved it. "Say it. Say you'll never leave me!"

He hit her again.

"Say it!"

She was bleeding. There was blood on her dress.

Look what you're making me do! Look what you're making me do!

"Say it!"

He hit her again. "Say it!"

She was lying on the floor. She made a sound, a muffled, unintelligible sound. More like a whimper. More like the sound his dog used to make.

He kicked her. "Say it!"

"Leave you . . ." she whispered, her hair covering her face, her back curled to him. "Never . . . leave . . . you . . ."

His arms and legs shook. He fell to his knees and pulled her to him, hugging her tightly. "My Sara. My little Sara." He dragged his fingers through her tangled hair. His hand came away sticky. "You love me so much. You love me so much. Do you hear me? Sara? Sara?

Under the glow of the red safelight, Nash stared into the developing bath. He gently rocked the tray, agitating the solution, watching as Sara Ivy slowly materialized.

He hadn't been able to sleep. After getting back into his jeans—not an easy feat for someone wearing wet boxer shorts—he'd picked up his car and gone straight to *Shoot the Moon* to process the negatives.

Somehow he'd managed to operate the camera even though he'd been in a trance. The picture was perfect. The focus was perfect. Depth of field just right. And Sara Ivy . . .

The camera had picked up things his eye and flustered brain had missed. The delicate perfection of her skin. Even though the photo accentuated the dark smudges under her eyes, the effect was haunting and sexy at the same time.

With a pair of tongs, he lifted her image from the developer, let the solution drain off, picked up a second pair of tongs and transferred the print to the stop bath. Thirty seconds later, he switched it to the fixer. Another minute and he was turning on the overhead white light.

He stared at the photo, experiencing a deep need. But along with that need came more disturbing emotions: She somehow managed to stir up an ache inside him, a tenderness he didn't want anything to do with. Looking at her picture made him feel vulnerable. Looking at her picture made him feel weak, human. For the first time in twelve years, he was afraid.

There was more going on than appeared on the surface. Rich, happily married women didn't try to kill themselves. Oh, sometimes they *pretended* to, but it was usually a carefully orchestrated act put together to restore hubby's flagging interest, to get a little romance going.

Sara Ivy, on the other hand, had meant it. She'd wanted to die. She had been angry at him for stopping her.

God. What the hell was going on? Why was he letting himself get involved?

She was married.

She was in trouble.

He wanted her.

No matter what logic he used, he couldn't deny the fact that he wanted her.

He blew out a breath and rubbed his burning eyes, trying to shake her off. He put her picture in the final clean rinse, ran fresh water and left the room, turning off the light and taking the set timer with him.

In his office, he sprawled out on the tattered orange sofa, not bothering to unfold it. He lay there in the dark until the timer went off. Then he made his way back to the darkroom, turned off the water, lifted the photo from the clear bath, and spread it out to dry.

By the time he made it back to the couch, night was almost done.

He watched as light crept between the slats in the blinds, watched as the black turned to gray, watched as the Chicago dawn came in, not on little cat feet, as Carl Sandburg had once put it, but with a yearning ache he couldn't quite define, and even less understand.

* * *

Nash was dreaming about rutabagas when the sound of a key in the lock brought him to partial consciousness. Knowing it had to be Harley or Tootie, he shifted on the couch, trying to ease his stiff spine, then settled back, hoping to get a couple more hours of sleep.

Without even trying to be quiet, Harley came in, rudely slammed down a stack of papers on the desk, and asked, "Have you seen the news?"

Nash groaned and rolled to his side, his face toward the back of the couch.

Behind him, Harley flicked on the television.

"Come on, Harley." Nash wrapped the pillow around his head. "Give me a break."

But even with the pillow, Nash could hear Harley flipping through the channels.

"Turn it down," he groaned. "Turn it down."

"I think you'll want to hear this."

The familiar voice of a local female newscaster blared from the set. "And when we come back, the story of the Sara Ivy beating and possible rape, a story that has Gold Coast residents fearing for their safety and the safety of their loved ones."

Nash shot from prone position to sitting, both feet on the floor.

"What . . . ?" he croaked.

"Sara Ivy's in bad shape," Harley said, restacking the papers and parking himself on the corner of the desk. "Happened early this morning. Guess she'd been drinking and decided to go for a swim. Left the house in the middle of the night, took a dip in Lake Michigan, then walked home. On the way back, somebody worked her over."

Nash swallowed, but it didn't do any good. The lump was still lodged in his throat.

The commercial ended. The anchor introduced the story, covering basically the same ground Harley had covered. Then they cut to a live interview with Donovan Ivy.

Microphones were jammed in his face. "Mr. Ivy, did you see or hear anything?"

Ivy shook his head, his expression dazed. His voice, when he finally answered, reflected shock.

"No."

He was a wreck. He hadn't shaved. His shirt was wrinkled, his eyes bloodshot.

"My wife . . . She's a remarkable woman. She somehow managed to crawl home, then tried to call nine-one-one. The telephone fell on the floor."

"And you completed the call?"

"Her call had been cut off, so I put another one through."

For the first time in twelve years, Nash felt like crying. Jesus. He should have known better. He should have seen her safely home.

"I believe we have a recording of that first nine-one-one call," the reporter said.

They waited, then Sara Ivy's recorded voice, a voice filled with terror, was heard. *"Help! Help me! Please!"*

Nash ran a trembling hand through his hair. "Jesus."

"The police suspect that rape was the motive. Do you know if your wife was a victim of rape?"

Donovan Ivy looked around, his face a mask of torture. "How can they ask the guy that?" Harley said. "And they say *we* have no feelings."

"I . . . uh . . . don't know." Donovan Ivy struggled to pull himself together. "They took some samples. They're running tests."

"What about the police officer who claims to have seen your wife that night?"

The question seemed to surprise him, throw him off. "I don't know anything about that."

"What is the extent of your wife's injuries?"

"Head trauma. That's what they're calling it."

"I understand there was a lot of blood."

"Please, please. Could we talk about something else?"

The reporters' ruthless questions brought back flashes of other such questions, of another time . . .

Nash squeezed his eyes shut, blocking it out.

Attack. Rape. Blood.

His fingers began to tingle. He started to get dizzy. He was going to throw up.

He was vaguely aware of Harley, babbling in the background, his voice seeming to come from the other end of a long tunnel. "That just got him thirty thousand sympathy votes. Hell, I might even vote for him now."

There was a hum in Nash's head.

"You know what I think?" The hum got louder and louder. *"I think he's bullshitting everybody. That's what I think. I think it's all an act."*

The hum became a roar.

"Hey, bud." Harley's voice came to him through that long tunnel. "Hey, man. You okay?"

Nope.

Goin' down.

Goin' down.

Nash tried to open his eyes. The room slanted. He shut them again. He tried to stand, staggered, and fell back against the couch.

Something was pressed against his face. Over his nose and mouth. A bag. A damn paper bag.

"Breathe," Harley instructed. "Just breathe normally."

Nash breathed. In and out. Little by little, the room cleared.

Sometime during his little spell of the vapors, Harley had turned off the television. Little by little, Nash came around, until he was well enough to hold the bag himself.

He was drenched in sweat. As wet as if he'd just gone for a swim in Lake Michigan. "Thanks," he said when he felt able to breathe without the bag. "Where'd you learn that trick?"

Harley shrugged. "I hyperventilate upon occasion."

Nash nodded. Of course.

"It's nothing to be ashamed of."

"Right."

Outside, on the street below, a horn honked. Another answered.

"Don't take the Ivy thing so hard. It wasn't your fault."

"You don't understand," Nash said. "I was with her last night."

Seconds passed.

Nash frowned. "Don't look at me like that. I didn't hurt her, for chrissake!"

"I know, I know. But don't let anybody know about this or Ivy will try to dump the blame on you."

Nash found himself talking, telling Harley what had happened.

When he was done, Harley said, "It wasn't your fault. Under the circumstances, I doubt she would have let you see her home anyway, so quit flogging yourself."

But Nash couldn't quit thinking about her. As the day went on, he stayed close to the television, waiting for updates.

That night, he sat on his tattered couch. In his hands, he held two photos of Sara Ivy. He stared from one to the other, one to the other.

In the first one, he'd captured her in a moment when she'd thought she was totally alone. Her back to the restroom wall, eyes closed, head back, throat exposed.

Bleak.

And the picture from the beach . . .

Radiant. Haunting. Sexy.

He'd accused her of living in an ivory tower, an ivory tower she'd tried to escape.

Attacked.

Beaten.

Maybe raped.

His hands trembled. He dropped the pictures. Then, elbows on bent knees, he ran the fingers of both hands through his hair. Jesus. Oh, Jesus.

The eyes see only what the mind is prepared to comprehend.
—Robertson Davies

Chapter Seven

The next morning, as Nash ate chicken pot pie and drank lukewarm instant tea while watching the news, an update on Sara Ivy came on.

"Although lab tests have shown that the only semen found in Sara Ivy's body was her husband's, a motive of rape hasn't been entirely ruled out. At this point, with the exception of the statements by Mr. Ivy, everything is speculation and will remain speculation until Mrs. Ivy regains consciousness. At that time, it is hoped she will be able to shed some light on the attack and give the police something that will aid the stalled investigation."

Next came an interview with Sara's doctor. He explained about brain swelling and fluid leakage and about how they had to keep her sedated until most of the danger was past.

The picture cut back to the live newscast and the seated anchor—a meticulously groomed woman of about thirty.

"Meanwhile," the woman read, "when urged by doctors and nurses to leave his wife's bedside for a few hours of much needed sleep, Donovan Ivy refused. And so he remains nearby, exhausted and rumpled, keeping silent vigil. When others offered to take his place, he said he didn't want his wife awakening to find strangers at her side."

The anchor picked up her papers, tamped them together on her desk, and said, eyes to camera, "I guess there are still a few good men out there."

Irritated, Nash flicked off the television. Donovan Ivy was managing to turn his wife's beating into a media blitz. Harley was right. This was going to get him some votes. Lots of votes.

A hum.

In her head.

Voices. Far away.

Noises. The deep, comforting rumble of a motor, like something in the basement of a big building. In her mind's eye, she visualized huge, shuddering, sheet metal ducts.

There was a light show behind her lids. Flashing patterns that shifted with the sounds, seemed to be part of the sounds.

Sara slowly opened her eyes.

Light.

White. Blinding.

She shut her eyes.

Later. She'd try again later. . . .

Later came.

And with it came the same disorientation, the same confusion. She opened her eyes again. Her lids were so heavy. So incredibly heavy . . .

White. Everywhere.

White walls. White ceiling. Blinding white light.

"Darling."

Donovan's voice.

The ceiling slanted. The room spun.

She tried to remember, tried to recall what had happened. She'd been drunk. She'd walked to Lake Michigan. She'd tried to kill herself. . . .

He had been there. He'd pulled her out. He'd saved her life. And what a life it was to save.

"Mrs. Ivy? How do you feel?"

She struggled to keep her eyes open. She blinked, struggling to focus.

Dr. Westfall. Theirs was a mutually beneficial relationship. He gave her the drugs she needed. In return, he was paid well for his services.

He'd taken care of her broken arm, taken care of her when she'd had her miscarriage. He'd been with her through bad times, so many that he was almost a father figure to her. He may have been a dotty old fool, yet his kindness had always been impossible for Sara to resist. For all his incompetence, she felt as if he really cared. And for Sara, that was something. That was a lot. Pathetic though he was, unethical though he was, she was glad to see him.

"It's nice to have you back," he said.

His kind, soothing voice, so like a minister's, or perhaps a funeral director's, made her weepy.

"There, there." He patted her arm. "Your husband has been very worried about you. We've all been very worried about you."

Then, to Donovan, "I'll leave you two alone a couple of minutes."

Alone? Panic fluttered. Panic threw itself against cement walls. *No. don't leave me alone with him.*

But it was too late. Dr. Westfall was gone. Donovan stood by her bedside.

"How are you feeling?" He leaned over the bed, placing a careful hand on her arm. "I've been so worried. When I found you on the front step, I thought I would die. What would I do without you?"

Found her?

"The police are doing everything they can to try to find the animal who did this to you."

Find the animal?

Once again, she struggled to remember. She recalled walking home. Someone had given her a ride. A policeman. Yes. She'd felt so brave. She'd planned to tell Donovan she was leaving. She *had* told him. And he'd beaten her senseless. Now he was trying to say someone else had done it.

He was insane.

Something she'd known for years.

Oh, God. It hurt to think.

She wouldn't let him do this. She wouldn't keep quiet this time.

"I'll send a message to your father to let him know you're all right. I'm sure he's seen the story on the news. In fact, why don't I call him?" Donovan picked up the bedside phone. "What's the number?" He waited. When she didn't answer, he pushed several buttons, put the receiver to his ear, saying, "I'll just call information."

He gave the operator the town, followed by her father's name. He jotted down the number, then pushed the disconnect button. "We wouldn't want to upset him, would we?" he asked as he dialed the number. "How old is he by now? Almost seventy, I'd guess. A prime candidate for a heart attack."

Her head hurt. Flashes of light moved across her vision. It was getting harder and harder to think.

What did he want? Why was he doing this? *He is threatening to hurt your father if you tell the truth.*

Yes. That was it.

Receiver to his ear, Donovan waited, listening. He covered the receiver with one hand. "Maybe you'd like to tell him yourself." He put the phone to her ear.

"Hello? Hello?"

A deep, comforting voice. Her father's voice. A voice she hadn't heard in years.

She pressed her lips together and shook her head.

"No?" Donovan asked in mock disbelief. He shrugged and placed the receiver back in the cradle just as Dr. Westfall returned.

"What? Crying again?"

"She's overwrought," Donovan explained.

"Poor dear."

"Hurt," Sara said on a half-sob. "I hurt."

"I'll give you something so you can rest." Dr. Westfall ordered morphine. When the nurse arrived with the drug, he rolled Sara to her side and stuck the needle in her hip.

"There," he said, pulling down her gown. "That should give you some relief."

"Yes," she whispered, hoping it would come quickly.

Within two minutes, her fingertips began to tingle. Her tongue felt thick. Sleep beckoned. And with it, darkness. Blessed, numbing darkness.

The next time Sara opened her eyes, she was alone.

Her head still hurt. Her vision was still blurred. But at least Donovan was gone.

Then, from the vicinity of the hallway, she heard footsteps.

She quickly closed her eyes, hoping whoever it was would think she was asleep.

She listened.

Quiet.

Nobody there.

Dazed by pain, confused by the lingering effects of the morphine, she tested her limbs, first lifting her arms. Something snagged—

"Hey, hey," a man's voice whispered. "Don't do that."

A hand touched her, gently putting her arm back alongside her body on the bed.

"You'll pull out your IV."

She slowly opened her eyes. In the glow of the fluorescent ceiling light stood Nash Audubon. From her drug-enhanced perspective, he looked like a vision from the afterlife, a shimmering, not quite real entity.

An angel.

The image was such a contradiction to how she thought of him that she experienced an unexpected urge to laugh. Instead, she smiled somewhere deep inside.

"You're—" The word came out a startling croak. She swallowed, licked her dry lips, then tried again. "You're . . . an . . . angel."

His sober frown broke into a smile that seemed a part of the light that surrounded him. And then he laughed. It was a rusty rumble that came from deep within his chest, a sound of genuine surprise and delight.

"Am . . . I . . . in heaven?" she wondered out loud.

Nash, wearing a faded denim jacket, the cut along his cheekbone a maroon scab, looked like freedom. His hair was wind-tossed, as if he'd been riding a motorcycle, or driving a car with all the windows down.

"If you're in heaven," he said, "then I'm in the wrong place."

She struggled to focus her mind, to make sense of his presence in her room. She must have gone to hell. That would explain everything. "There are . . . bad angels," she ventured.

He laughed again.

The sound made her feel warm.

Something blossomed in her once more. This time, the smile reached her face.

Pain.

It knifed through her head.

She gasped and squeezed her eyes shut. Not dead. Definitely not dead.

"Where does it hurt?"

He touched her brow. He slid his fingers across her skin, magically finding the spot. "Here?"

She gave an almost imperceptible nod.

He smoothed his fingers across her brow, barely skimming her skin. His touch was soothing, somehow easing the pain.

Finally, when she dared to open her eyes again, she asked, "You're here for a story, aren't you?"

He drew away, and his expression sobered. "I came to see you."

To see her?

Don't be nice to me. It makes it harder. It makes everything harder.

Under any other circumstances, she would have called his bluff. Came to see her. How ridiculous.

Instead, to her horror, she felt a flutter in her chest, in her throat. It would be nice if he'd really come just to see her. She closed her eyes.

Don't cry. Don't you dare cry in front of him.

A tear slipped from under her eyelid and rolled down the side of her face.

"I'm sorry," he whispered. The pain she'd felt in her head had somehow gotten into his voice.

He touched her free hand, lifting it. And she noticed that the pads of his fingers weren't heavily callused like her father's, and they weren't soft like Donovan's. They were firm, tough.

Something brushed her fingers. Something soft. Warm.

A careful touch. A reverent touch.

Nash Audubon's lips.

"I'm sorry—" His breath caressed her knuckles. Then he grew still, as if listening.

"Bye, Sara."

He laid her hand back down. She heard the sound of movement, then silence.

A little later a firm footfall sounded in the distance, outside the room, followed by Donovan's voice. "There was no phone call for me." He spoke to someone in the hallway, using the tone of voice he always used when addressing waiters, waitresses, clerks, tellers.

"I'm sorry, Mr. Ivy."

"Next time, get your message straight."

Nash sat in the office of *Shoot the Moon*, watching the late news update on the Ivy beating.

"When Mrs. Ivy regained consciousness, she could only say she never saw the person who attacked her. Even though a suspicious car had been spotted three nights in a row near the crime scene, even though the Ivys have a security system, no clues to the identity of the perpetrator have been found. Even the officer who came forward and claimed to have seen her that night could not be reached for comment. We were told he's been transferred to another city.

"So now, five days after the brutal attack, Mrs. Ivy is being released from the hospital to return home." The anchor confronted the camera. "A home that used to be her haven, her place of refuge. But no more."

The live broadcast cut to a remote recorded earlier that day. As the broadcaster once again went over the details of Sara Ivy's attack, the screen showed Sara leaving the hospital.

Nash jumped up, grabbed a videotape, shoved it in the VCR, and pushed the *record* button.

His eyes flashed back to the screen.

Sara Ivy. Walking down the steps. Her husband's arm around her. She'd lost weight. Weight she couldn't afford to lose. And the way she carried herself, with an incredible weariness—she seemed beaten down. Defeated. Not the woman he'd seen on the beach, the woman who had stood so defiantly before him and demanded to take her picture.

Her eyes.

Her eyes were dark, lonely pits. *She looks so sad.* He couldn't handle seeing that sadness.

What was wrong with him? He could remember a time when other people had been able to turn him inside out. But that had been long ago, before life had made him what he was now.

Nash watched as the Ivys paused near the limo, watched as Donovan Ivy opened the door for his wife. She looked up at him, then away.

Nash watched as she got into the car, watched as Donovan slid in behind her, watched as they drove away.

When the piece was over, Nash stopped recording, pushed the rewind button, and watched it again.

Something was wrong. Something bothered him. Something more than the way she looked. Something more than the unhealthy circles under her eyes.

When the tape ended, he played it again. And again. With each replay, his hands knotted tighter. But as many times as he watched it, he couldn't figure out what was bugging him, couldn't figure out what didn't seem quite right, so he simply chalked it up as another figment of his unhealthy infatuation.

Fashions, after all, are only induced epidemics.
—George Bernard Shaw

Chapter Eight

Sara looked through the Chicago phone book, but could find no number for Nash Audubon. She called information.

No listing.

She looked up the number for *Shoot the Moon*, and dialed it.

And if *he* answered? What would she say? Would she beg?

A man's recorded voice came on the line, a voice she didn't recognize. Kind of young, kind of California. "I'm not here. Leave a message."

She hung up and tried again later. This time someone answered, but it wasn't Nash. It was the voice from the answering machine.

She didn't speak.

"If you're another jerk calling about that article in last week's *Moon*—"

Sara cleared her throat and broke in. "I . . . I . . . ah, was looking for Nash."

"Nash? Why?" the voice asked suspiciously. "You a collection agency? Parole officer?"

Sara let out a sigh. "No, I'm neither of those things."

"Hang on."

She heard a clatter, then footsteps that faded into

the distance. The man shouted Nash's name. A minute later Nash was barking into the phone.

She pulled in a breath.

"Hello?" he repeated with growing irritation.

"This is Sara Ivy," she finally said.

Silence.

"I ... was wondering ..." She swallowed and gripped the receiver tighter. "About the picture you took of me on the beach."

She couldn't wait to get the conversation over with. Her words came out one on top of the other. "I want it. I'll pay you for it."

She was playing right into his hands, leaving herself wide open to blackmail, but she didn't know what else to do. She couldn't let him put that picture in *Shoot the Moon*.

She waited and waited and waited—so long that she began to think they'd been disconnected.

He finally spoke. "It didn't come out."

"What?"

"The picture. It didn't come out. The film got wet or something."

She sank into a nearby chair, knees trembling.

Thank God. Oh, thank God.

Some women drank to take their minds off their lives; some cleaned. Sara did both.

She dug through her closets, deciding to get rid of about a quarter of her gowns, most of them ones Donovan had picked out. She wasn't allowed to wear any of them more than four times, only once if the gown had been purchased for a big occasion such as the literary auction.

She had recently heard of a place on the South Side called Two Timers that sold used clothes.

Since Donovan didn't allow her to drive or take mass transit, she had to hire a taxi. Early in their marriage, she'd had a chauffeured car at her disposal, but Donovan had quickly decided a car made it too easy for her to leave the house, gave her too much freedom.

At Two Timers, the cab driver, an elderly man with pictures of his grandchildren on the dash, was kind enough to help carry in the boxes.

Sara thanked him and gave him a generous tip before he left.

"Wouldn't want a job, would you?" joked the shop owner, dragging Sara's boxes across the gritty wooden floor.

"Are you looking for someone?"

The woman straightened, pushing her woolly, gray-streaked hair from her face. "Been looking for a year. Nobody wants to do volunteer work, especially in this part of town."

"I might be interested."

"You?" The woman snorted. "It's dirty work, and the clientele aren't very uptown."

A few years ago, Sara had applied for a job at a nursery. The building had smelled like damp earth. There were shelves of seeds. There were greenhouses full of live plants. It had made her think of home.

When Donovan found out, he'd been furious, saying that no wife of his worked, that no wife of his needed to make money.

But volunteer work. He might feel different about volunteer work. . . .

That night over dinner, with a burning stone in the pit of her stomach and the hand that held her fork shaking hard, she told Donovan about the opening at Two Timers.

"A used clothing store?" He looked across the table at her, the candlelight flickering over his features. He was dressed in a white oxford shirt and sand-washed khaki slacks, the epitome of casual, sexy male elegance. "Volunteer work?"

Her pulse raced. She could hear her heart pounding. Carefully, she put down her fork, not on the china plate where it might clatter, but on the tablecloth. Then, hiding them from his eyes, she gripped her hands together in her lap. "Yes."

"For the homeless?"

She swallowed and nodded.

Ever since her hospitalization, Donovan had been especially nice to her, not just publicly, but privately. And so far, he hadn't wanted sex.

Yet she knew better than to relax. For him, anger seemed to be a cumulative thing. The longer he went without blowing up, the more unpredictable he became.

"I think that's a good idea," he said.

She relaxed her clasped hands, her palms stinging where her nails had bitten into them.

He was going to let her go!

Inside, she was dancing, singing.

Freedom! Every day, she would have eight hours of freedom.

"But not full-time," he said. "That wouldn't look good."

Her heart plummeted. Was he going to give her something, only to take it away?

"Afternoons?" she asked. "Maybe twelve to five?"

He lifted his glass of wine to his mouth, a thoughtful expression on his perfect features. "Five o'clock? That's kind of late. The days are getting shorter. It will soon be getting dark around five."

"I'm not sure they'd want me if I worked any less."

He put down the glass. "How many days a week are you talking about?"

"I . . . I don't know. Five?" Go for it. "Six?" She knew seven was unthinkable. Even if the store were open, Donovan would never allow her to work on Sunday. They always went to church together on Sunday.

"Three. No more than three."

She was careful to hide her disappointment. Three days. Only three days. But three was better than none.

She patted her mouth with her napkin, pretending to wipe at food she'd not eaten. She knew better than to let him see how much getting out of the house meant to her, knew if he had the slightest inkling, he would take it all away.

She placed her napkin over her plate. "I can see what the owner says. If that isn't satisfactory, then I won't do it."

Marilyn's need was so great that she was willing to take anyone who could breathe, for any amount of time.

"If I had what you spend on cab fare, I could retire," Marilyn told her when Sara had been there a week.

"My husband doesn't want me to drive downtown," Sara said, making excuses for Donovan, pretending he was a good husband. Luckily, he hadn't insisted on a limo, deciding that a cab would appeal more to the "lower class."

"That's nice of him." Marilyn dug through a plastic laundry basket looking for the mate to a sock. "When I was married, my husband wouldn't have cared if I'd walked through Cabrini Green to get home."

"You're single?" Sara asked with envy.

"Divorced four years and loving it."

"Kids?"

"All grown up. Got a girl going to beauty school, and a boy in the navy."

"That's nice," Sara said with a wistful smile.

"Nice now, but they put me through some bad times. Drinking. Smoking dope. Worrying about whether or not they were practicing safe sex. The teen years are hard all the way around. Most kids don't know what they want or who they are when they're eighteen. They think they do, but they don't."

"I was very young when I got married."

"Well, sometimes things work out okay."

"Yeah, well . . . I don't know."

"Not so okay?"

This was supposed to be her time away from her real life. Sara wanted to be someone else while she was at the thrift shop. She wanted to forget about her life with Donovan.

"Just the same problems everybody else has," Sara said with a smile.

Marilyn nodded.

Much of the donated clothing consisted of evening wear—not practical for many of the store's patrons who needed winter clothes. But the evening wear kept the store in the black. Women who had heard of expensive designer gowns selling for a fraction of the price made their way to the little shop.

The homeless made up the rest of the clientele, with their selections given to them free, or, if the person happened to be extremely proud, purchased for a small sum.

In a short time, Marilyn was leaving Sara to run the store by herself. She'd been at the shop two weeks when a reporter for the *Chicago Journal* stopped to do a story.

"You'll have to wait until Marilyn gets back," Sara told him.

The man took a picture of her, then explained. "It's you I want the story of, not the shop."

She thought about Nash Audubon, and how he'd passed as a legitimate reporter.

"Your husband isn't going to like it if I don't do the story."

"My husband?"

And then Sara realized the interview had been orchestrated by Donovan. Of course. What would look better than to have his wife doing volunteer work?

"Where shall we meet next week?" Sara asked as the reporter closed his tablet. "The Jerry Lewis Telethon? Habitat for Humanity?"

He laughed, not realizing she was angry.

"Aw, now ain't that sweet," Harley drawled, folding the newspaper he'd been reading. He tossed it to Nash, who caught it with both hands. "Now he's got his wife hawking wares in one of the most dangerous sections of Chicago. I always knew he was a nice guy."

Nash shook open the paper, and quickly scanned the article and its photos.

Harley was talking again, but Nash wasn't listening. He was too busy noting the location of Two Timers.

Sara moved through the shop, straightening, buttoning, picking up, making sure the clothes were in the right places.

Cold, damp, November air clung to the wooden floor. It crept up the hem of her jeans, curled around her bare ankles.

Should have worn socks, she told herself. But the

change in weather had been a surprise. Two days ago it had been in the seventies. Now, a few days after Halloween, they were predicting freezing temperatures for the early dawn hours.

The street-front window was covered with condensation. Through the drips, she could see a bit of gray sky, and it looked as if the forecasted snowflakes were beginning to fly.

Snow.

She felt a small, quiet thrill. Life?

The bell above the door jangled, drawing Sara's attention.

A man. Wearing a black wool baseball cap. Bent against the cold. Brushing snowflakes from the shoulders of his leather jacket.

She was alone, and Sara couldn't help but feel apprehensive. She had heard too many ugly stories about this area of town. Nonetheless, she squeezed through the racks of clothes and made her way to the front.

The lighting was bad. Two days ago a fluorescent bulb had burned out and had yet to be replaced. Now, even though it was early afternoon, the winter sky had cast the shop in shadow.

The man pulled off his cap, revealing dark shaggy, *familiar* hair.

Nash Audubon.

She stopped, a hand against the rough fiber of a wool coat, her body blocked in by the tightly packed clothes.

She hadn't seen him since the hospital. And sometimes she wondered if she'd really seen him then. She'd been so full of morphine that the five days she'd spent in bed seemed no more than a drug-induced dream.

He slapped his cap against one leg. "You alone?"

He frowned as he looked past her, into the darkness at the back of the store.

She tucked her hair behind her ear, and noticed that her hand trembled. She quickly dropped it, made a fist, then clasped both of her hands tightly together.

Darvon.

She was careful not to take any during work. It dulled her head too much, but sometimes the craving came over her. She would feel a tense ache in her back and neck, she would feel a headache coming on, and she was tempted.

She watched as Nash moved deeper into the interior of store, his eyes quickly taking in and dismissing several racks of clothing.

"Are you looking for something?" she asked.

He glanced at her, then back at the clothes. "Leisure suit. Looking for a leisure suit."

"Leisure suit?"

They couldn't *give* away leisure suits. In fact, Marilyn had just been talking about the wasted rack space and the possibility of throwing out the really unpopular garments.

"Maybe something with a pattern," he said. "Paisley perhaps."

"Paisley." A paisley print leisure suit. Okay.

She moved to the back of the store. "There might be something here," she said, trying to shove the clothes aside. Dust drifted up in her face. She sneezed. And sneezed again.

Bless you.

Excuse me.

Bless you.

With her nose still tickling, she continued her search, more careful this time as she pushed the hangers along the metal rod.

Everything she saw was unsightly. Marilyn was right. They needed to do some serious weeding.

"I'm sorry. I don't think—"

"Here."

He shot forward, the single word an exclamation, or a greeting.

He slapped his cap back on his head and dug out a dark brown leisure suit trimmed with heavy white thread. He hooked the hanger over the rod, freeing both hands. "Or how about this?" He pulled out an off-white ribbed knit, looked it over, then hung it with the brown.

Then came a navy-blue-and-red plaid. He brushed at the shoulders with the side of his hand, stirring up the smell of musty clothes and vintage sweat.

As soon as he left, she was going to tackle the entire back section of the shop.

"What do you think?"

He lifted the suits with an index finger under the hooks. He fanned the suits out in front of him, leg extended.

"I don't know . . ."

One at a time, he tucked the suits under his chin.

She took a couple of steps away, hoping he would follow. "We might have something else up front."

He stood where he was, admiring the suits, turning them this way and that. "It'd be hard to beat these babies."

So much for the idea of trying to coax him to a different section of the store.

"I'll have to try them on," he announced. "That way, you can help me choose." He held up his last selection. "I like brown, but it's hard to beat plaid, don't you think?"

She gave him a weak smile and made a helpless gesture with one hand. "The dressing room is over there." She indicated a little cubbyhole with a baby blue plastic shower curtain strung across the opening.

While holding the suits, he struggled out of his jacket. "Here," he said, handing it to her. "Will you hang onto this?"

She took the jacket, still filled with the warmth of his body, and folded it over one arm. He was moving to the dressing room when the bell above the door jangled.

"Gonna be frost on the pumpkin tonight," said an old woman who stopped by at least twice a week.

Many of the customers were regulars. They came to chat, or they came to look over the merchandise, or they came for the hot coffee Marilyn always kept on hand.

"Got anything new?" the woman asked, rocking from side to side on arthritic ankles as she made her way through the crowded shop.

Sara knew little about her except that her name was Ruthie and she loved clothes with color and shine. "A sequined blouse came in yesterday."

As soon as Sara had spotted it, she'd quickly tucked it away for Ruthie. Now she rounded the glass-topped counter, draped Nash's jacket over a chair back, then dug through a huge, soft-edged cardboard box until she found the blouse.

She spread it out on the counter. Even in the dimly lit shop, the sequins sparkled.

"*Ah.*"

Sara smiled at the reverence in the woman's voice, watched as she ran knotted fingers across the textured fabric.

"Isn't it beautiful?" Ruthie asked. "Look how it catches the light."

"I thought you might like it," Sara told her. "Shall I put it in a sack for you?"

"Thanks, hon."

Sara had no idea what Ruthie did with the clothes she carried away from the shop. Many of them wouldn't even fit her massive figure.

"Isn't this great?"

Sara and Ruthie looked up to see Nash standing in the center of the shop, stocking feet apart, arms spread wide.

The jacket sleeves hit him a good four inches above the wrist. Between his white socks and the hem of his pants was about three inches of hairy leg.

He should have looked a total fool, and he *did* look a fool, there was no question about that, but not a *total* fool. He also looked . . . adorable.

Ruthie didn't even try to contain her reaction. She put a hand to her chest and laughed. She hooted. She *howled*.

"What?" Nash looked insulted. "Is brown not my color?"

"Oh, that's precious." Ruthie shook her head from side to side, bosom heaving, eyes watering.

Sara had her fingers pressed tightly against her lips.

With both hands braced at his waist, Nash said, "I'll have you know that last year I was voted best-dressed man in Chicago."

Then he stomped off, back to the dressing room.

Sara and Ruthie looked at each other. Their brows went up. Their lips formed a circle, and they burst out laughing.

"That man is precious," Ruthie said, rubbing her eyes. "Just precious."

"Babies are precious," Sara informed her. "Puppies are precious."

The woman shrugged and gathered up her bag. "Grown men can be precious, too. Thanks, hon." She winked at Sara, then left, chuckling as she stepped out the door.

Nash made another appearance. This time he was dressed in his own clothes, his cap tilted, his hair pulled back from his forehead. He tossed the suits on the counter. "I'll take them all."

"Going for that best-dressed award again, huh?" Sara asked as she rang up Nash's purchases.

"Clothes make the man."

The cash register was ancient, with round ivory buttons that were cracked and yellowed, and a lever that had to be pulled down in order to engage the punched keys.

"Three dollars."

He dug around in the front pocket of his jeans and finally pulled out a wrinkled bill. He took his time smoothing it out, then placed the curled currency in Sara's outstretched palm.

One dollar.

Then he pulled out another bill and proceeded to smooth it, just as he had the first one. He finally placed the second one in Sara's hand, a hand that was now noticeably shaking.

By the time he'd added the third bill to the stack, she could feel sweat gathering under her armpits. A trickle ran down the middle of her back, stopping at the waistband of her jeans.

She stuck the money in the cash register. Once the drawer was shut, she pressed the back of her hand to her upper lip, to the beaded perspiration.

Her nerves were tight. She needed something to calm them. She shouldn't have tried to go cold turkey. She shouldn't have—

He reached across the counter and grabbed her

hand, holding it in his firm grip. A grip that was familiar.

"You okay?"

His blue eyes held the same earnest quality they'd held the night at the Renaissance, when everything he'd spoken had been a lie.

He may have pulled her from the lake, and he may have come to visit her in the hospital, but he couldn't be trusted.

"It's a little hot in here," she said, knowing she should try to pull her hand away.

He grabbed her other hand and pressed them together, enfolded them in both of his.

"You're cold."

He rubbed his hands gently over hers, the friction quickly warming them.

Her gaze moved from their hands, up the buttons of his flannel shirt, past his chin, his lips, his nose, to stop at his eyes—and there she saw the same smoldering light she'd seen that night at the beach, when she'd stood brazen and almost naked before him.

She tugged.

Surprisingly, her hands slid free. Surprisingly, he let her go. She wasn't used to that where a man was concerned. Where superior strength was concerned.

Flustered, she turned and pulled a plastic bag from a nearby box, all the while aware that he was watching her every move.

He watched as she folded the clothes. When she had trouble getting them into the thin plastic grocery bag, he held the edges open and she slid the folded suits inside.

He looped his fingers through the handles and lifted the bag off the counter. "Bye, Sara."

She nodded.

He was walking toward the door, when he stopped and turned.

"What would you have been willing to give me if that picture had come out?"

Now he was back to the old Nash Audubon. "Are you talking blackmail?"

"I'm just curious, that's all."

Her fingers gripped the edge of the countertop. "I guess you'll never know."

"No?"

"No."

She couldn't see his expression, silhouetted as he was against the light of the window, but she could feel his eyes on her.

And then his voice came from the shadows.

"Even if the picture had come out," he said, "I wouldn't have run it."

She would have liked to believe that, but she knew better.

He waved his package. "Take care."

Yes. "Take care."

Two minutes after Nash was gone, she remembered his jacket. She grabbed it from the chair and ran out the door. She looked up and down the sidewalk, then across the street, but could see no sign of Nash Audubon.

Nash looked over his left shoulder, then pulled the Fairlane away from the curb, the blast from the heater hitting him full in the face, the air more cold than warm.

Thoughts came one on top of the other.

It wasn't a good place for her.

Not a safe place.

None of my business.

After her recent attack, you'd think that husband of hers would have more sense.

None of my business.

She was too thin. When she talked, her voice trembled, her hands moved nervously.

None of my business.

But she'd joked with him, and she'd smiled at him.

And he would see her again.

After all, she had his jacket.

What is there in thee, Moon! that thou shouldst move
My heart so potently.
—Keats

Chapter Nine

CSeveral days later Sara sat at the kitchen table, drinking her morning coffee, when Donovan hurried in, straightening the knot in his tie. On his way to the coffeepot, he paused to put his hands on her shoulders and brush his lips against her cheek, then continued on.

"There's been a good response to your job," he said, pouring coffee into his cup.

Donovan was in a good mood. He'd been in a good mood for three days. How much longer would it last? And when it was over, would he explode?

And *why* was he in a good mood? Was he seeing someone?

She hoped so.

"Maybe I was a little hasty in saying you could work just three days a week."

She was careful to hide her excitement. Was he going to allow her to spend more time at the shop?

How little it took to please her now, she thought wryly. Years ago, a job in a used clothing store would have been a drudgery. Now she lived for the time she spent in the little shop. When she wasn't downtown at the store, she counted the days and hours until she'd be there again. And when she was there, she tried to hang on to every second, wishing it wouldn't slip away so fast.

Without taking time to sit, Donovan scanned the counter. "Where's the Sweet'n Low?"

Her heart pounded. She'd forgotten to put it back in the customary place when she was finished with it. "Here." She pushed the bowl with the packaged sweetener to him.

He picked out a pack, shook the granular down, tore the paper and poured the contents into his coffee.

Even though she didn't want any, she reached for the jelly. Without looking up, she said, "The store is open late every Friday." She spooned out some jelly and dropped it on her plate. "I'm sure Marilyn could use the extra help."

"Tonight?"

She picked up her knife and carefully spread jelly on toast she probably wouldn't be able to eat.

"How late?"

"Until nine."

He thought a moment. "Nine? That would work out perfectly. I have a business meeting that will last until ten or eleven."

She wanted to laugh. She wanted to shout and clap her hands. Instead, she kept her head down and continued to spread jelly on the cold triangle of toast. It wouldn't be wise to let him see her happiness.

After Donovan left, Sara wanted to head for Two Timers immediately, but she forced herself to wait. Donovan had spies everywhere, and it wouldn't do for her to be seen leaving early. Who knew what he might suspect?

On the way downtown, she chatted with the cabdriver. He told her about his family, about how he was going to night school. Upon arriving at the shop, she gave him way too much money and told him to keep it, then rushed into Two Timers.

One look at Marilyn and the excitement Sara had been struggling so hard to contain exploded. She grabbed the older woman by both hands and jumped up and down like a schoolgirl who had just been told she could stay up an extra hour.

"I'm staying until nine," she announced giddily, pumping Marilyn's arms. "Isn't that wonderful? I can stay till nine o'clock!"

Marilyn laughed. "Calm down, girl! Stay *where* until nine o'clock?"

"Here! I can stay here!"

"Here?" Marilyn looked at her with a Girl, are you crazy? expression.

Sara didn't care if she was acting totally out of character. She had a glorious nine hours of freedom ahead of her.

Before heading downtown to Two Timers Nash decided to shower and shave. Spruce up. With a towel slung low around his waist, he stood in front of the sink, going through the medicine cabinet. He pulled out a dust-covered ceramic container of after-shave that looked as if it had been excavated from a dig. He finally managed to get off the rusty cap. He took a whiff, almost gagged, then dumped the contents down the drain. He'd have to go au naturel.

Then he dug out a pair of scissors and trimmed the hair on both sides of his head, around his ears. The back he left as it was, partly because he liked it long, partly because he didn't think he could cut it himself.

Plan A. He would be charming.

It had been a long time. Did he know how to be charming anymore? Did he have any charm left in him?

Back in his office, he slipped into jockey shorts, a pair of jeans that weren't too worn-out, and a blue chambray shirt. He hoped the heat from his body would steam out the wrinkles.

He couldn't stay away from her; it was that simple. He'd tried, but he'd found himself mooning around like some lovesick teenager. He'd stared at her pictures so many times that he could conjure up both shots in his mind—total recall.

But that wasn't enough. He needed to see her, talk to her. Touch her.

When he got to the shop, it wasn't Sara behind the counter. It was a formidable-looking woman with hard eyes, and frizzy hair that stuck out in every direction. She was wearing a black polyester sweat suit with white lint all over it.

"Can I help you find something?" she barked.

"I . . . I . . . ah . . ." His gaze moved through the shop, searching, not finding.

No Sara.

"I left my jacket here the other day," he said, his voice vague, his mind distracted.

"So you're the one. Sara said you might be stopping by to get it." The woman strode across the wooden floor, boards creaking. She bent, grunted, then came back, holding his jacket.

He took it. "Thanks." Sara. Where was she? He shifted his jacket from one hand to the other.

The heater that hung from the ceiling kicked on. Hot air blew in his face.

Plan B. Time to go to Plan B.

Did he have a Plan B?

He slipped into his jacket. He straightened the collar. He shoved his hands into the front pockets of his jeans. Killing time. Playing for time.

A plan gone awry. That's what he had.

He'd pictured himself coming in. Sara would be alone in the shop, like before. He'd turn on his charm. The evening would pass before they knew it. Suddenly it would be time for her to close. That's when he would offer to give her a ride home. On the way, he would ask her if she wanted to go out to eat. . . .

He walked backward. "Well, thanks."

When he reached the door, he pushed against the metal handle. The door swung open. He turned—and practically ran into Sara Ivy.

"Nash," she said breathlessly, looking up at him in total surprise. Her cheeks and lips were flushed from the cold. Her breath was a soft cloud.

"I see you got your jacket," she said. She was bundled in a long green wool coat. She wore red gloves. Outside, it was snowing again. She had snowflakes in her dark hair. In her hands, she held a large cardboard pizza box.

He stepped to one side, holding the door open for her. He followed her in.

"Sorry, Marilyn. They didn't have anchovies, so I got sausage on the whole thing." Sara slid the box across the counter.

She tugged off her gloves, stuffed them in her pocket, then she shrugged out of her coat.

"Can you stay for pizza?" she asked Nash, making him realize he was standing there, as if waiting for an invitation. "No, I—"

"Oh, come on," Marilyn said. "What man refuses food?"

"No, really—"

She wasn't listening. She was already tossing out paper plates and napkins like a Las Vegas dealer.

At the same time, Sara was shoving things around under the counter. She finally found what she'd been looking for: three foam cups. She lined them up on the counter. One tipped over. She straightened it, knocking over another.

"They're full of static electricity," she said, laughing, giving up, letting them roll around on the countertop while she opened a liter of cola.

Nash stepped forward. It looked as if he was staying to eat pizza. "I'll hold while you pour." He picked up one of the cups, feeling a small electrical charge against the palm of his hand.

And so he found himself perched on a wobbly stool, sharing a sausage pizza with Sara Ivy and her intimidating friend.

Sara was different tonight. He had seen her a total of six times, and each time she surprised him. Each time she wasn't what he'd expected. Tonight, she seemed full of suppressed excitement. Radiant. Her eyes were bright, her cheeks and lips red, her face was open, friendly.

He found himself watching her, studying her. The way she moved. The way her hands floated when she talked. The delicate line of her jaw and cheekbone. The way the light fell on her. Her exotic fragility.

I saved her life, he found himself thinking, not with arrogance, but rather dreamlike awe.

They talked. They ate. They ate and they talked. At some point, Marilyn left to wait on a customer.

They talked about winter. They both liked it.

Snow. Had he ever skied? No? Snowshoeing? He'd snowshoed? How wonderful.

They talked about Chicago. Sears Tower. Big Stan. Big John.

She'd never been in either? She had to be kidding.

"Do you think Chicago really means city of the big smell?" he asked.

"Shoulders. Isn't it city of the big shoulders?"

He loved the El at night. She'd never ridden it. He couldn't believe it. "Never?"

"Never."

"What about Resurrection Mary? Ever driven up Archer Street to see her?"

"The ghost? No. Have you?"

"Oh, yeah. Lots of times. Did a piece on her last fall."

"Have you ever actually seen her?"

"Well . . . no."

They talked about movies. He knew she loved musicals. He had planned to tell her he loved them too. But in the end, he found he couldn't lie.

"I hate them," he admitted, his words surprising himself. "Unless you count *Rocky Horror*. I've seen that at least twenty times."

"I've never seen it."

"Never?"

"Never."

"What a wasted youth."

She smiled.

And he smiled.

"Time to close up." Marilyn's voice came to them from the other side of the shop.

Like somebody waking from a dream, Nash looked around, wondering how much time had passed, hardly believing it when he spotted the clock on the wall. 9:10.

Sara let out a gasp, jumped to her feet, and started picking up cups and napkins.

With Nash's help, the counter was clean in two minutes.

"How about a ride home?" he asked, shoving the trash into a sack, looking up at her. He slowly straightened, his heart pounding with a strange intensity. He felt the way he used to feel as a kid, when confronted with a girl he had a crush on.

"Ride?" she asked, as if she hadn't heard him right. She was suddenly agitated. "No, no. I don't think so. Thanks anyway."

"Sure?"

She nodded. "I don't need one."

The roller coaster he'd been on derailed.

For a brief time, he'd forgotten something very important. Sara Ivy was married.

Do you love him?

He thought about the nights he'd been on stakeout, sitting in his car, looking up at her window, watching the lights go out.

He had to stop the insanity now.

This was it. Last time.

Like a last cigarette.

Last drink.

Last look at a place you were leaving for good.

Last time.

He told her good-bye. He left the shop by himself. He drove back to *Shoot the Moon* by himself. On the way, he flicked on the radio and cranked up the volume, the bass rattling the windows, thumping in his chest.

If he didn't watch out, he'd start thinking. If he didn't watch out, he'd start feeling. If he didn't watch out, he'd fall in love. No way in hell could he let that happen. No way in hell.

A clever man commits no minor blunders.
—Goethe
If you're going to screw up, screw up big.
—Nash Audubon

Chapter Ten

Friday came around again. Every time the bell above the shop door jangled, Sara looked up, hoping—

No, last time he'd come for his jacket, she told herself.

He wouldn't be back.

Ding, ding.

She looked up.

Nash.

Wearing his brown leather jacket and faded jeans. A black T-shirt. His hair was different. She'd noticed it last time. It was cut above the ears, but long in back. She liked it that way. The slash across his cheek had healed to a red line. He would probably have a scar for the rest of his life, but it wouldn't look unsight—

"Hi."

She had been slipping a flannel shirt on a hanger. Now she grasped the hanger with both hands. "Hi."

With his hands deep in the front pockets of his jeans, he looked around, rocking on his heels.

The phone rang. She jumped. "Excuse me." Then, "I'll get it!" she shouted to Marilyn in the backroom.

She hurried, answering on the third ring. Someone wanting to know if they were open.

"Busy night?" he asked after she'd hung up.

"A little."

He cleared his throat, looked around, then back at her. "I was wondering . . . if you'd like . . ."

The heater kicked on, drowning out his words.

"What?"

"Party," he said. "Would you like to go to a party?"

A party? A million things ran through her mind at once. A party. She didn't do parties. What kind of party would Nash Audubon go to? It didn't matter. She would love to go anywhere with him.

"I couldn't." She turned away and slowly hung the shirt on the rack. She smoothed it over and over.

"Why not?"

Marilyn took that moment to make an appearance. "Yeah, why not?"

I'm married. I'm afraid. I can't. "I'm working."

Marilyn tucked a felt-tipped pen behind one ear. "Go ahead. I can handle the shop. Always did before."

Why was Marilyn encouraging the impossible? "I won't know anybody," Sara said lamely.

"If you don't like it, we don't have to stay," Nash said. "Say the word, and we'll go somewhere else. Say the word, and I'll take you home."

A party. With Nash Audubon. How dangerous. How terribly, terribly dangerous.

And unthinkable. Out of the question.

Sara signaled to Marilyn and both women walked to the back, heads together. "Marilyn, I can't possibly go anywhere with him," Sara whispered once they were out of earshot.

Marilyn shrugged. "Why not?"

"*Why not?* I'm married. That's why not."

"What's wrong with going somewhere with a friend? A friend who just happens to be a guy? If I asked you to go to a party, you'd go, wouldn't you? Being married wouldn't keep you from it, would it?"

"This is different."

"I don't see any difference. Go on, girl. If your idea of fun is spending nine hours moving smelly clothing around in a shop in the bad part of town, then you *need* to get out and party."

Sara thought about what Marilyn had said, then slowly turned and left the backroom.

She found Nash lounging against the counter, idly turning the rotating earring display. As soon as he saw her, he straightened, a look of expectation on his face. "So . . . ?"

"I have to be home by ten."

He relaxed and smiled a slow, pleased smile—a smile that took her breath away.

Before Sara could change her mind, Marilyn grabbed her coat and helped her into it, then practically shoved her out the door. "See you Monday," she said. Then lower, for Sara's ears only, "I'll cover for you."

There was no place to sit.

Sara stood by the open passenger door of Nash's faded green car, looking at the seat, or the place where the seat should be.

"Hang on a minute."

Nash gathered up handfuls of clothes and papers and magazines and trash and threw it all in the backseat. He clicked his tongue and shook his head. "That maid's getting lazier all the time."

He wadded up a flannel shirt, brushed off the passenger side of the seat, then gave an elegant sweep of one arm.

"*Entrez-vous.*"

What was she doing? she wondered as the car moved down the street. If Donovan were to call the store, if he were to find out she'd left, let alone left with Nash . . .

Nash maneuvered through turns and traffic, moving through the streets like a taxi driver. "I've got to stop by *Shoot the Moon*," he said.

She tensed, his words an unpleasant reminder of what he did for a living.

At *Shoot the Moon* she was honored with a grand tour.

Once inside the door, Nash grabbed a Blackhawks cap off the coathanger, slapped it on his head, and led her down the hallway.

"Here we have Harley's office." He pushed open a door to reveal a room that was neat as a pin. Plants hung from the ceiling. On the desk was an old Royal manual typewriter. Beside it, tidy stacks of papers. *In* and *out* trays, with the *in* almost empty, the *out* almost full. A wind-up clock, ticking loudly.

"Harley is paranoid about electromagnetic fields," Nash explained. "He types everything on the manual, then somebody else has to enter it in the computer for him." Nash turned off the light and closed the door.

"And this is Tootie's office." He opened another door. "Tootie's working late tonight because she's taking tomorrow off. Wave to Tootie."

Sitting behind a desk, almost hidden by a mountain of paper, was a wrinkled old woman. She was hunched in front of a computer screen, cigarette dangling from the corner of her mouth, her eyes squinted against the smoke.

Sara waved.

Tootie waved.

"Can't tell Harley and Tootie are related, can you?" Nash said. He closed the door. "She thinks smoking's medicinal."

"I heard that!" Tootie shouted. As soon as the words were out, she started coughing a dry smoker's cough.

"And to think she's only thirty-two."

"I—*cough, cough*—heard that too! I'm *eighty*-two, smart-ass!"

They moved on down the hall, back the way they'd come. "And this—" He opened another door. "—is my office."

A hand to the middle of her back, he coaxed her inside.

The first thing she noticed was the ragged orange couch. She hadn't seen one like it for twenty years. The second thing she noticed was that Nash's office was dreary. Neglected. Not messy, like Tootie's, but ... transient. Nothing on the walls. In one corner was a tiny microwave. Next to it, a coffeepot and a counter cluttered with canned food. Tuna. Soup. Nothing that would spoil. Nothing a person had to worry about.

He propelled her deeper into the room, toward a desk stacked with papers. In the center of the desk was a computer. He flicked a switch. The machine hummed, then made a series of sounds until pictures came up on the screen.

He moved the mouse, then clicked. "We don't do any of the actual printing here," he explained, leaning down, squinting at the screen. "Everything goes on a floppy and it's run down to a printer on a Hundred-thirty-eighth." He clicked a few more times. Articles in newspaper format came up. "Here's something I've been working on for next week's paper. It's a story about a group called Joggers Anonymous. They can't quit jogging."

"Is that bad?"

"Only for the jogger. Here's another one I'm calling 'Life's a Bitch, Then You Die.' "

Sara looked at the screen and read:

Another Chia Pet plunges to her death from a twenty-story apartment window. "She was so sweet," the heartbroken owner said. "Never a problem."

"Ohhh," Sara said, her voice full of sympathetic laughter. "That's so sad."

Nash shrugged. "We don't make the news; we just report it." He shut off the computer and straightened.

"Almost forgot." He crossed the room, opened a closet, and pulled out a plastic grocery bag. "The reason we stopped here in the first place."

A grocery bag. Very much like the one she'd given him at the shop. *Exactly* like it, in fact.

He dug inside—and out came a handful of leisure suit. "Which one do you want to wear?" he asked. "Harley took the brown, so that leaves the cream and the plaid."

"Is this for an article?" she asked. "Leisure suits anonymous, perhaps?"

"They're for the party." He shrugged out of his leather jacket and exchanged it for the plaid. The suit had looked bad before, at the shop. But at least it had been ironed. Now it was full of wrinkles, which Nash, as he lifted his arms to admire himself, actually seemed taken with.

He picked up the cream-colored suit and held it out to her. "This one's a little smaller."

She took the suit. He wanted her to put it on?

She held it up. She turned it. It didn't look dirty.

"There's a bathroom down the hall. It has a mirror. Not a big mirror, but a mirror."

"What kind of party is this?"

He looked at her and smiled. "Leisure suit bowling."

Sara had bowled only once before in her life, and that had been at a classmate's birthday party. She'd been ten, just about the age when embarrassing things were always magnified a million times. All she could remember was the humiliating experience of tossing the ball at the people sitting behind her. Whatever had happened after that had been a blur, blocked out the way traumatic experiences sometimes were.

When they arrived at Lakeside Lanes, people were already bowling.

The place had a bar atmosphere with dim lights, beer advertisements, and a smoky haze. Balls flew down varnished wooden alleys, crashing into pins, tossed by people dressed in leisure suits.

Sara and Nash walked up to the front counter and ordered bowling shoes from a balding, big-bellied gentleman in a starched bowling shirt.

"Gillette party," Nash informed him.

Without batting an eye at their attire, the man slapped a couple of pairs of shoes on the counter.

They carried their shoes across the carpeted entryway and found a place to sit at a low counter.

Bowling alleys never changed, Sara thought as she sat down in the orange plastic chair.

She wiggled her feet into a shoe that had, over the years, lost all suppleness. The strings had been broken and retied, the soles were hard and bumpy.

"How's the fit?" Nash asked, shoes on and ready to go.

"Like a wooden shoe."

He laughed. "The ultimate in comfort."

Then it was time to pick out a ball.

"What weight do you use?" he asked.

They stood in front of a wooden contraption that housed rows of dull black balls.

"I have no idea." She put her fingers in one of the balls and tried to pick it up. It didn't budge. She tried another. The holes were spaced too far apart.

"Here." With one hand, he tested the weight of a ball. "Try this one."

"It feels about right."

"If it's too light, you won't get as many strikes."

"I don't think we need to worry about that."

They found an empty lane.

"Let's take a couple practice shots," Nash said, placing his bowling ball in the metal return area, then sliding into the molded scorekeeper's seat.

Meaning Sara was supposed to go first.

She turned her ball, looking for the finger holes. She found them. She stuck in her fingers.

"Ever bowled before?" Nash asked suspiciously.

"Once. When I was little."

He got up out of the chair and came to her side. "You live in Chicago, but you've never been to the Sears Tower, and you've never ridden the El. Now you're telling me that you've bowled only once in your life?" He shook his head, and she wondered if he was teasing her. It had been such a long time since someone teased her that she wasn't sure.

He supported the ball with one hand. With the other, he arranged her fingers. "This one doesn't go in a hole, this one does. Feel better?"

"Thanks. I can do it."

"Never said you couldn't."

She stepped into the launch area, or release area, or whatever it was called. The last thing she wanted was for this to turn into one of those activities where the man wrapped his arms around the woman so he could show her how it was done.

Ah, never played pool, little lady? Never played miniature golf?

She glanced to her left, to see how the others were doing it. She put her feet together. She lifted the ball, supported it with both hands—and felt her pants begin to slide. With her left hand, she grabbed her waistband and held on. With the ball now held in one hand, she aimed. She rolled the ball down the alley. It got sucked right into the gutter, like metal drawn to a magnet.

All that work for a gutter ball.

"Whoa," Nash said from the scorekeeper's chair. "Hold everything."

"I am. That's my problem."

He stood, opened his jacket, undid his belt, slid it from the loops, and handed it to her.

She wanted to put on the belt by herself, but in the end she had to accept his help. She held the waistband of her pants while he wrapped the belt around her, leaving three inches of fabric sticking out the top. He finished by knotting the belt at her waist. "That should do it."

"And here I always thought leisure had something to do with comfort," she said.

"That was before polyester."

Their eyes met.

She couldn't pull hers away. Her heart began to hammer.

Beyond what was happening between them, balls clattered. People shouted, laughed.

He smiled, and she felt warmth flow through her veins. But that warmth was quickly replaced by terror. *This shouldn't be happening.* "I shouldn't be here," she heard herself confess in a tight voice.

"Sure you should."

But she saw something flash in the depths of his eyes. An awareness, as if he, too, suddenly found himself looking at the big picture, as if, for a fraction of a second, he'd stepped outside himself long enough to experience a stab of doubt, as if he, too, wondered where this was leading. . . .

She pulled her gaze away and quickly looked past him, desperate for a diversion. Coming toward them was a young man with the most beautiful long hair Sara had ever seen. And he was wearing what looked like the brown leisure suit Nash had purchased at Two Timers, except that it had been modified. The pants had been cut into shorts and rolled above suntanned knees. On his feet were white socks and leather sandals.

"That's my boss," Nash said, following the direction of her gaze.

This sweet-faced *boy* was Harley Gillette, disreputable owner of *Shoot the Moon?* A thorn in the side of the city of Chicago?

When Harley reached them, Nash made introductions. Harley smiled an angelic smile and shook her hand. "Glad you could come. And I'm glad you brought Nash. I was afraid he'd be a no-show. And we can't have a proper party without last year's best-dressed winner in attendance. He's got to pass the crown."

Someone shouted his name. Harley looked over his shoulder, waved, then swung back to Sara. "I've been trying to talk the owner of this place into letting us body-bowl, but so far he says no."

"Body-bowl?" Sara asked.

"You put on a crash helmet and throw yourself down the lane."

"Sounds like fun," she said dryly.

"I thought so." He shifted his weight from one foot to the other.

He's shy, she thought, intrigued.

"So," he said, with a shrug of his shoulders, "there's all sorts of food and stuff to drink in the back room. And bowl as long and as many games as you want."

And so they bowled.

From ceiling speakers, rock music blared while balls crashed into pins and people yelled and laughed and had fun. Somewhere amidst the chaos and noise, Nash gave her a few pointers, but not in an overt way. They came as suggestions, or comments on what he'd found worked for him.

Everything was moving so fast, hardly allowing time for thought. As soon as Sara was done with her turn and sitting down, it was time to get up again.

After a few frames, she learned that if she stood slightly to the right of center, she could keep the ball from going into the left gutter. And if she stood even more to the right, she sometimes knocked down a few pins.

Fifteen minutes into the game, she had her sleeves rolled up, a piece of string holding back her hair.

There were red arrows painted on the wooden floor, and if she stood on a certain mark, then took three steps and released the ball, she could sometimes get a lot of pins.

And one time, during the third game, she knocked down all of them!

A red light in the shape of a crown flashed above the lane. She screamed and clapped and jumped up and down in her size-seven saddle shoes and bundled leisure suit.

And when she turned around, Nash was sitting in the scorekeeper's chair, grinning at her, making her heart give a sudden leap, making her breath catch.

"Good thing you're wearing my belt," Nash said, his eyes shining, laughing.

She slid into the round plastic seat beside his and picked up the pencil as he moved into position to take his turn. As he leaned over to grasp the ball, air from the hand dryer blew the hair back from his face. The sleeves of his plaid jacket were several inches too short. Bare arms stuck out.

He took his stance—wide, short pant legs flapping, scrunched white socks above white-and-blue saddle shoes. He stood, feet together, back straight, ball braced in both hands, and aimed. Then released.

The ball went straight, but at the last minute, it veered to the left, clipping the corner pins, knocking down three.

"Nash is having a bad night."

The voice came from over her shoulder. She turned to see Harley examining the score sheet, his shining hair brushing the table.

"He usually does better?"

"Lots."

Her earlier suspicion resurfaced. What did Nash want from her? Why was he being so nice? "So he's playing badly on purpose," she said, the thought sobering.

"Mmm, I doubt that. He's not that chivalrous. I'd just say you probably make him nervous."

Harley smiled his sweet smile, patted her hand, and

straightened. Two minutes later, he was leaning against the shoe counter, microphone in hand.

"For the next two frames, everyone has to bowl left-handed!" he announced.

Then, five minutes later, "For the next two frames, everyone has to bowl with two hands."

After that, it was backward.

By the time it was over, Sara's chest hurt from laughing so much.

"I don't know when I've ever had so much fun," she gasped, trying to catch her breath.

"The magic hour is approaching," Harley announced. "The time when the crown is passed to the new leisure suit king, so get those votes in."

The magic hour? Sara's eyes scanned the walls, looking for a clock, finally spotting one at the end of the alley, near the first lane. 9:55.

Oh, God.

Oh, God.

She picked up her purse, took two steps, then remembered her shoes. She dropped into the nearest seat and began tearing at the laces, pulling them into tight knots.

"Had enough?"

Nash, crouching in front of her.

"I have to go." She frantically worked at the laces. "I have to go."

He brushed her hands away, calmly untangled the mess she'd made, and loosened her shoes.

She kicked them off, shoved her own soft loafers on her feet, grabbed her purse and coat, and ran for the door.

She was searching the street for a cab, when Nash showed up behind her.

"What the hell are you doing?"

"A cab," she said breathlessly, beginning to walk down the dark street, hoping to find a cab stop.

"I'll take you."

He didn't understand. She had to go. She had to leave *now*.

She heard a door slam. Heard an engine turn over. And then Nash was pulling up next to her, leaning across the seat and throwing open the passenger door.

"Get in."

She got in and quickly shut the door.

He pulled away, tires squealing.

"Your shoes," she said when she saw he was still wearing the bowling shoes.

"Grand theft bowling shoes."

When she didn't laugh, he added, "As much as I'd love to own these little jewels, I'll take them back later."

"Oh, my God."

"Now what?"

"My clothes."

She turned around. On her knees, she hung over the seat and pulled the bag containing her clothes from the backseat.

"I'll stop someplace—"

"No! *Keep driving.*"

She pulled off the jacket and threw it down. She turned and dropped into the seat. Her fingers went for the belt. She tugged at the leather knot.

"Oh, shit." She tugged some more. It wouldn't come undone. "I can't get it off! No, don't stop! Don't stop!"

With one hand on the wheel, while the car careened down the freeway, Nash tried to help her. She slapped his hand away.

"Just drive. *Drive.*"

She got it undone. Without unzipping the pants or removing the belt, she kicked off her shoes and slid out of the huge pants. Then she grabbed her jeans, turning them this way and that, finally finding the right way. She shoved her legs in, one after the other. She stood, her feet on the floorboard, her shoulders braced against the back of the seat, and tugged up her pants. She buttoned them, zipped them, then shoved her feet back into her shoes.

"Christ. What happens if you get home late? Do you get grounded?"

"Just drive."

"Yes, ma'am. Anything you say, ma'am."

They turned onto Lakeview Boulevard. One more minute and she'd be home.

Another turn and they were on Sara's street.

"Stop the car."

He kept going.

"Stop! Stop the car!"

He slammed on the brakes and pulled to the curb. "Your house is two blocks away."

"I want out here."

"I'm not going to dump you out two blocks away. Not after what happened to you a few weeks ago."

She grabbed her coat and purse and opened the door. Gone was the woman he'd bowled with, and the woman who had shared her pizza with him. She was once again the cold socialite, the rich bitch.

And then it hit him. She was just having fun with him.

Suddenly he saw everything clearly for the first time since he'd pulled her from the lake. Here he'd been mooning over her for days—hell, *weeks*—and she was just having fun with him.

What a relief.

What a goddamn relief.

He could play this game. He knew how. He understood the rules.

He could have her. He *would* have her, no strings attached.

So much for taking it slow. So much for the let's-get-to-know-each-other bull. So much for charm. They were both adults. They both knew what was going on. "Let's cut the crap," he said, his right arm draped over the back of the front seat. "I want you. I wake up wanting you. I go to sleep wanting you."

Without waiting for her reaction, he leaned forward, opened the glove compartment, dug around for a business card—a *real* business card—and handed it to her. "If you ever feel in need of . . . well, male companionship, you know where to find me."

He couldn't see her face. All he knew was that she was very still. Then she straightened and slammed the door.

As he watched her run up the street, he smiled. And the smile was a heartless smile, a smile devoid of emotion.

Would she come?

After using a line like that?

Not likely.

Not damn likely.

She comes more near the earth than she was wont, and makes men mad.
—Shakespeare

Chapter Eleven

When Sara got home, Donovan wasn't there. She raced through the house, tearing off her clothes. Upstairs, she tossed the clothes in the hamper, quickly threw on a pair of pajamas, and dove into bed.

An hour later, Donovan showed up.

She pretended to be asleep as he slid into bed beside her, smelling of cheap perfume and whiskey.

He didn't touch her.

He didn't say a word.

Thank God, she thought to herself as she struggled to keep her breathing steady. Thank God.

Sara took no interest in cooking, or decorating, or gardening. Why should she? The place they lived, or rather where they slept and ate, wasn't a source of happiness or security. The house was Donovan's domain, not hers. It was a showplace, not a home.

Nonetheless, she was able to fill her days, dividing her time between the shop and the Literacy Foundation. She attended meetings and fund-raisers, and although she was around many different people, she kept her distance, never becoming overly friendly. It wouldn't do for anyone to invite her and Donovan for dinner. It wouldn't do for her to have to reciprocate.

But no matter how busy she stayed, Nash's blatant confession kept coming back. *I want you. I wake up wanting you. I go to sleep wanting you.*

His words had both thrilled and terrified her. But what he'd said next had been a drenching with ice water.

You know where to find me.

What arrogance!

She hated him.

God, how she hated him.

It had all been a ploy. All of it. His visit to the hospital. His visit to the shop. The bowling party. He'd only invited her in hopes that their evening together would end in bed.

She should have known that being nice didn't come so easily to someone like him. He wasn't nice simply for the sake of being nice.

All along, she'd wondered what he'd wanted from her, suspecting that it was another sordid story for his sordid paper. She'd never dreamed he'd wanted *her.*

Never dreamed he'd wanted sex.

Sex.

That's what it all came down to. Men used it to dominate. To conquer. To control.

You know where to find me.

Damn it, he'd made her *like* him. And then he'd insulted her thoroughly, as only someone like Nash Audubon could insult a woman.

His face had been so smug, so sure.

You know where to find me.

What nerve!

What gall!

Days passed.

Little by little, Sara found her anger toward Nash

dissolving. Every once in a while, she would catch herself thinking about the fact that he wanted her, and strangely enough, that thought would make her feel good, feel a little powerful, in a world where she had no power.

Sometimes she would pull out his business card. Even though she had the address and telephone number memorized, she would look at it. She would run her fingers across the raised ink, admiring the simple lettering.

She would never go.

Of course she would never go. But she couldn't keep from thinking about it.

What would it be like? To be with him?

He would be masterful. Forceful. He would scare her. She didn't want to be scared.

No, she would never go.

She wanted him to come, to stop by the shop. Deep down, she waited. Deep down, she hoped.

But he didn't come.

Two weeks before Christmas, on the way home from work, she took a cab by *Shoot the Moon*. Rectangles of light shone from some of the third-floor windows. Which room was his? The corner? From the outside, it was hard to tell.

The driver asked if she wanted him to stop.

"No."

She gave him the address she shared with Donovan, then leaned back in the seat. The cab moved through the darkness, past decorated shop windows, beneath strung garlands and Christmas lights. Taking her home.

She didn't *desire* Nash, she told herself. Desire had nothing to do with it. Anyway, Donovan had killed all desire in her. Sex was something she feared, something she dreaded. Something she *loathed.*

So why did she so often catch herself thinking about being with Nash? *Like that?*

Maybe because he'd brought it up. Maybe because he'd put the idea in her head by admitting that he wanted her. Or maybe she thought the touch of someone else would erase some of Donovan's taint.

Whatever was going on in her head—it was beyond logic.

And little by little, she felt herself succumbing.

She *needed* to see him. Talk to him. Be with him.

The day came when she decided he'd won. She was ready for the trade-off. Sex, for his company.

On the Friday evening before Christmas, Sara put her plan—pathetic though it was—into motion.

"I need to get a little more shopping done before Christmas," she told Marilyn.

All afternoon they had served hot cider and doughnuts to their regular customers, and now things were winding down.

"Take the evening off," Marilyn insisted, just as Sara had hoped.

Sara cleared her throat. "If Donovan calls, will you tell him that I'm shopping?"

"Sure, honey. Be careful."

There was no fooling Marilyn.

The cab driver let her out at *Shoot the Moon.*

"Want me to wait?" he asked, eyeing the decrepit warehouse.

She paid the fare. "That won't be necessary."

When she stepped from the cab, a damp, bone-chilling wind took her breath away. It lifted the hair from her head. It stung her eyes.

She stood on the street corner, clutching the collar of her wool coat to her throat, watching as the cab's red taillights disappeared.

"This is insane," Sara said under her breath. Then she told herself what she always told herself when faced with a moment of difficulty. She lived with Donovan Ivy. What could possibly be worse?

She turned and faced the four-story brick building. This was it. There was no turning back.

You know where to find me.

She moved across the wide, uneven walk, to the rusty metal door.

She knocked.

She waited.

No answer.

She knocked again.

With the cold wind biting her bare wrists and face, she walked around the corner of the building. Head tilted back, she looked up at the third floor and saw lights. But then, maybe they were left on all night.

Why hadn't she told the driver to wait? If Nash wasn't at *Shoot the Moon*, what would she do? How could she possibly catch a cab in this part of town? There were *no* cabs in this part of town.

She tried the door again. She jiggled the knob. She shoved with one shoulder. She pounded with her fist. Then she turned her back to the door, her arms folded at the waist, and stared out at the street.

There wasn't much traffic. A few cars moved up and down the four-lane. One slowed, then went on.

A minute later, she knocked again.

Behind her, a car slowed. She glanced over her shoulder. The same car that had driven by before.

Panic began to build. Just when she'd decided she'd better start walking, the warehouse door swung open.

Standing there, bare-chested, wearing nothing but a pair of gray jogging pants, was Nash. His hair was wet. Droplets formed on tapered strands to trickle down his chest.

"Sara."

His voice.

It brought comfort and it struck terror at the same time. He sounded surprised. And puzzled. Maybe a little pleased. She hoped to God a little pleased.

He pulled her inside. The door closed behind her, automatically locking.

"I was taking a shower." He motioned somewhere up and behind him. "I thought I heard a knock."

She'd seen him partially dressed before, at the beach, but she hadn't been in any condition to notice much. Tonight, because of her mission, her senses were fine-tuned to things sexual, sensual.

He wasn't big. Not like a body-builder. Not like Donovan. But he was solid. Hard-looking. His skin, where it lay in contours across sinewy muscles, had a smooth, burnished quality.

He lifted both hands and pulled his dripping hair back from his face, revealing dark armpits within the framework of woven muscles.

She had planned to cut to the chase, to simply say she was here to do it. Instead, she found herself gripping the leather strap of her purse with both hands, forcing herself to look him directly in the eyes.

"Do you still—" She swallowed. Heaven help her, she could hardly breathe. "Do you still . . . want me?"

His arms dropped to his sides. He stood there a moment, surprise registering in the depths of his turquoise eyes. He took half a step. Without a word, he reached out and lifted one of her gloved hands. He turned and pulled her after him, up the two flights of stairs to his office.

Once there, Sara hovered nervously near the closed door while he dug through a duffel bag, pulling out a white T-shirt. He straightened, slipped one arm in a sleeve, then the other. His head went through the neck-band, and, with both hands, he pulled down the shirt, his hair leaving wet spots.

Why was he dressing? she wondered, her heart slamming.

She watched as he moved barefoot about the room. He picked up a can of cola from the counter. "Something to drink?" he asked.

She ran a tongue across dry lips and shook her head. Why was he drawing this out? She would lose her nerve if he didn't hurry up.

He looked at the can, put it down, then went on to something else. "Gatorade?"

Again she shook her head. It wasn't a smooth left and right movement, but a series of jerks.

To cover her nervousness, she concentrated on her gloves, pulling them off, stuffing them into her pocket. Then she unbuttoned her coat and slipped it from her shoulders. She was looking for a place to put it when Nash jumped forward and took the coat from her. He went to the closet, dug out a hanger, and hung it up. When he turned back to her, the coat silently slipped from the hanger and fell to the floor.

She didn't think it worth mentioning.

Her eyes moved to the digital clock on the desk. 8:03. His gaze followed hers, and when she looked up their eyes met.

"We don't have much time," she heard herself say, vocalizing the unspoken words.

That galvanized him into action. He grabbed the cushions from the couch and tossed them on the floor. Then he pulled out a double bed. It unfolded with a creak and a banging of metal.

White sheets.

Clean.

Two horizontal creases where the mattress had been folded.

He snapped his fingers as if he'd just thought of something. "Wine. I think I have a bottle of wine around here somewhere."

She hadn't expected preliminaries. She didn't *want* them, but maybe a glass of wine would help.

He rattled around in one of the cupboards and came back with two paper cups and a green wine bottle with a twist-off cap.

He handed her an empty cup, put the rim of his cup between his teeth, freeing both hands so he could open the bottle.

He poured hers, then his.

"Happy holidays."

"Happy holidays."

The cup was of thin paper. She had to be careful holding it so the sides wouldn't collapse.

She took a sip. Not bad. Sweet, and warm. Very warm. She could feel it burning in her belly. She took another sip.

He crossed the room and locked the door.

Good idea.

"Lights off?" His hand hovered over the switch.

"Yes."

Definitely.

Scared. She was scared to death.

He flicked the switch.

Light from the street cut through the blinds, making striped patterns of light and darkness across the floor, across the bed. Too light. It had to be darker.

"Won't they close more than that?" she asked.

He crossed the room, briefly struggled with the blinds, then shrugged his shoulders, giving up.

She put down her drink on the filing cabinet and walked to the window. Grasping a white cotton string in each hand, she pulled in opposite directions. The blinds closed a little more.

Leave. Get your coat and get out.

She swung around. "I don't know anything about you." She spoke into the darkness as she moved her hand across the file cabinet, searching for her cup, finding it. Now she was the one who was stalling. "You could be married for all I know."

"I'm not."

"I am."

"I know."

"And that doesn't bother you? Sex with a married woman?"

He laughed.

Her eyes were beginning to adjust, enough for her to make out his shape perched on the corner of the desk.

His voice cut through the darkness. Flat. Emotionless, the words coming slowly, giving them added impact. "Some people say . . . I have no conscience."

If she had been scared before, she was terrified now.

Yes, she could believe people said such a thing about him. Didn't she believe it herself?

"Why did you come, Sara?"

So composed. He sounded so composed, while she was a wreck, while she was falling apart. She took another drink of wine, finishing it. She put the empty cup down on the file cabinet. "I don't know." There was a slight tremor in her voice that she didn't think he'd notice. He didn't know her that well. He didn't know her at all.

"Boredom?"

"No."

She wouldn't tell him that she'd been thinking of him, that she couldn't get him out of her mind. She wouldn't give him that kind of satisfaction. "Well . . . yes. I suppose boredom might enter into it."

"That's what I thought."

He sounded almost relieved.

On the desk, the clock let out a low hum, the green numerals glowing, counting down the time, time that was quickly slipping away.

"It was something I had to do."

"You mean an obsession?"

"I don't know. Maybe."

"I have obsessions."

He stood. He moved toward her. He poured more wine in her cup, then lifted the bottle to his mouth and took a long swallow.

She drank the wine like medicine. And when she was done, she put the empty cup aside and began to undress.

Nash took another swallow of the cheap liquor, shuddered, capped the bottle, and looked up to see Sara tugging her sweater over her head, dropping it to the floor.

Without taking his eyes from her, he set the bottle aside. How many times had he thought of her over the past two weeks? How many times had he almost driven to the shop, or down her street, only to stop himself at the last minute?

And now, here she was.

Standing in front of him. Taking off her clothes. Acting as if she did this everyday, as if this were some kind of business arrangement.

He wanted her. God knew he wanted her. And he had even issued the challenge, but suddenly everything felt wrong.

"Do you still want me?" she whispered.

He let out a low groan. Hadn't he dreamed of this every day? Every night?

Behind him, the clock made a grinding sound, the way it did on the hour and half hour.

Eight-thirty.

He was about to be noble, about to suggest that maybe this wasn't a good idea, when she unhooked her bra and let it fall to the floor.

His eyes had adjusted to the darkness. And even though she had closed the blinds, he could see the shadow of her breasts, see the dark circles of her nipples.

Instant erection. Blood pulsed through his loins, making him stiff and hard.

Next came her jeans.

Then her panties.

The paleness of her skin glowed in the semidarkness. He could see a dark triangle between her thighs.

She lowered herself to the bed until she was lying on her back, her dark hair fanned out on the pillow, her breasts thrust upward, the skin across her ribs taut. Her flat stomach. Her hipbones.

"Hurry."

Her voice was husky and tight. *Urgent.*

He had always enjoyed foreplay. He liked to take a woman to the edge, to pleasure her with his hands and mouth and tongue before burying himself between her thighs. There was nothing more erotic than a woman experiencing an orgasm while he was tasting her. He liked to be right there when her body tensed, when she shuddered . . .

But Sara wanted no more than the basic act.

He pulled off his T-shirt, then, briefly impeded by his throbbing erection, he slid his jogging pants down his hips and thighs, kicking them free.

Air kissed his hot naked skin.

Two narrow bands of light fell across her body, revealing her in teasing, taunting patches. A throat. A rose-tipped nipple. A hipbone.

And then he noticed that she hadn't taken off her socks.

He smiled. One knee braced against the mattress, he picked up her foot. He ran a hand down her leg, stroking her from knee to ankle. He tugged off her socks, then rested the soles of her bare feet against his thighs. He ran his fingers over her calves, her knees. Then, cupping an ankle in each hand, he moved her feet from his thighs to his hips.

He had expected her to open immediately, but she didn't. He placed his hands on her knees. "Sara?"

She opened.

She turned her face to the side. He could see the tendons in her neck. He could see her parted lips.

"Hurry," she whispered, breathlessly. "Hurry."

He lowered himself between her legs. On the way, he kissed her stomach, then moved up her body, until her breasts were crushed against his chest, her stomach to his stomach, the tip of his penis poised to enter her.

Blood hammered in his head, but through it a gnawing voice said, this wasn't making love. He didn't know what the hell it was, but it wasn't making love. They'd never even kissed.

She was using him.

He felt her hands against his buttocks, felt her spread fingers dig into his flesh as she urged him to take her.

Sweat dripped from his face, falling on her. Blood pounded, pounded.

So what? So what if she was using him?

While his engorged erection throbbed, while sweat dripped from his body, a shudder went through him. He thrust. Long. Hard.

Nothing.

No penetration.

Her body shifted with the force of his unsheathed thrust.

Breathing ragged, he lifted his hips, allowing himself access with his hand. He ran his fingers through her triangle of hair, then he slipped a finger between her soft folds. He frowned. He stroked her again, deeper this time. Again, he frowned.

She was dry. As dry as a desert.

He raised himself on his elbows, his knees between her thighs, his abdomen pressed against hers. With his chest rising and falling, he searched her face. Their positions had shifted enough so that a thin band of light fell across her delicate features. And he could see that her eyes were squeezed tightly shut.

What the bloody hell?

When the moon's in the full, then the wit's on the wane.

Chapter Twelve

Instead of being hot and wet and melting, she was dry, her teeth clenched, her body rigid and braced for an unwelcomed penetration.

"Don't stop."

"You can't just expect . . . me . . . to tear into you."

"It doesn't matter."

He pushed himself away. "Christ, this is impossible." He sat up, his back to her, his feet on the floor, elbows on his knees. He ran his hands through his hair. He rubbed his face. "Christ."

He was sweating. His breathing was rapid and shallow. His heart was beating like a hollow drum.

He sat there for a couple of minutes, waiting for his blood to cool, the silence in the room oppressive, the silence directly behind him oppressive. Outside, a few blocks away, a siren howled, then faded into the distance.

He didn't get it. What the hell was she after? What kind of game was she playing? It was obvious she didn't want to have sex with him, that she was forcing herself.

His gaze dropped to his jogging pants on the floor. He snatched them up, stuffed his legs into them, and pulled them on. Standing, he searched through the darkness for his T-shirt.

He found it. He put it on. Turning, he said, "I don't know what the hell—" His voice caught.

She was lying on her side, facing the window, clasped hands under her head, knees drawn up, eyes open wide, staring at nothing. Crying. Soundlessly.

Oh, Christ.

He was a man with no heart, no conscience, but suddenly he ached with an ache that was unbearable. An ache that tightened his throat and stung his eyes. An ache he remembered but had never wanted to experience again.

"Sara."

He dropped down beside her, the mattress dipping, springs groaning. He reached for her, a hand hovering over her naked hip, finally settling on her shoulder.

Her skin was like ice.

He tugged at the woven blanket, pulling it free of the mattress. He covered her, her body a slight mound beneath the heavy fabric.

For once in his life, he was at a total loss. He didn't speak. He didn't know what to say.

She pulled in a trembling breath. The sound seemed to fill the quiet of the room, adding weight to the ache in his chest. And then, she spoke. Quietly, emotionlessly, her very lack of feeling a reflection of her measured control, of words doled out with utmost care.

"I thought I could be somebody else. At least for a little while."

He had no idea what to do, but he found himself pulling her into his arms. He held her, and he rocked her. He breathed in the scent of her. He stroked her hair, letting the satin tresses slide through his fingers.

Instinctively he knew that this was the real Sara Ivy. Not the socialite with her expensive gowns and jewels, not the hard woman who had snubbed him.

And the woman on the beach—she, too, was Sara Ivy. Defiant. Brave. Sexy.

That one drove him crazy.

But this one . . . this one broke his heart.

Time passed. The clock on the desk made its old familiar grinding sound.

Nine o'clock.

Sara lifted her head from his shoulder and let out a sigh. "I have to go."

Feeling strangely fragile, he let her slip out of his arms. Her body left a warm, invisible imprint on him.

She stood, gripping the blanket under her chin. "Don't watch me dress."

He had seen her naked body. He had a photo he stared at almost daily, a photo he'd lied to her about.

He turned. He walked toward the windows. With one finger, he pushed at the blinds. Metal popped, bent, making a triangle he could look through.

The full December moon. Low in the sky, blurry, as if a storm was moving in.

"Don't go," he said quietly, without turning around.

"I have to."

"Why?" He didn't want to think about her going back to Ivy. "If you had a satisfying marriage, you wouldn't have come here."

She didn't say anything. No agreement, no denial.

He couldn't figure her out. Why would a woman stay in a marriage that was no good? Some women did because of kids, but she didn't have any.

That left money.

He made it a point to avoid intimate conversations, but suddenly he wanted her to talk to him, wanted her to explain things.

Rather than suffer the intrusive glare of a sixty-watt bulb, he opened the blinds, letting in just the right amount of light.

Behind him, he heard her move, heard the soft whisper of her shoes as she crossed the room.

He turned.

She was dressed and slipping into her coat. Her clothes seemed to have given her strength. Some of that cool, aloof control was back.

She went to the phone and called for a cab.

Anger—or was it fear?—leaped in him. "What happens if you get home late?" he asked, his voice bordering on sarcasm. "Does he cut off your allowance?"

She silently considered him.

For the last several years, he'd prided himself on the fact that he knew more about life than anybody. It was an arrogant assumption. Suddenly that truth was never more apparent. As she stared at him, the foundation of his self-assurance wobbled, and he experienced a moment of doubt.

He had a sudden image of himself, standing next to a yawning precipice, ready to tumble headlong.

"Yes," she said with a smile that hinted at self-mockery.

He remembered that this was the woman who had tried to kill herself.

"He takes away my allowance."

They were talking around the problem, talking around what had just happened, or hadn't happened, between them.

"I don't get it," he said, frustration getting the best of him. He wanted solid answers. "Why did you come here? To spite him?" Then he had another thought, a thought that fit more with his original opinion of Sara Ivy. "Or was it to get yourself dirty, only to find you couldn't go through with it?"

She looked away, some of her newly regained composure slipping. "I . . . I, ah . . ." She swallowed. She pressed her lips together. "I was willing to make a trade," she said so softly he hardly heard her. "At least I thought I was." She shrugged her shoulders and let out a nervous little laugh. "Sex just doesn't seem to be a good means of barter for me." She clasped her hands together. "Perhaps if you'd wanted something else, anything else, it might have worked."

"What are you talking about?"

"Sex. That was your ultimatum, wasn't it?"

The room slanted.

What had happened to him? How had he gotten so heartless?

There had been a time when he'd been more naive than Harley. There had been a time when he'd been a nice guy, too. And he'd been hurt. And he'd decided to get tough or be eaten alive. But this . . . Oh, God.

"I have to go."

Her words came to him through a thick haze.

"W-wait." Shaking, he grabbed a sweatshirt, then managed to stuff his feet into a pair of sneakers. "I'll walk you."

They made their way down the stairs, then down the hallway.

Outside, the moon was completely obliterated by snowflakes drifting earthward. They were huge—like tissue-paper cutouts, floating on the still air.

Sara's face was lifted to the night sky. "Snow." Her voice held the wonder of a child.

He watched as wet flakes kissed her cheeks, her hair, her eyelashes, melting against her skin. When she looked back at him, she was smiling. Not the self-mocking smile he'd seen earlier, but a soft, slow, real smile.

The wall he'd put up, the barrier he'd worked so hard and so diligently to build, crumbled.

And he knew, in that second, from that point on, that nothing would be the same.

He would never be able to look at the world with the same detachment, the same distance, the same lack of emotion that had been so hard to come by.

They hadn't made love. Their bodies hadn't joined, but *something* had happened. She had somehow, some way, touched his soul.

He, who had sworn never to love anyone again, watched her with a feeling of helplessness. He watched as snowflakes continued to fall on her face and hair and eyelashes.

A benediction.

He took one faltering step, then another.

Ever since the night on the beach, he'd known that he had to have her, possess her. But now everything had suddenly turned around.

Now he wanted more.

He stopped directly in front of her. Slowly, her face was drawn to his. Her smile faded. A question came into her eyes.

Slowly, carefully, he took her face in his hands, cupping her cold cheeks against his warm palms, watching as their breaths mingled. He lowered his head, watching as her eyes fluttered closed, as her face lifted to his.

His own eyes closed. And then there was just the softness of her lips.

Her hair slid over his wrist. Her hands came up around his neck.

He pulled her closer, bulky coat and all, his mouth moving over hers. Her lips parted, inviting his tongue. And when he slid it against hers, his heart pounded, his body throbbed.

A horn honked.

Reality.

A hand to her chin, he broke the kiss. Her eyelashes fluttered. She looked dazed, slightly disoriented.

"I'm sorry about what I said the night of Harley's party." His voice came out tight and strained and a little lost. "I sometimes say things I don't mean, just because . . . well, because I'm an ass." He brushed a finger across her bottom lip. "Come and see me anytime. We can play Monopoly. Or watch TV. Do you like to look at stars? I have lawn chairs set up on the roof of *Shoot the Moon*."

Honk.

She blinked, glanced over her shoulder, then back. "I have to go."

He wanted to extract a promise from her. He wanted her to tell him that she'd be back, that he would see her again. He loosened his hold and she slipped away.

She ran to the cab.

He followed, closing the door for her once she was inside. As the cab pulled away, he could see her watching him through the glass.

She lifted her hand in farewell.

Pathos. A word Harley had dug out of him, its meaning just now truly hitting home.

He lifted his own hand, the slow, lingering gesture mirroring hers.

How could one simple movement hurt so much? How could it be so bittersweet?

Back inside *Shoot the Moon*, Nash moved around in a daze. He picked up the cup Sara had used. He started to throw it away, then stopped himself. Instead, he put it on the desk.

He picked up the wine bottle, then put it back down. He turned on the TV. Ten minutes later, he realized he was staring blankly at the screen, so he shut it off.

Inside him was a hollow ache, a kind of loneliness he hadn't felt in years.

An hour later he picked up the phone and called information. Then he put in a call to his ex-brother-in-law.

"Matt. How's it going?" Nash asked as soon as he recognized the voice at the other end of the line.

"Christian. My God."

The shock in Matt's voice was no surprise.

"Where are you calling from?"

Nash's answer came without hesitation. "Atlanta." A lie that would serve them all.

"I-It's good to hear from you."

"Do you have Maureen's number?"

"Maureen?" All friendliness vanished. "Maureen remarried a long time ago," Matt said in a cautious, suspicious voice.

Matt was a good guy. Nash didn't blame him for wanting to protect his sister. "I know."

"She's got two kids." A touch of sympathy now.

"Girls?" Nash finally managed to ask, his voice almost failing him.

"Girl and a boy."

No ages, no names. Nothing personal. That was okay. Nash didn't want to know anything about her new life.

"Christian, she's happy. Why stir things up?"

He and Matt had hunted together, watched football together. Together, they'd shingled a roof on a cold, blustery winter day. Back when life was normal, when life was life, when bad things happened to strangers.

"Hey, you're talking to the guy who helped you put

in your septic system," Nash said. "You're talking to the guy who rushed you to the emergency room when you fell off the roof." His voice dropped, became more serious. "I just want to talk to her. I just want to tell her . . . that everything's okay. That I don't blame her. For anything."

Silence.

Nash knew just what he thought. "Matt," he said quietly. "I'm not crazy."

"It's over. Let it go."

It was Nash's turn to be quiet. Then, finally, "Nobody knows that better than I do. That's what I want to do. Let it go."

Matt gave him the number.

After hanging up, Nash stared into the dark. Twenty minutes later, he picked up the receiver and punched in the Seattle number Matt had given him.

Ring, ring.

He pulled the receiver from his ear and held it over the cradle, ready to hang up. Before doing so, he stopped, then lifted it back to his ear.

"Hello? Hello?"

Maureen.

Years fell away.

"Hi, Maureen," he said quietly.

There was a long pause, then, "Christian? Christian, is that you?"

"Yeah. Yeah, it's me."

"Where are you?"

"It's probably better that you don't know. How are you doing?"

"I'm fine."

Two strangers. Two strangers who had once been intimate, who had once shared their lives. He didn't know what to say, didn't know why it had been so important that he get in touch with her after so many years. She was a different person. So was he.

"I'm glad you called," she said. "I've wondered. I've worried . . ."

"I hear you're married."

"We have two children. A girl and a boy. And my husband—he's a doctor."

Nash swallowed. "I'm glad for you."

There was a pause, neither knowing what to say.

"Christian, are you okay?"

"I'm fine."

"I had to go on with my life. You understand, don't you?"

"I know. That's what I wanted to tell you. I don't blame you for divorcing me. Twelve years is a long time to wait for someone. And even without the years, it wouldn't have been the same. It wouldn't have worked."

"No . . . it wouldn't have. I'm glad you understand. When you got out, I wanted to be there, but my husband didn't like the idea. And I'd just had a baby . . ."

Nash thought about the day of his release from prison. A gray winter day. He'd been driven to the train station, handed a ticket to Chicago plus three hundred dollars in cash, and turned loose. Not a high point in his life.

"And later, I tried to find you."

"It's okay." He took a breath. It was getting easier to breathe. "I didn't want to be found." It hadn't been hard to disappear.

"Maureen?"

"Yes?"

"What we had once. It was good, wasn't it?"

He heard her quick intake of breath. He wished he could take back the words. He'd upset her. He hadn't meant to upset her.

"Yes," she said, her voice breaking, "It was good. It was damn near perfect."

He exhaled. That's what he'd thought. That's how he remembered it. But sometimes a person's memory got things screwed up.

"Do you have a Christmas tree?" he asked, needing to get on firmer ground. "I remember how you always had to have a real one."

"Yes," she said, his question giving her time to pull herself together. "I remember how you loved Christmas. How you used to get as excited as a kid."

He smiled. "Remember that first Christmas Eve? When we slept under the tree?"

"We were so young."

The memory was too intimate. He'd crossed a line he shouldn't have crossed. "Yeah, we were. Well, I gotta go."

"Wait—Christian?"

"Mmm?"

"I have something I want to say."

He waited.

"I once told you that what you did was wrong, that you had just made the nightmare all that more impossible to bear." Her voice was tight, winding higher and higher. "I'm sorry," she said. "I was so angry. You threw everything away, even me. At a time when I needed you the most."

Emotion was unleashed. All the pain, fear, anger, guilt, poured out. "I *hated* you for that. I hated you for abandoning me. But now I know I was wrong. It's no excuse, but I was out of my mind with grief." Her voice reached a trembling pitch. "Our little girl. Dead. And like that."

She fell to silence, and he sensed that she was crying. He heard her blowing her nose, heard her sniffle.

He waited, listening.

"I want to tell you that you did the right thing," she said when she could continue. She sounded calm now, with only a hint of tears. "Do you hear me? You did what you had to do. And you shouldn't have been sent to prison, you should have been given a damn medal."

"Don't make me into something I'm not." His voice was deep, coming from a throat that burned like fire. "They give medals to heroes."

"Yes," she said, all trace of hysteria gone. "Yes, I know. And Christian, I saved everything. Baby clothes. School pictures. Birth certificate with her little footprints. When you're ready . . . if you ever want anything . . ."

Somehow Nash told Maureen good-bye. Somehow he hung up. And when the receiver was securely in the cradle, he laid his forehead against his crossed arms and, for the first time in twelve years, he wept.

I, a stranger and afraid,
In a world I never made.
—A.E. Housman

Chapter Thirteen

The bell jangled. The heavy glass door swung shut. Frigid lake air immediately filled the shop, bringing with it Nash Audubon.

He stood just inside the door, his shoulders hunched against the cold.

Four-thirty.

Almost time to close.

Almost dark.

Behind him, the muted orange of the setting sun played upon the frost that grew in lacy patterns on the window.

Sara hadn't expected to see him again—and she'd told herself it was better that way. But if she'd known he was coming, she could have rehearsed, would have practiced what she should say. His surprising appearance had her thoughts in a jumble.

Nine days had passed since she'd made such a fool of herself in his office. With each passing day, the memory of that night had become more and more humiliating. She wanted to erase it from her mind, but it was always there, always growing.

She watched as he took off his wool cap, as he raked back his shaggy hair, then repositioned the cap on his head. His feet, in leather hiking boots, shifted on the scratched, dull surface of the wooden floor.

His smile, when it came, was crooked and slow. "Hi."

"Hi."

Intimate.

There was a feeling of awkward intimacy to their encounter. Two strangers who had shared a bed, whose naked bodies had touched.

"Need a ride home?" he asked quietly.

Don't tempt me. Please don't tempt me. "I can't."

"Is that your answer to everything? I can't?"

Almost always, she admitted to herself with a familiar sense of self-loathing. She looked down at her knotted hands. "I can't."

Her voice was dead.

He stepped closer, close enough for her to feel the cold emanating from his jacket. He looked into her eyes, and she felt herself begin to weaken.

He took her hands. Roughened fingertips smoothed her white knuckles.

Why was he here? She had already proven that she couldn't give him what he wanted from her.

"Come on," he whispered, the lowness of his voice too seductive.

Life fluttered somewhere deep inside her.

"I can't," she repeated. But this time the words meant nothing.

"It's cold out," he explained. "I was in the neighborhood and thought you might not want to wait for a cab." He shrugged and looked over his shoulder, at the world behind him.

She had feared seeing him again. And here he was, acting as if nothing had happened, making it much too easy for her.

* * *

He waited while she closed up. He followed her around. He asked if he could help.

He, who had kissed her as she'd never in her life been kissed. With tenderness, and heat, and magic.

No. She'd mistaken the tenderness. And the magic. And most likely the heat.

She took the drawer from the cash register, locked it in the fireproof file in the back room, turned down the heat, turned off the lights, and headed for the front door, where Nash was waiting.

He helped her with her coat, unfolding the thick collar and tucking it around her neck.

"No gloves?" he asked.

"I forgot them." They were in the shop, but she was too flustered to go back and get them.

"No hat?"

She shook her head. In the shop, too.

He pulled off his gray wool cap. "Seventy percent of body heat escapes through your head," he said, slapping the cap on her. He tugged at the bill, adjusting it. And then they were stepping out the door. And she was pulling the key from her pocket.

He tried to take it from her, but she jerked her hand away. "Quit being so nice to me," she said, suddenly, alarmingly close to tears.

He put up both hands and took a step back. "Okay, okay."

She tried to stick the key in upside down. She had to turn it over and try again. This time it went in. She turned the key, praying that the recalcitrant lock would work the first time. Her prayer was answered, and a second later she was pocketing the key and they were moving up the street, side by side.

Five minutes later, she was hunched in the passenger seat of Nash's battered car, her breath a cloud, her nostrils and eyeballs stinging from the cold, her fingers and toes numb.

Beside her, Nash turned the ignition and pumped the gas pedal.

Nothing.

He tried again.

Still nothing. Not even a click.

"Been meaning to get a new battery." He shouldered open his door and got out.

She couldn't see through the frosted-up windshield, but she heard the hood open. Heard him mumble, heard him slam the hood shut. With a fingernail, she scraped at the frost that had built up on the inside of the glass.

The driver door opened and Nash slid in beside her and tried again.

Nothing.

It was getting late. She had to go. She had to get home before Donovan. "I'd better catch a cab." She was scooting out her door when Nash stopped her, a hand on her arm.

"Let's take the El."

In the distance, she could hear the train rattling along the tracks.

"What about your car?"

"It'll be okay here for a few hours. I'll get a battery and come back."

"I think I'll just take a cab," she said through frozen lips.

"There's nothing like the El at night."

"That's what I hear."

Her teeth were clenched with cold. Her voice was shaking. "That's w-why sane people don't r-ride it."

The El, especially after dark, was a dangerous place, or so she'd always been told.

"It's one of those things you're supposed to avoid," she said. "Like dark alleys."

"Hey, I'm not asking you to lick cold metal. I'm asking you to take a ride on the night train. It's the best seat in the house, I promise."

It was on the tip of her tongue to say I can't, when she caught herself. She hesitated, giving him time to come up with another reason for taking the El.

"It's quicker than a cab," he offered. "Don't have to fight traffic."

That did it.

Next thing she knew, they were hurrying down the street to the nearest elevated station.

While they waited on the platform with the crowd of rush-hour travelers, Nash turned her around so they were face to face. "Here," he said. "Put your hands under my jacket."

She couldn't. She couldn't reach for him, touch him.

In the dim light of the station, they were just two people among many. He took her frozen hands and slid them inside his open jacket, around his waist.

He was hot, radiating heat like an atomic reactor. He smelled like leather and wool and outdoors. His breath was a warm cloud against her cheek, his arms strong.

Safe.

Standing outside the train station, on a dark, wintry Chicago night, in a place she'd been warned never to go, she felt safe. For a brief moment in the chaos of her ugly, shameful life, she felt safe.

The train pulled into the station. The doors slid open. People hurried aboard.

Sara and Nash were able to get a window seat that faced east.

The doors closed. The train lurched, then moved smoothly away from the station. Inside, the artificial light washed everything in lime green. The molded plastic seats, the graffiti, the weary faces. The floor was littered with trash, with paper cups, candy wrappers, and newspapers. Flyers had been glued to the walls.

Jesus Saves.

No Spitting.

Vegetarians Don't Eat Their Pets.

Love is a Four-Letter Word.

Outside, the lights of Chicago flew past, keeping time with the *click, click, click* of the El's metal wheels.

Sara saw the city from a totally new perspective—a story and a half off the ground. Areas that during the day were dingy and unappealing were now, under the glow of city lights, different.

The artist in her, a person who had died years ago along with her self-respect, stirred. The view from the train car was magic. Poetry. Cinematic and surreal.

Scenes flashed past with dizzying speed. Buildings were close. Buildings were far away.

Close.

Far.

Close.

Far.

A rectangle of light. A kitchen. People.

Life.

Wabash Avenue bathed in purple light.

The Wrigley Building, drenched in gold.

"Chicago," Nash said with a hint of the same wonder she was feeling. "A great city. A city with character. History. Did you know the zipper was invented in Chicago?"

"How about Twinkies?"

"Cracker Jack."

"Roller skates."

"Spray paint."

"Pinball."

"Pinball?"

"Yeah."

The ride was over way too soon. When the train began to slow for the station, Sara got to her feet and Nash moved to follow.

She put a hand to his shoulder. "Stay."

"I'll walk you home, then catch a train back."

"No. Please." She couldn't keep the desperation out of her voice.

The train pulled to a stop. The doors opened.

"Good-bye." She stepped out.

Nash followed.

The doors closed and the train pulled away. They were the only two on the platform. Gold Coasters didn't ride the El.

"I'm not letting you walk home alone. That maniac could still be out there."

What would Nash think if he knew her shameful secret—that she lived with the maniac? She shared his bed.

"That was in the middle of the night," she said, pretending the story Donovan had told the press was true, hoping to sound convincing. More than anything, she didn't want Nash to know of the ugliness that went on behind the doors of the Ivy estate. Let him think anything but the truth. "Plus they've beefed up the police patrol. Please." She begged him with her eyes. "The neighbors. You can't."

His hands were shoved deep into the pockets of his jacket. He looked away, up the street that led to her house. Then he looked back at her. He pressed his lips together and nodded.

Thank you.

She relaxed slightly, then remembered his cap. She took it off and held it out to him.

"Keep it."

"I can't."

He smiled at her words, and she smiled back.

"Really." She continued to hold the cap out to him. "I can't."

There was something going on between them that was more than his having wanted to sleep with her, and her having wanted his company. Something she would have liked to explore, but knew she couldn't. Maybe in another life.

It was in her head to tell him that they couldn't do this again, but her throat tightened. The words wouldn't come.

A train approached from the north. It pulled to a stop. Without taking his cap, Nash gave her a quick smile and jumped into the last car just as the doors were closing.

It lurched. She watched as he made his way to the back. At the last window, she thought she saw a raised hand.

When she stepped in the front door, Donovan was waiting.

"Where have you been?"

"Work."

"You're late."

She tried to remain calm. She checked the anniversary clock on the mantel. "Ten minutes. That's all. I had a customer just as I was closing and didn't get out of the shop until late." Lies, lies. Donovan had made her a master at lies.

"Where did you get the cap?"

"At the shop."

He jerked it from her head and threw it on the floor. "Never wear anybody else's clothes. Do you hear me? *Never!* I get clothes for you. *New* clothes."

She tried to look casual as she took off her coat and hung it in the closet. She wanted to pick up Nash's cap, but she didn't dare. She would get it later.

"Why don't I get you a drink," she suggested.

Donovan couldn't be swayed. "What kind of late customer?" His eyes took on a look of anger that made her knees weak. "Are you seeing somebody?"

How ironic, that in all the years of his unfounded suspicion, she had never as much as looked at another man. Until now.

"Of course not." She kicked off her shoes, went to the bar, grabbed the ice bucket, and headed in the direction of the kitchen. "I'll get some ice and be right back."

He came with her.

"What if I said I had you followed?"

Followed! How stupid of her. It was exactly something he might do. But then, he could also be lying.

With her heart beating madly, she stood in front of the refrigerator and pressed the ice machine button. Cubes tumbled into the bucket. She released the button.

Silence.

Admitting the truth wouldn't save her. Her only chance was to lie more, in hopes that he, too, was lying. "Then I would say that should satisfy you," she said evenly. "Then you should know I haven't been seeing anyone."

She walked past him, back to the bar, her feet sinking into the plush white carpet. She got out two glasses, dropped in some ice, then filled the glasses with Scotch. She held a glass to Donovan, and when she did, her hand shook so hard the ice rattled.

He grabbed the drink, swallowing the contents in one gulp. Then he stared at her. She could see a pulse beating in his temple. He clenched and unclenched his jaw.

She downed her own drink.

Years of dealing with Donovan set her mind into quick, self-preserving motion. "I've been thinking that maybe I should quit at the shop," she said casually, hoping her words would placate him rather than make him angrier. "I don't like not being here when you get home."

His eyes narrowed, and her heart hammered all the more furiously.

He crossed to the bar, refilled his glass, then hers. He drank his down. She did the same.

Then he came to stand in front of her. He brought up his hand. It was all she could do to keep from flinching.

He ran his fingers through her hair. When he came to a tangle, he tugged, ripping past it.

Then he put a hand to her throat. He rubbed his thumb over her Adam's apple, his fingers pressed into her flesh. He bent his head and placed his wet lips against her neck, directly under her ear. He sucked. He was giving her a hickey, staking a visible claim.

She squeezed her eyes shut.

His mouth moved to another spot, then another. When he was satisfied, he raised his head. "Tomorrow you stay home. For good. I want you to stay home for good. You're going to take care of me now."

She swallowed. She nodded.

He straightened, his hands on her shoulders. She opened her eyes to find him staring at her.

"You're not crying, are you?" he asked, suspicious once more.

"I'm crying because I'm happy," she said, wondering if he was vain and egotistical enough to fall for her terrible acting.

She could feel some of the tenseness leave him. He began to fondle her breast, then he frowned, bringing up a subject they had fought over several times. "There are a lot of good plastic surgeons in Chicago who could give you nice big boobs."

Placating being her only goal, she said, for the first time, "I'll think about it."

That pleased him.

He examined her hair, fingering it as if it were second-rate fabric. "And maybe a permanent. And some different makeup. With some help, you could be attractive." He pressed his lips to hers, then shoved her away. "Go upstairs and put on a sexy dress. We're going out."

Life was back to normal.

After showing her off as his possession, they would return home for thirty minutes of degrading sex. After that, he would fall asleep and she would be left wide awake to face herself.

They went to a comedy club. There was a comedian from New York whose name sounded vaguely familiar to Sara, but she didn't keep up with such things. Donovan got them a front table where he proceeded to keep the waitress hopping, bringing him drink after drink.

It was a raunchy crowd, a loud crowd, the comedian's act extremely vulgar. Once Sara leaned over to Donovan and suggested they leave, but he waved her words away. He was having a good time, laughing loudly at the jokes.

Halfway through the show, he pulled Sara onto his knee. Across the room, photographers were taking pictures of the comedian. Cameras flashed. Sara's eyes seeked out the source, anything for a diversion.

Staring at her, camera in hand, was Nash.

Donovan must have felt her stiffen, because he looked up, then followed the direction of her gaze.

With eyes never leaving Nash, Donovan slid his hand into the front of Sara's spaghetti-strapped gown and slowly squeezed her breast.

He wanted Nash to take a picture of them.

After what seemed an eternity, Nash slowly lowered his camera and slipped into the crowd.

Chapter Fourteen

She was drinking again.

She was drunk again.

It wasn't a sloppy kind of drunk. No, she had reached the perfect place every serious drinker, every drug addict sought but rarely achieved. That enviable level that could be compared only to being stone cold sober.

Sara's movements were precise, her vision clear. And yet she was numb. Blessedly, blissfully numb.

She stood in the master bedroom, staring out the latticed window, at Donovan's world below.

Earlier, a gardener had trimmed the shrubbery that ran along the black iron fence surrounding the property. Another person had put new bulbs in the lights that lined the curved drive.

The pool was empty now. In the spring it would be filled, but no one would swim in it. It was for looks, like everything else.

Shortly after she and Donovan had married, Sara had dreamed of having children. She had imagined taking them places. To the beach. On picnics. Swimming lessons. Music lessons. School programs.

There would be wet kisses. Stuffed animals. A warm little body to hold close.

A miscarriage.

She had tried to convince herself that it had been

for the best. She'd told herself that her motives were selfish. She had been looking for someone to care for and love, for someone who might love her in return.

She hadn't thought about Donovan, hadn't thought about the terrible injustice of bringing a child into his world.

For the best. The miscarriage had been for the best. And yet, in her mind, she often pictured the child she'd never had, the child she'd lost. . . .

Beside her, the telephone rang.

Sara slowly turned away from the window to stare at the ringing phone.

It was probably Donovan, calling to check on her, calling to make sure she was where she should be.

Pick it up. Pick it up.

On the sixth ring, she lifted the receiver to her ear. She paused, then, "Hello?"

"Sara."

Nash.

Even with half a bottle of bourbon in her system, the sound of his voice still made her heart slam. It somehow managed to cut through the haze, the numbness.

"I went by Two Timers. Marilyn told me you weren't working there anymore."

"I quit."

"Why?"

Because I was scared. For me. For you. She pulled in a tight, stabilizing breath, preparing to lie. "I got tired of it."

She braced herself for some comment that had to do with her social station, or her not being able to cut it in the real world. Her boredom. It didn't come.

"Can I see you? Can we meet somewhere?"

She put a hand to her trembling mouth. She

blinked and looked up at the ceiling, then squeezed her eyes shut. She thought about the ride on the El. She thought about the bowling party. The leisure suits.

He likes to lie on the roof and look up at the stars. Oh, God. There was more to this than the places he'd taken her, the freedom he'd given her a taste of. It was about him. *Him.* She didn't know if she had the ability to recognize love when she saw it, but she was terribly, terribly afraid that was the emotion she was feeling for Nash.

"Sara . . . ?"

She drew another shaky breath. With her shoulders hunched, an arm pressed to her stomach, she opened her eyes. "I can't."

"Harley's dad has this cabin up north in Michigan," Nash said hurriedly, as if expecting her to hang up any second. "He lets me use it sometimes. Come away with me for the weekend."

Come away with me for the weekend. Oh, God.

"We can go up on Friday and come back on Sunday. Tell—" There was a short pause. "Tell *him* you're going to visit relatives."

"I *can't.*" This was agony.

"Tell him your sister's having a baby. Tell him you have to go to your father's surprise birthday party. Tell him your best friend is getting married. Anything. Tell him anything."

What he was suggesting only served to remind her of how little he knew about her, and how small and confined her world was. A prison of her own making. What would have been simple for most people was impossible for her. She had no friends. She had no family.

Come away with me for the weekend.

He may as well have asked her to scale the tallest mountain. To fly to the moon.

Through the window, she caught a flash of movement. Outside, the automatic gates swung open. Donovan's black limo was rolling in.

Sara gripped the receiver with both hands. "I have to go."

"I'm not giving up."

"I have to go."

"You'll think about it? Tell me you'll at least think about it."

"Yes." Anything to get off the phone, to make sure he didn't call back as soon as she hung up. "I'll think about it."

The receiver clattered. Outside, the limo disappeared into the garage.

Two minutes later, Sara heard Donovan's footsteps on the carpeted stairs. She heard him coming down the hall.

He was supersensitive to her every nuance. He could read her better than she read herself. To him, she was transparent. He could see all the way to her brain, read her every thought.

To block the signals, she had to do something, had to look busy or he would suspect—She had to—

She ran to the bathroom and closed the door—quietly, so he wouldn't hear. But she didn't lock it. She'd learned never to lock anything. There must be no secrets, no privacy.

She turned on the water. She wet her hands. Hot. Too hot.

The door burst open.

Donovan filled the doorway, his face set in angry, stony lines. "Who were you talking to?"

"No one." Her breath came quickly, like a heartbeat. "No one."

Inwardly she flinched, knowing her repeated denial only gave validity to his suspicions.

"I saw you. In the window. When I came up the drive."

She turned off the water. She picked up a towel and went through the motions of drying her hands. "A solicitor," she said. "That's all."

She hung the towel on the rack. She folded it just so, in order for the monogram—the letter *I* entwined with green ivy—to show. She straightened it. She straightened it some more.

"You're *lying!*"

He grabbed one arm, jerked her around to face him, then grabbed her other arm.

"Who-were-you-talk-ing-to?" Each syllable was punctuated by a shake.

Here it comes, she thought with the part of her mind that analyzed things from a safe distance.

She wouldn't cower. She looked directly into his rage. "Nobody!"

He shook her and shook her.

"Was it Cray? If it was, I'll *kill him.*"

"No! No, it wasn't Cray!" Why did he keep insisting on dragging Cray into this?

"Maybe I should call him. Maybe I should ask him over. We could have a little *ménage à trois.*"

She pressed a hand to her churning stomach and gripped the marble counter with the other. "I-I don't want to see him."

He let go of her arms and shoved. And shoved again.

Then he slapped her, palm open so as not to leave any marks. He slapped her face, her arms, the side of her head, hitting her until her ears rang.

With a strange inner calm, she watched the scene from afar.

Then, with one small attempt at self-preservation, she lifted a bent arm to deflect his blows.

That movement seemed to send him over the edge.

He swung, this time with his fist, aiming at her face. She closed her eyes and tried to dodge him. His knuckles made contact with her jaw, the force behind the swing knocking her backward, her head striking the marble countertop.

The room spun. Light patterns flashed behind her eyes.

I can't pass out. I can't.

That was her last thought before everything turned black.

When she came to, the bathroom was dark. The floor was cold and hard.

She lay there, listening.

Silence.

She was alone.

Slowly, she pushed herself to a sitting position, her back to the tub. The room tilted. Her stomach heaved.

She managed to get to her feet in time to throw up in the toilet, then she stumbled into the bedroom and fell across the bed.

"You've got to quit drinking so much."

Donovan's words slowly sifted into Sara's half-conscious brain.

"Here, let me help you."

She forced herself to open her eyes. Standing over her was Donovan, one of her nightgowns in his hand.

He helped her out of her clothes and into the gown. Then he tucked her into bed.

"I'm going to call Dr. Westfall," he said when she was settled.

The scene was familiar. This was the phase that always came after the beating. While he was never contrite, he was always concerned, treating her like an ill, half-witted child.

For the moment, she was safe.

When the doctor buzzed the gate, Donovan, waiting near the intercom, pushed the remote button that automatically opened the gate.

"I'm sorry to have to get you out like this," Donovan said as he let the doctor in the front door and escorted him upstairs to the bedroom.

"She's drinking again?"

"When I got home from work, she was unconscious on the bathroom floor. She must have fallen and hit her head."

The doctor examined her.

"A slight concussion would be my guess. An X ray would probably be a good idea."

"That won't be necessary."

"It's up to you."

The doctor put a hand to her chin and turned her face toward the light. "A bruise on her jaw. Must have hit it when you fell," he told Sara. He patted her arm in a fatherly fashion. "You'll live."

Donovan knew Sara wouldn't say anything. And he could always shut up the old man with money. Westfall was a fool, and fools were easily manipulated.

Donovan stepped into the hallway with the doctor, making sure the door was left open a crack so Sara could hear their conversation.

"It's sad to see someone so beautiful with such problems," Dr. Westfall said. "Your wife needs help.

Have you thought any more about a rehab center? There are places that are discreet."

Donovan nodded and pulled at his bottom lip. "I'm afraid she wouldn't stay."

"There are institutions, as we've discussed."

Donovan turned, put a hand to his forehead and made a distraught choking sound. "I'd hate to think of her in a place like that."

"It might be the only solution. One of these days, I'm afraid she might injure herself more seriously. . . ."

Donovan waved his arm in a helpless gesture. "I thought she was better. She had a job downtown. She was drinking less. But then she suddenly quit her job, and slid right back. I wish I'd seen it coming. I *should* have seen it coming."

"Don't blame yourself. It's hard to predict these things." The doctor shrugged into his coat. "She needs to continue with the Valium and Darvon."

Donovan nodded, then let the doctor out, thanking him for coming. On the way back up the carpeted stairs, he thought about Sara and smiled grimly to himself.

He knew how to keep his wife in line. If the threat to her old man wasn't enough, then he would have her institutionalized. With the good doctor behind him, it would be easy to put her away.

And of course he could always reprimand her, although she seemed to have developed a tolerance to pain. His hitting her was never something he planned. It just happened.

He loved her.

He wouldn't share her. It was that simple.

Upstairs, she looked small and pale in the king-size bed. Donovan sat down beside her and pulled her into his arms. "Baby, baby. We'll work this out. I love you. You know I love you."

His wife didn't say anything. She didn't lift her arms to him. Instead, she just lay against his chest like a rag doll.

He felt a spark of anger at her lack of response, but he managed to push it to the back of his mind. She was simply too exhausted to react, he told himself.

From the bed, Sara could hear the shower running, could hear Donovan humming. A few minutes later, he strode into the room, his nude body dry and tan.

He sat down beside her on the bed. "How are you feeling this morning?" he asked, stroking her hair.

It had been four days since Dr. Westfall had come. During that time, Donovan had brought her flowers and carried her meals to her on a tray.

"I was thinking about picking up some champagne tonight," he said, continuing to play with her hair. "Maybe we could soak in the Jacuzzi. We haven't done that in a long time."

No, and they hadn't had sex in over two months. And the more days that passed, the more repulsive the idea of sex with Donovan became. The thought of having him on top of her, *in* her, made her ill. She would rather be beaten.

When she didn't respond favorably to his suggestion, he frowned. "You're not having your period, are you?"

The temptation to lie was great. It was a way out, but if—no, *when*—he discovered her lie, things would be worse. She kept her head bent so he couldn't see her swallow. She hesitated, afraid that if she spoke, her voice would tremble.

"Just a little headachy, that's all," she finally managed.

His frown deepened.

A headache rated only second to a period.

"Take something for it."

"I will."

His face relaxed. He got up, walked over to the full-length mirror, and looked at himself.

His muscles were getting unnatural, his body taking on an almost freakish quality.

He was hairless, except for his armpits and groin. Some time ago he'd started having his body waxed. That seemed to be when his sexual interest in her had begun to wane—and she had begun to hope that he was seeing someone else.

Apparently satisfied with his appearance, he started dressing, his movements slow, as if he were deliberately putting on a show, as if he were trying to entice her. After he'd tucked in his shirt and straightened his tie, he came back to her side. With his hands, he massaged her shoulders, her neck, then her temple, drawing small circles. "Poor baby. You rest today, and tonight Papa will make you feel better."

He pressed a kiss on the top of her head, grabbed his jacket off the chair, and went humming down the hallway.

As soon as he left, Sara started drinking.

Three hours later she reached for the phone.

Chapter Fifteen

 Ring.
Something ringing.
Door?
Alarm?
Phone.

In order to get everything to the printers in time, Nash had been up most of the night. Now he struggled to open his eyes a crack. Lying on his back on the low, fold-out bed, he groped across the floor, his hand finally coming in contact with the telephone cord. He reeled it in, knocking the receiver off the cradle. He picked it up, and lifted it to his ear.

"Yeah." His voice came out a croak.

At first he thought the line was dead, then someone spoke.

"I'll go."

Sara.

He sat up. "What?"

"I'll go," she said. "To the cabin. With you."

Before he could formulate an answer, she told him to pick her up at the Silver Spur Tap on English Avenue. Then she hung up.

The traffic on the North Side was bad. Nash drove by the Silver Spur, hoping she would be waiting outside. No such luck.

He ended up having to find a parking garage, then walk two blocks to the bar.

It was one of those dingy places that was taller than it was wide, wedged between a corner market and a gym.

He could hear music before he opened the door. The old kind of honky-tonk. Belly-rubbing, western wail. Inside, through the haze of cigarette smoke, he spotted her, sitting near the end of the bar, elbows on the counter, glass to her mouth, oblivious to her surroundings.

Her oblivion gave him time to look her over.

She was dressed a little weird, wearing her green coat, which was normal, but underneath . . . The coat was unbuttoned and hanging open, exposing what looked like a pink, knee-length dress. Under that, she wore black stirrup pants, the stirrups unslung and hanging over bare Achilles tendons. The quarter-inch heels of her slip-on dress shoes were hooked over the bottom rung of the barstool. On her head was his cap, tilted back at a rakish angle.

He watched as she finished off her drink like someone who'd been in the business a long time, watched as she set the empty glass back on the bar top, her movements careful and heavy.

With a sinking feeling, he realized she hadn't called him because she'd wanted to see him. She'd called him because she was drunk.

Wasted.

Run.

Turn around and run, you dumb ass.

He didn't move. People bumped him from behind as they squeezed past.

He watched as she ordered another drink.

The bartender refilled her glass and placed it back in front of her.

Nash moved reluctantly forward, his feet sticking to the floor, the smell of stale beer filling his sinuses.

"You really need to get yourself a hobby," he said, sliding onto the empty bar stool next to hers.

Without taking her attention from her glass, she laughed. A low, throaty sound. Then she turned and looked him full in the face. Her cheeks were flushed, her lips red, her eyelids heavy, covering the upper part of her pupils, doing a reverse sunset.

"You," she said. "*You* can be my hobby."

He should have been insulted. Instead, he was intrigued. Turned on. It was all so bad. So seedy.

When the moon is full, you howl.

She asked him if he wanted a drink. He shook his head.

She finished hers, ordered a pint of bourbon to go, and then she was sliding off the stool, leading him through the smoky bar, to the door.

"Car's two blocks away," he explained once they were outside. He waved his hand in the direction of the parking garage.

She walked beside him, her hands buried in the pockets of her unbuttoned coat, green tails flapping in the frigid winter wind.

Anybody else would have been cold. Anybody else would have been trying to keep her teeth from chattering. She was past that.

"Wait."

He stopped her. He made her turn to face him.

She stood staring calmly at him while he struggled with the buttons of her coat. It would have helped if she'd taken her hands out of her pockets, but she didn't. It was double-breasted. He didn't bother with the inside button, but finally managed to get two of the outside ones fastened.

"Okay."

He took her elbow and steered her in the direction of his car.

It was where he'd left it, tires and all. The hubcaps had been ripped off long ago, so he didn't have to worry about them.

He fished the key from the front pocket of his jeans and unlocked the door. He didn't normally open car doors for women, but he thought that maybe in a situation like this, he should. But she beat him to it. He gave himself a mental shrug, rounded the car, unlocked his side and slid into the driver's seat.

He pumped the gas and turned the ignition. The engine kicked over. Then he was backing out. He threw the car into drive, and they were on their way.

"Lucky for you I just put in a new thermostat," he said, slapping the heat lever to high.

She tossed his gray cap in the backseat. "I'm lucky all right." She slumped down in the passenger seat, one bent knee braced against the glove compartment, then reached into the pocket of her coat to produce the pint of bourbon. "Just can't get that silver spoon out of my mouth." She unscrewed the cap and lifted the decanter to her lips.

"Let me guess. You're the designated driver, right?"

She slid even further down in the seat, took another long swallow, capped the bottle, and stuck it back in her pocket.

This wasn't going at all the way he'd planned. She wasn't the Sara he'd been dreaming about. This one was tough. Hard. About as high as somebody could get.

"Why don't I just take you home?" he suggested, pulling away from a stoplight.

"You offered a weekend. I want a weekend."

"How about coffee? Food?"

"Don't want to lose the buzz."

"Buzz? How about roar? How about a freight train? A jackhammer? A fucking sonic boom?"

"Shut up and drive."

"If you don't want to go home, we could just stop somewhere and rent a room for an hour. You're too wasted to know where you are anyway. Beach or flophouse, what's the difference?"

"This is even more romantic than I'd dreamed."

"Or how about I drop you off at the Betty Ford Clinic? How would that be? Feel in the mood for a little detoxification?"

"Drive."

"Or would that be fornication?"

No reaction.

"How about moderation? Ever heard of that word?"

She wasn't receiving. He was having a conversation with himself.

They took I-80 east, around the tip of Lake Michigan. She wanted to stop to pee in Gary, Indiana. He told her to forget it. He wanted to live a little longer.

Once they got to Michigan, they stopped twice. Once for the can and gas, once for another pint of booze. How the hell could someone so small put away that much booze? Her liver had to be the size of California.

Nash had once read an interesting article about Truman Capote being so drunk he had to be poured out of a plane. The description of poured had stuck in his mind. It was so visual, so perfect. Now, after fifteen years, he could finally put that description to good use.

By the time they reached Harley's cabin, Sara had reached the liquid state.

And really, Nash thought, he'd had enough.

He put the car in park, turned off the ignition, and stared through the windshield at the log cabin. There wasn't another road or house in sight. There were no streetlights or electric poles. No sign of life. Six, maybe ten inches of untouched snow lay on the ground. Snow that wasn't blackened by exhaust, or tracked up by human feet. It covered the cabin's pitched roof. It lay in the creaking, bobbing branches of the huge pines that towered over the cabin. In the distance, through a grove of leafless saplings, was the icy blue of Lake Michigan.

He was two hundred miles from Canada, twenty from the nearest 7 Eleven, and sixty from a town with a sizable population. With Sara Ivy.

And he couldn't help but think that it seemed sacriligious to bring someone along who was too wasted to enjoy it.

Then he had another thought, this one more positive. Maybe this would do it for him. Maybe a weekend with Sara Ivy would get her out of his system once and for all. For good.

"Come on, Truman." He shook her shoulder, trying to wake her from her drunken stupor.

"Don't call me names," she said, batting her hand against the inside of the door, finally finding the latch, turning it, shoving with her shoulder.

It didn't open.

He reached in front of her and pulled up the lock. "I've found this works rather well."

She shoved—and tumbled out onto the ground, into the snow.

He sighed, got out his side, slammed the door, then rounded the car to help her.

She was on her hands and knees, buried to her

thighs and elbows, her coat spread out behind her, a half-empty bottle of bourbon wedged in the snow.

He bent down to grab her by one arm.

She jerked free.

He let her go.

She struggled to push herself to her feet. Her ass went up first, then the rest of her finally followed, until she was standing, until she stood *swaying* in front of him.

Her coat was unbuttoned again. Her black pants were stuck with snow, the knees packed with hardened clumps. Her shoes, her ridiculous shoes were filled with snow, her bare ankles bright red from the cold. And now he realized her dress looked suspiciously like sleepwear.

He didn't know where the laughter came from. It took him totally by surprise. He didn't think he had that kind of spontaneity in him anymore, but suddenly he was laughing. Hard. The kind of laughter that stole his breath. The kind of laughter that made his lungs hurt in a good way.

He was still laughing when a huge snowball hit him full in the face.

His breath caught. He sucked in snow. He coughed. He choked.

He picked up a handful of snow and threw it back. He took a step, snagged his foot on a hidden limb, and fell over backward.

Snowballs pelted him.

"Don't laugh at me!" she screamed. "Don't you dare laugh at me!"

He kept laughing.

"Stop it!"

She bent down, picked up two handfuls of snow, and threw them at him, hitting him full in the face.

The temperature was probably just below freezing, but wet was wet and snow was snow, and cold was cold.

He'd had enough.

He scrambled to his feet. Without hesitation, before she had the chance to reload, he charged, taking her down, his body meeting hers knee to knee, hip to hip, chest to chest.

She grabbed another handful of snow and shoved it in his face. He shook his head, wiped the snow out of his eyes, then grabbed both of her hands and braced them on the ground over her head.

He lifted his chest from hers and ran his gaze down the front of her, to where their bodies pressed compactly together. "Are you wearing pajamas?"

Melting snow from his warm face fell on hers.

Her expression was defiant. "Do tabloid journalists eat yellow snow?"

He laughed again. "My favorite kind."

She blinked, then glanced down at herself, surprise registering in her face when she focused in on what she was wearing. "Yes. I sleep in this."

"That's what I thought."

They were both breathing short and fast, their mingled breath creating a steamy vapor between them.

It was crazy.

He was freezing.

She had to be getting cold.

But when the moon is full . . .

"You are one crazy broad," he said.

Slowly, slowly, he lowered his head, letting go of her hands, bracing his elbows on either side of her face.

His wet lips touched hers.

Icy.

Cold.

Like the snow.

The chill of her nose.

The warmth of her tongue.

He felt her arms go around him, her hands on his shoulders, fingers pressing through his jacket.

He moved his mouth over hers. He sucked her lips. He sucked her tongue.

He got so hard for her he hurt, a sweet, sweet ache pressing against his jeans, a sweet, sweet ache he wanted to put inside her.

She moaned and tugged at his coat. He tried to slide a hand beneath her, to pull her closer. His fingers met cold snow.

For a minute, he'd forgotten where he was, forgotten they were lying outside, forgotten he had snow down his shirt and in his shoes and in his pants.

He let her go.

He got to his feet, then busied himself brushing the snow from his clothes. When he looked back, she was still lying there, watching him, her cheeks a bright red, her lips and the tip of her nose red.

"Come on. Let's go inside," he said, his body throbbing for her. He didn't want to have any time to think about this.

Seeming unaware of his crucial need for her, she stayed where she was.

"I'm going to make an angel," she said.

"What?" He pulled at the waistband of his jeans, trying to adjust things, make himself more comfortable.

"An angel."

She made sweeping motions with her arms and legs, then stopped, sat up, and looked behind her. Apparently not satisfied, she lay down and resumed flapping her legs and arms. "Come on," she said breathlessly. "You make one too."

"Nah."

"Come on. I won't go inside until you make one."

Christ Almighty.

He hunkered down beside her, thinking facedown would be the way to handle his immediate problem. Instead, he sprawled out on his back and proceeded to flap his arms and legs, the snow stinging his already cold wrists and ankles, the towering evergreen creaking, swirling above their heads.

I am fearfully and wonderfully made.
—Psalms 139:14

Chapter Sixteen

She stumbled twice going up the steps, but she didn't seem to notice. Once on the porch, Nash leaned her against the wall, fished out Harley's keys, unlocked the door, and, hand to her shoulders, directed her inside. He closed the door behind them and hit the light switch. He let go of her, crossed the room and turned up the heat. Then he plopped down on the cedar bench just below the thermostat.

He closed his eyes and rested his head against the wall. Under his feet, in the basement below, the furnace kicked on.

She'd worn him out.

He heard her footsteps.

"Bathroom's that way," he said, motioning behind him without opening his eyes.

Her intoxication had certainly put a different twist on the situation. The thing to do would be to turn around and head back.

He was almost asleep when he felt something on his knees. He opened his eyes to see her kneeling between his legs, running her hands up and down his thighs. He could feel her hands through his jeans, and those hands were cold.

He was cold. And whether or not she knew it, *she* was cold, and, due to the fact that her blood was now about ninety-proof, it could take a little more than sex to warm her up.

Feeling irritated and protective toward her at the same time, he got to his feet, pulling her up after him. She clung to his waist, swaying slightly, tilting her face toward him, as if expecting a kiss. An invitation he couldn't ignore.

With his arms around her, he bent his head until his lips touched hers.

Cold.

She burrowed closer, working her hands up the back of his jacket, the chill following the same path.

He brought a hand down to cup her bottom, lifting her against him. Her mouth opened under his and he slid his tongue past her teeth.

Cold as ice.

He was more than reluctant to break contact, but he pulled away, his arms still around her, keeping her snug against his groin. "Let's get you into a warm shower."

In the bathroom, he turned on the wall heater. Instant radiant heat.

She stood in front of it, her hands extended. "Feels good." Then she turned to him, running her hands across his chest. His pulse quickening, he reached under her gown and hooked his fingers in the waistband of her pants. His fingertips skimmed her flesh as he slid her pants down her hips.

She wasn't wearing underwear.

He groaned, closed his eyes, then opened them.

She was staring up at him. "Touch me."

He walked her backward until she was against the wall. He worked a leg between hers, then he slowly raised that leg, lifting her from the floor. She gasped and grabbed his shoulders to steady herself. Her eyelids fluttered closed, then open. A pulse beat frantically in her neck.

Light from the ceiling fell across her face, shadowing her dark lashes, the smudges that were always in evidence under her eyes now exaggerated, the gray of her eyes cloudy, blurred with sensuality.

He hesitated.

She turned her face, a question in her gaze—and he saw a bruise running along her jaw.

"How'd you get that?" he asked, tracing a finger along the discoloration.

Her eyes shifted from his. She lifted a tentative hand to her face, her voice trembling along with her fingers.

"I was drunk," she said, suddenly seeming more focused, as if the subject had brought her back to reality.

He was getting in deeper and deeper. He didn't want to care, didn't want to think about what she was doing to herself. But he did care. And he couldn't stop himself, couldn't ignore her problem. "Sara, Sara." He loved to say her name. It drifted over his tongue like a soft breeze. "What makes you so self-destructive?" he whispered, pressing his lips to the madly beating spot on her neck. "Let me help you. I want to help you."

She stiffened. "I think—I think—"

He lifted and lowered his leg. He could feel her moist heat through the denim of his jeans.

"What do you think?" he asked, his voice husky.

"I think . . . I'm ready to take a shower now. By myself."

Was it his destiny to be forever tormented by this woman? Did she get a buzz out of dragging him to the edge, only to push him away?

He lowered his leg until her feet touched the floor. She pushed a stray lock of hair behind her ear, and as she did, he saw that her hand trembled. The irritation he was feeling instantly crumbled. He left her alone.

With shaking hands, Sara locked the bathroom door.

Nash's comment about her bruise had brought her around, had sobered her. It wasn't the only bruise she had. On the soft inner flesh of both arms, she had circular marks—perfect fingerprints that she wouldn't be able to say had been caused by a fall.

She would put him off until dark. He wouldn't see her bruises in the dark.

Her heart was still hammering when she stepped into the shower. She let the warm water run over her face, her hair, her body, soothing her, relaxing her, making her feel sleepy.

Ten minutes later, barefoot, aware of her nakedness beneath her gown, she stepped from the bathroom, a towel wrapped around her hair.

Nash was sitting on the couch, his back to her, a beer bottle resting against his thigh. Without turning around he said, "I started a gas fire upstairs."

She looked behind her, then followed the wooden stairs to a cozy little room with a slanted roof, an antique white iron double bed and a small paned window. Outside, darkness had fallen.

She shut off the light, found the control for the fireplace, and turned it down so nothing but a dim glow illuminated the room. Downstairs, she heard the sound of the shower.

"Sara."

She was lying on her side, a pillow under her head, heat from the fire warming her face.

Sleepy. So sleepy. She was no longer drunk, but she wasn't completely sober, either.

He repeated her name.

But the heavy languidness that had invaded her bones couldn't be shaken.

She felt the towel slip from her head. Damp hair fell against her face.

The bed shifted. She felt him next to her, a hip perhaps. Then something touched her scalp . . . and trailed through her hair.

A comb.

He was combing her hair.

The fire, her sleepiness, the alcohol still in her bloodstream, all combined to make the scene take on a sleep-drugged, incredibly sensual, dreamlike quality.

When she was little, she liked to have her hair brushed. She and her sister used to take turns brushing each other's hair. It had felt good. Soothing.

But this. *This.* Never had a man brushed her hair. It was innocently erotic, full of a sweetness she wanted to both deny and embrace.

She rolled to her back, her head on his lap. She could hardly remember the events that had brought them to this point. There had been the numbing loneliness, the overpowering need to see him, talk to him. There had been her phone call. . . .

This shouldn't be happening. This shouldn't be happening. . . .

In the subdued glow of the low fire, his face was cast in shadow.

He spoke. "You are so beautiful."

She wanted to believe him. He sounded so earnest, as if he truly meant it, but she knew better.

His hand slid up her bare leg, skimming her thigh.

"Do you always run around without underwear?" he asked, a barely detectable hitch in his voice.

"I forgot it," she said, all of her concentration on his hands.

One of them slid across her abdomen, his fingers threading through her silky, tangled curls. "That way, you entirely avoid the car wreck/clean underwear problem, hmm?"

"Yes," she said breathlessly.

"That was supposed to be funny. You can laugh."

"I don't laugh."

"Everybody laughs."

His head came down. She felt his breath against her cheek. Then slowly, ever so slowly, his lips made contact with hers. Softly. Just a brush. Then his tongue outlined her lips, a sinful, seductive trick.

Her arms had been lying limply at her sides, but now she reached for him, pulling him closer, loving the play of his muscles under the cotton of his shirt.

His tongue slipped deep inside her mouth . . . and his fingers slipped inside the moistness between her legs. And she forgot about the *why*'s and *why-not*'s. Just this once, she told herself. Don't think past the moment.

She gasped, allowing his tongue deeper penetration. She arched her back, deepening the kiss of his fingers.

They were both needing air when he straightened. "We don't have to do this," he said breathlessly.

She sensed that he was fighting for control. "I want to." And it was true.

This time was different. She wasn't afraid. This time had nothing to do with a bargain.

He fumbled for the hem of her gown. She sat up and raised her arms so he could tug it over her head.

She stretched, her body tight, her stomach contracted.

He stood and stripped off his clothes.

She fell back on the bed, watching him, until he stood naked before her, his body bathed in golden light and soft shadow. He was contoured muscles, broad shoulders, narrow hips.

"You have hair on your chest." Her voice sounded husky and strange.

"Don't look if you don't like it."

"I like it. It's sexy."

"Good."

He came to her then, pressing his weight down on her. His skin was hot and satin smooth, his muscles hard. He kissed her—open-mouthed kisses. He sucked her lips, her tongue.

"You drive me crazy," he whispered, moving down to kiss her throat, then her breasts.

His mouth was wet and hot, and when he pulled the tip of her breast deep into his mouth, she moaned and arched against him. His teeth scraped her rigid nipple again and again.

"You are so sweet, so sweet."

She, who had never really enjoyed the touch of a man, was curling, swirling, fainting, drowning. She was hot. Tight. Filled with pleasure, pain. She was someone else. Someone with no ties. Someone with no yesterdays or tomorrows.

And that lent her the freedom to let herself go as much as Sara Ivy could let go.

She grabbed his shoulders. She grabbed the bed. She twisted beneath him.

He moved lower. His hands slid beneath her bottom, cupping her buttocks. He lifted her. She felt his warm breath, felt his hair brush her inner thighs, and then his mouth found her.

His tongue dipped, circled, dipped with torturous skill. She could feel his breath, his teeth, his lips. Devouring. Licking. Sucking. Driving her closer and closer to the edge.

Something not right.

Something too good.

Something too . . . too—

Sweet.

An ache.

A mindless, sweating, gasping . . .

Ache.

"Nash!"

Her voice was a plea. But it was already too late. She was falling. She was drifting. She was flying away. "Stop. Stop . . ."

Her body bucked.

Every muscle in her body contracted, and contracted, and contracted.

She cried out in pleasure. And she cried out in fear.

A weakness invaded her arms and legs. When she could finally move, she scrambled to the head of the bed, crouching there on her knees. She grabbed a pillow and hugged it to her. "Why did you do that?"

He was braced on his hands and knees, sounding as if he'd just run a marathon. She could see he was surprised and perplexed by her reaction to his lovemaking.

"Y-you scared me," she said.

His expression softened. "Sara, I'm sorry." He looked at her in such a tender way she thought her heart might break.

As he watched her, as he waited, she gradually became aware of her body. The way her breasts felt engorged, her nipples tender. She could still feel the imprint of his hands on her bottom. She could still feel a coiling heat, a throbbing between her legs.

He came a little closer, moving on his hands and knees. He reached out and grasped the corner of the pillow. He gave it a gentle tug. Not enough to pull it from her grip. She made that decision.

She let go and the pillow was pulled aside so that she was kneeling naked before him in the glowing firelight.

"Sara," he said, a catch in his voice that sent another kind of thrill through her, "I want to be in you."

His bold words, spoken in a rasping voice, a passion-filled voice, warmed her. She felt his need. She wanted him in her.

"You won't do that again," she asked, scooting down on the bed as he tucked her beneath him.

"Love you with my mouth?"

She nodded.

"Not unless you want me to." He lowered himself, and when his flesh touched hers, she was surprised to find that he was sweating and shaking. The velvet heat of him pressed hotly against the softness of her abdomen, sending an erotic bolt through her belly.

She relaxed her legs.

She opened for him. An invitation.

She felt a shudder run through him. His hips spasmed. He groaned.

"Sara, Sara. I'm sorry."

With one thrust, he buried himself in her, filling her, stretching her with his length, his thickness. His lips found hers. And then he began to move.

She didn't know why he'd apologized for something that felt so wonderful. "Sorry . . . for what . . . ?"

Their bodies were wet and slick, and in the back of

her mind she felt vaguely surprised that it didn't hurt, that he moved so easily.

"Like to—" He laughed a little, a breathless burst of air. "—take it slow." Faster and faster he pumped, his breathing ragged against her ear, their bodies sliding, slipping.

The roar in her head was back, the sweet, hot ache. Mindless sensations were building in her, this time familiar, the very sensations he'd evoked with his mouth.

He thrust, driving into her again and again, until shudder after shudder went through him.

"Sara," he whispered hoarsely against her neck. "Sweet, sweet Sara."

She may have cried out, she didn't know. She may have moaned. She may have held him tightly as they both found fulfillment. She only knew that for a moment, for a few magical seconds in her otherwise shameful life, she realized total contentment.

"The X-factor," he mumbled a little later, the weight of his body heavy on her.

"Mmm?"

"The X-factor. It's when everything comes together perfectly. With pilots, it can mean the difference between life and death."

He rolled off her, and she felt a chill against her skin where his body had been. Before she could begin to feel sad, he pulled her close, tucking her against him. He felt for her hand, lifted it, brushing his lips across her knuckles, making her feel sad anyway, making an ache blossom in her chest.

"Serendipity," she whispered.

Nash woke up on his stomach, the heat of Sara's limber body moving across his back, settling on top of him. He could feel the soft globes of her breasts just beneath his shoulder blades, he could feel the heat between her thighs pressed to his bottom, a smooth leg on either side of his hips.

He grew stiff.

She bent closer and nibbled his earlobe.

His breath caught. He quickly rolled over, keeping her on top, his hands on her thighs. He pulled down her head and kissed her, hotly, desperately, his hands moving over her shoulders, the curve of her back, her bottom, her thighs.

"Let me taste you again," he begged.

"It scares me."

"Why?"

"You're too good."

"Too good?"

"You make me lose control. I don't like to lose control."

"That's what it's all about—losing it."

"I don't know . . ."

He knew she'd liked it, knew he could pleasure her more if she'd only let him. "If you want me to stop, I'll stop."

She rolled over, so her head was on the pillow. He kissed her face, then her breasts.

"I don't know what to do."

"You don't have to do anything. Here." He took both her hands, lifted them above her head and wrapped her fingers around the rails of the bed. "Just hang on."

Her position put an arch in her back and gave him unhindered access to her full, rose-nippled breasts. He cupped them, drawing pleasure from their weight. He moved his hands in a circle, her nipples burning the center of his palm. He rubbed, moving from her breasts to her ribcage, lifting her with both hands. Lifting and releasing, lifting and releasing. And then he moved down.

He pressed his lips to her navel, her abdomen, then lower . . . to her hot, throbbing flesh.

He felt a shiver run through her.

He didn't want to break contact, but he remembered his promise.

He looked up. "Okay?" he asked, his breathing as erratic as his heartbeat.

"Yes." The word was a whisper. A sweet, sweet yearning.

He kissed her.

She moved her hips ever so slightly, a signal. A sound came from deep in her throat.

He kissed her again. This time he left his lips there. His tongue moved against her swollen skin.

She shifted. She was making pleasure sounds, stirring his need. She arched, bringing herself closer. Her hands flailed for him.

"I need you," she gasped, her hands digging into his hair, alternately pushing him away and pulling him closer, as if she didn't understand the desire thrumming through her veins. "Need to hold you."

Without taking his mouth away, he shifted his body so she could touch him if she wanted to.

He took her with his mouth.

Licking.

Sucking.

He felt her hands on his hips. She pulled him close. He felt the sweetness of her breath against his flesh. A wracking shudder went through him. Followed by another. Her lips touched him, velvet to velvet. He moaned and she cried out, arching against his mouth, again and again and again.

Hope is an echo, hope ties itself yonder, yonder.
—Carl Sandburg

Chapter Seventeen

Nash woke to gray winter light that cast the tiny room in gloom or cozy shadow, depending upon one's perspective. Looking through the small window, he saw that snow was falling, thick and heavy.

He lay there, hardly daring to breathe, the dark head nestled against his chest stirring up a tender ache he wanted nothing to do with. Long-forgotten emotions moved through him, a longing for something that could never be.

The white sheet was pulled up under her arms. During the night, the blankets had slid to the floor, not needed.

They'd spent the night together, but he really didn't know her any better than he had that first time he'd seen her, standing across the crowded suite of the Renaissance.

At that time he'd had the strange notion that he'd like to wrap her in a blanket and take her someplace warm. Someplace safe.

He rubbed the stubble of his jaw, keeping movement to a minimum, not wanting to wake her. He would go downstairs and make coffee. Did she like coffee? What about food? What did she like to eat? *Did* she eat?

He knew *nothing* about her.

Except that she drank too much.

Except that she was married.

Except that she'd tried to kill herself. And that he'd stopped her.

He slid out of bed.

She turned toward the warm spot where he'd been, her knees drawn up, one hand under her pillow, one hand curled, resting on top.

Watching her, he slipped into his gray jogging pants and white T-shirt. In the dim light, he could see the bruise along her jaw, the smudges beneath her sooty lashes.

There it was. That pang. That ache.

He wanted to help her.

But who was he to think he had any answers, any solutions? He was running from life too, just in a different direction. And he understood that oblivion was sometimes the best way, the only way.

He went downstairs and started the coffee.

While water dripped through the filter, Nash looked in the freezer and found a package of frozen eggs. Harley's old man ran a tight ship.

Nash defrosted the package in the microwave, heated a skillet on the stove, then poured the package contents into the sizzling pan.

It wasn't like him to think past the moment, but he kept finding himself dwelling on their return trip.

He didn't want her to go.

In particular, he didn't want her to go back to *him*, to Ivy.

So what are you saying, old boy? That you want her to move in with you?

No, no. He didn't want *that*, he tried to tell himself. God, no.

But for her to go back to Ivy . . .

He was making toast when he heard a footfall in the room above his head.

His heart beat an irregular rhythm, then settled.

Hurried footsteps sounded on the stairs.

She was running.

The toast popped out. He caught both slices, dropped them on a plate, then grabbed a butter knife.

Sara flashed past the doorway, the pink of her nightgown a blur. The bathroom door banged, then she was back, her black pants in place under her gown. "I have to go," she said breathlessly. She hopped around, putting on one shoe, then the other.

"I thought we'd head back tomorrow."

"I have to go *now*."

She was the most frustrating woman he'd ever met. One moment, shy, almost backward, the next as spoiled and demanding as a child.

"Sit down and eat something first."

"There isn't time." She rushed from the kitchen. A moment later, she returned, coat in hand. She shrugged into it. She buttoned it. She stood in the doorway waiting.

"Have you looked outside?"

She glanced over her shoulder, in the direction of the living room, then back at him, question on her face.

"It's snowing," he explained.

She raised both arms in an impatient gesture. "I don't care if it's raining cows. I'm leaving."

The scrambled eggs were done. He turned off the heat and removed the pan from the burner.

"How do you propose to do that?" He rested one hip against the counter. "Dogsled?"

"Ha, ha, ha."

He was hurt, goddamn it, he realized. Hurt.

He had romanticized this whole thing. He had envisioned their having a tender breakfast together, then maybe a shower. He had even been thinking of trying to talk her into not going back to Ivy.

What a sap.

When he fell, he fell big-time.

They'd had their night. She was done with him. She couldn't wait to get away.

How ironic that he of all people should have a woman hurt him this way. If she had been anyone else, he would have been more than happy to get rid of her. Hell, he would have had the car running and the driveway shoveled before she'd even gotten up.

He deserved this. He really did.

He was thinking what a pathetic bastard he was when he heard the sound of an engine turning over.

Son of a—

He ran out of the kitchen and through the living room. He jerked open the front door in time to see his car burrowing through the snow in the direction of the two-lane.

He ran out on the porch, remembered he was barefoot, and ran back in the house. He shoved his feet into his workboots, grabbed his coat, and hurried outside.

Brakelights.

Under cover of the porch, he stopped. He heard a familiar revving sound as she tried to rock the car back and forth.

Stuck.

He was amazed that she'd made it as far as she had.

He zipped his coat, shoved his hands into his pockets and watched, a front-row seat. And he couldn't deny that he felt a certain amount of satisfaction with the result of her little attempt at desertion, even if it did mean his car was stuck.

The engine died.

He heard the grind, grind, grind as she tried to re-start it. Once the engine was warm, it flooded easy as hell.

When nothing happened, she got out and stood staring at his car.

He brought his hands together in a slow, sarcastic motion, palm to palm.

Clap.

Clap.

Clap.

She looked up, and even though the length of a football field separated them, he could almost see the glint in her eyes.

She threw him the finger.

He stopped clapping so he could laugh. He laughed loud, so she would hear him.

Slamming the car door, she swung around and started walking the opposite direction, trudging through the deep snow.

He let out a sigh, bracing his hands on his hips. Did he have time to go inside and get a pair of socks? He hated to think of walking through the snow without socks.

For all its depth and heaviness, she was making headway.

He let out another sigh and plunged down the steps after her.

He should have had the advantage, since he jogged, since he was dressed more appropriately, since he hadn't put away a gallon of booze, since he'd eaten something in the last twenty-four hours, but she seemed to have desperation on her side.

She was bounding through the trees like a flushed deer.

He paused in his pursuit long enough to cup his hands to his mouth. "Truman!"

She didn't slow.

But her direction quickly became skewed. No longer was she heading for the highway. Instead, she'd veered off course and was heading toward the lake, barreling blindly through saplings. Staggering. Tripping. Falling. Getting up again. Always getting up again.

When she reached the top of the rise that would reveal the beach and water below, she stopped.

From a hundred yards away, he saw her falter.

Lake wind tugged at her hair. It whipped her coat about her legs.

She lifted a hesitant hand to her face, as if to brush the hair from her eyes. She looked behind her, back the way she'd come, then turned once again toward the lake.

As he watched, he saw her collapse, falling to her hands and knees, defeated.

He moved steadily in her direction, sometimes running, sometimes walking, loath to face her, yet needing to make sure she was okay, knowing she wasn't.

When he reached her, he looked down, and his heart contracted. "Y-You've lost a shoe."

She followed the direction of his horrified gaze, to where her bare foot was half buried in the snow. Slowly, she lifted her face to his. It was wet with tears, and she looked so goddamn lost it broke his heart.

"I'll see that you get home."

Wind-driven snow battered him. Behind them, Lake Michigan roared in on whitecaps to crash against icy shores.

"It's r-really b-beautiful h-here, isn't it?" she asked through frozen lips.

"I'll see that you get home," he repeated.

She made a small, distressed sound and shook her head, as if it didn't matter, as if it was too late.

A couple of yards away, he spotted her shoe. He scooped it up, dumped out the snow, and stuck the shoe in his pocket.

Then, kneeling down beside her, he braced her hand on his shoulder while resting her foot against his thigh. He brushed off the snow, then wrapped his fingers around her icy foot, trying to warm it.

She seemed past feeling discomfort. She didn't even seem to notice the cold.

"What have I done?" she whispered to herself. "What have I done?"

His throat hurt so much he didn't think he'd get the words out. "Mistakes happen," he said thickly. "If he loves you . . . If you love him . . ."

He heard a strangled sob.

Unable to look at her, he shifted to a crouch, hands on knees. "Hop on."

"W-What?"

"You can't walk barefoot through the snow. Come on."

Gingerly, she leaned against his back. Before she could change her mind and move away, he grabbed both her legs and straightened. Her arms quickly went around his neck.

Piggyback he carried her, heading toward the cabin.

Experience enables you to recognize a mistake when you make it again.
—Franklin P. Jones

Chapter Eighteen

Sara sat on the couch, pants rolled above her knees, feet in a bucket of lukewarm water.

"You're just damn lucky you weren't out there any longer or you would have ended up with frostbite," Nash said. "And damn lucky the temperature wasn't any lower."

She removed her feet from the water and began to dry them. Nash tugged the towel from her hands, knelt down in front of her, and briskly rubbed her feet. "I want you to know I wouldn't do this for just anybody."

Her feet dry and warm, blood tingling in her toes, she curled up in the corner of the couch, quilt around her shoulders. He left with the towel and bucket to return a couple of minutes later carrying two plates.

"I'm not hungry."

He put one of the plates on the table in front of her. "You do have a digestive system, don't you? Or are you on a liquid diet?"

"Funny."

She looked at the plate.

Reheated eggs. Soggy toast.

Her stomach lurched.

"Eat, or I'll force-feed you."

He plopped down across from her in an overstuffed chair, picked up his fork and plate, and dug in.

His hair was ruffled. He needed to shave. He looked rough. He looked safe.

She wished she could know him better. She wished they had never met. She found herself fantasizing about what it would be like to wake up next to him every day.

He glanced up and saw that she wasn't eating. He wagged his fork at her. "I'm not kidding about the force-feeding."

With absolutely no appetite, she picked up the plate. She stuck the fork in the eggs. She took a bite. Then another.

"This wasn't supposed to happen," she said, swallowing.

"What?"

"You. Me."

"You called, remember?"

"You put the idea in my head. And anyway, when I called I was a little—" Her words trailed off. She had no desire to verbalize her weakness.

"I used to live in this house where I hit my head on a beam every time I went into the basement," he said.

She didn't miss a beat. "Let me guess. You finally learned to duck."

"No, I quit going into the basement."

"A little extreme."

"Maybe." He got to his feet. "More?"

She looked down at her plate, surprised to find it empty.

"No. Thanks."

He gathered up the dirty dishes and headed for the kitchen.

Two minutes later, she found him at the sink, up to his elbows in dish soap.

She picked up a towel and started drying.

As if by silent agreement, there was no more mention of last night, or of Sara's flight of panic that morning.

As they worked, he made small talk. Small talk over dishes. An oasis—or was it a mirage?—of homey comfort in the midst of chaos and confusion. He told her the cabin belonged to Harley's dad. "His old man is James Gillette."

"The newspaper mogul?"

"None other."

She didn't get it. "How can someone who grew up in a newspaper household produce a tabloid like *Shoot the Moon*?"

"Harley's got this thing about broadsheets. He hates 'em. He had the chance to head some big paper in Springfield, but he turned it down."

"To do a tabloid." Half question, half statement.

"Gotta have your priorities."

They finished the dishes.

Priorities. She knew all about priorities.

Nash let the water out of the sink, dried his hands, then grabbed his coat and shrugged into it, adjusting the collar. "I'm going to walk to the highway and see if I can find somebody with a four-wheel drive or snowplow or something who'll make a path for us."

She wanted to stop him. She wanted to tell him to stay, to lock the door to keep out the world. But there would be no escaping Donovan. And every second Nash spent with her put him in more danger. Every second she was gone was a threat to her father, her family.

"Wait here and make sure the gas is off, the thermostat is turned down and the door locked."

Nash stood at the door, hand on the knob.

I will remember this, she thought. *Years from now,*

when you're looking up at your stars, and I'm staring out the window of Donovan's house, I'll remember this, and that memory will comfort me.

He looked as if he were about to speak, then maybe thought better of it. A ghost of a smile played about the corners of his sensuous mouth, then he shook his head just slightly, as if clearing it, as if he didn't get her, as if he didn't get any of it. And who would? Then he opened the door and left, a blast of cold air hitting her, chilling her to the bone, to the soul.

On the way to the highway, Nash stopped by his stranded car. It still smelled faintly of gasoline. Another hour and it should start.

He tossed his duffel bag in the backseat, then began walking.

Snow was still coming down, covering their earlier footsteps. It would have been a good day to stay inside, making love in front of the fire. . . .

Dream on.

At the highway, he was ignored by vehicles flying past, splattering him with brown slush. Finally a four-wheel-drive truck with a rusted-out body and monster snow tires pulled onto the shoulder. The passenger door flew open.

Behind the wheel was a kid of about seventeen dressed in brown duck coveralls, green Northern boots, and a plaid wool cap, the screams of Aerosmith's Steve Tyler hitting Nash full in the face.

"Need a lift?"

Nash hopped in. The condition of the floorboard instantly told him he was riding in a chore truck. Hot air blowing from the heater stirred up the smell of cow manure, something Nash, being a city kid, had experienced only a few times in his life.

"Just pulled somebody out of the ditch along I-80," the kid said, obviously enjoying the bad weather. "This lake-effect snow can hit before you know it. One minute it's sunny and the road is dry, the next it's bumper-car time. I'm Danny."

"Nash."

"You from around here?"

"Chicago."

"Chicago? Man, I try to stay away from that place."

"It's bad everywhere. Ever see the movie *Deliverance*?"

Danny laughed.

They chitchatted. Danny told Nash he was trying to figure out what he wanted to do with his life.

"I'm still working on that one," Nash said.

They reached Nash's car and found the snow had been cleaned off the windows and Sara was waiting behind the wheel.

"Wife?" Danny asked.

Nash let out a snort. "Hell, no."

"Girlfriend?"

"Not even that."

"You're old enough to be my dad, you don't know what you want to do with your life, you have a woman with you who isn't your wife or your girlfriend, but you're looking at her like she's the last glass of water in the middle of a baking desert, and somebody's getting ready to dump that water on the ground."

Was he so easy to read? Did he really have it that bad? Here he'd hoped last night would have been enough to get her out of his system. Instead, she seemed more a part of him than ever before. He knew the softness of her touch. He knew how her skin smelled. He knew how she tasted. He knew the feel of her body under his.

He knew she loved somebody else.

Her husband. Not unusual for a wife to love her husband.

Danny dug out a pair of cloth work gloves from under the pile of clothes and trash that littered the seat. He tossed the gloves to Nash. "You're more of a mess than I am."

Nash slipped on the gloves and laughed. "You're a regular smart-ass."

Danny pointed his chin in the direction of the truckbed. "There's a tow chain in the back. I'll get turned around while you hook it to your car."

Nash found the chain buried under a bunch of hay. He pulled it out, metal clanging against metal, knocking into empty feed buckets.

While Danny maneuvered the truck into position, Nash crawled under his car, snow working down his shirt and pants. He attached one end of the chain to the axle. With Danny in position, he hooked the other end to the truck's bumper hitch.

Nash cupped his hands around his mouth. "Start the car!"

The engine turned over.

"Put it in gear!"

Sara nodded and pulled down the gearshift lever.

Danny inched the truck slowly forward, until the chain was taut. He gave it a little more gas, then a little more.

With a lurch, the Fairlane jumped forward. Then the car was moving smoothly behind the four-wheeler.

Danny stopped, then reversed slightly in order to give the chain some slack. He jumped out and unhooked one end from his truck, while Nash wiggled back under the Fairlane to unhook the other.

"Thanks," Nash said, handing the heavy wet chain and gloves back to Danny.

"You shouldn't have any trouble if you follow my tracks out."

"If you're ever in Chicago, look me up. I'll give you a tour."

"Take care."

Nash brushed the snow off himself as best he could, then slid behind the steering wheel while Sara moved across the seat to the passenger side.

An hour later they were out of the lake-effect snow and driving on dry pavement.

Two hours after that, Nash was taking the off-ramp that led to Sara's part of town.

Halfway up her street, she asked him to stop. He pulled to a curb. How many times had they enacted this scenario? Three? Four?

He waited.

"This can't happen again," she said. "Don't call me."

No good-bye. Or, I'm sorry. It was great, but we both have our lives to lead. Just, Don't call me. As if he were disposable. As if she'd had her fill, her thrill, and was done with him. Finished.

He swallowed. Hard. He kept his eyes trained straight ahead, down the street that led to her house. "No sweat."

"If you find out I'm working someplace, don't come there."

He was getting kind of sick of Chicago. The cold. The snow. The wind. Maybe he'd move. Maybe he'd go south. "What if you're trying to swim to the middle of Lake Michigan?" he asked. No, he wouldn't mess things up for her, make things harder. He'd just get out of the picture completely.

A thoughtful pause. Then, "Let me go."

The door handle turned. Hinges creaked.

Go then. Just get the hell out.

She didn't. Instead, she closed the door.

"You never really liked me, did you?" she asked.

He knew what she was doing. Trying to relieve any guilt she might be feeling about using him. Using him up.

It was in his head to tell her he'd been crazy about her, infatuated, maybe even a little in love—just to hurt her the way she was hurting him, but then he realized he couldn't do that to her.

"No," he said woodenly, deciding to let her off the hook. "I never really liked you."

"It was all a game, wasn't it?"

A game. Was that what she wanted it to be?

"I had a bet with somebody." He congratulated himself on his quick thinking. He could swim through black water. Hell, he could swim through mud.

He heard her indrawn breath.

"A bet?"

She twisted around in the seat. He sensed that she was looking at him. He could feel the heaviness of her gaze.

"To see if you could screw Donovan Ivy's wife?"

There was a roar of pain, of denial lodged way down inside him. He was afraid if he opened his mouth it would come ripping out. His head turned until he was staring back at her. And he realized how simple it would be to make her hate him. How painfully simple. "You said it, not me."

She recoiled.

Martyring himself, he watched her. He finally found

his voice. Thank God it sounded normal enough. A little raspy, but she wouldn't be able to detect anything unusual. She didn't know him that well.

"There were different kinds of bets," he said, twisting the knife a little deeper into them both.

She swallowed. She ran a tongue across her lips. "Different kinds?"

Hating him would make it easier for her to walk away, to go back to the man she loved. "Depending on the sex."

She stared and stared. "Sex?"

A subject they had avoided all day. Her fear of him. Her eventual trust. Her eventual response. So sweet. So damn sweet.

"Yeah, there was traditional—or, I guess a professional might say, vaginal."

Heartbeat.

"The typical, white-bread, boring stuff."

Heartbeat. Heartbeat.

"Then . . . there was oral."

Heartbeat, heartbeat, heartbeat.

"Then there was oral, both partners."

Something flickered in the depths of her dark-lashed eyes, and he thought of a pebble tossed in a lake, creating circle after circle after circle.

"Money," she said flatly, with emotionless acceptance.

That was what hurt the most. That she wasn't really surprised. That she'd expected no better of him.

"That makes you a prostitute," she added.

He rolled that around in his head, willing to play the game, a distant part of him amazed at the turn things had taken, another part numb to it all. "Yeah. I guess it does."

As he watched, mesmerized, horror-struck by the

whole impossible situation, the blood drained from her face.

There, he thought. *You got what you wanted, you're free.* But he felt no satisfaction, only pain.

She let out a choked gasp, blindly searching for the door handle. She found it, tumbled out, and ran up the sidewalk, in the direction of home.

Nash forced himself to breathe shallowly. Had to surface slowly. Had to get acclimated.

He finally put the car in gear and turned around in the middle of the street, tires screaming.

heavenless hell and homeless home
—e.e. cummings

Chapter Nineteen

Trying to pull herself together, mind numb, body on autopilot, Sara stepped into the house and closed the door.

She stood there, eyes closed, head tipped back, both hands behind her on the doorknob.

Nash.

Don't think about him, don't think about him at all.

But she couldn't stop herself. She had sacrificed everything to be with him, *everything*, only to discover it had all been a sham, all been for nothing.

Don't think about him.

Gradually, little by little, she became aware of the silence in the house.

Safe.

For now.

Donovan wasn't home. Maybe he wasn't even back from his trip.

Yes!

She latched onto that idea, she clung to it.

Yes! Yes!

Maybe he didn't even know she'd been gone!

Maybe—

"Sara?"

Terror jumped in her throat as her husband's voice drifted from somewhere beyond the kitchen.

How old is your father now? Doesn't your sister have children? Wouldn't they be in school? Wouldn't they walk home by themselves?

She willed her feet to move, one step, then another.

It used to be his threats that kept her tied to him. But more and more, to her shame, it was also her lack of self-worth. She deserved whatever he did to her.

It wouldn't be so bad. She'd been through it before. Lots of times. She could go through it again. In two hours, it would be over and Donovan would pamper her. He would tell her how much he loved her.

And really, could the physical pain be any worse than the pain of Nash's words?

Oh, God.

Don't think about that. Don't think about that.

"Sara?"

No way out.

Donovan's voice came threading through the kitchen, coming from the direction of the solarium, the hot tub.

Like someone in a funeral procession, she continued her slow march, one jerky step after the other. Down the hallway. Through the kitchen.

The door to the solarium was ajar. She could smell the chemicals in the whirlpool, feel the humid heaviness of the air. Through the door, she saw Donovan, relaxing in the tub.

Maybe he didn't know. Maybe he didn't care.

"Did you forget about our date?" he asked.

Her gaze shifted from his face to a bottle of champagne near his elbow, then back.

Waiting for her. He was waiting for her.

Beside the ice bucket were two champagne glasses.

She swallowed. Her body, from her feet up, slowly turned to lead.

"Come, darling. Take off your coat."

With the finesse that was so much a part of him, he twisted off the wire, popped the stopper, poured the bubbling liquid into the two glasses, and extended one toward her.

She couldn't move.

No way could she move.

He waited, glass extended.

Move. Play the game.

Maybe everything will be okay.

Maybe he won't hurt me too much.

The message somehow got through from her brain to her feet. She shuffled forward, the soles of her shoes making a shushing sound on the tile.

"Did you forget our date?"

The stem of the champagne glass slid from his fingers to hers. Liquid splashed the back of her hand.

He lifted his glass.

Cheers.

His eyes were bloodshot. His normally clean-shaven face was shadowed. Even his chest was stubbled.

Without taking his eyes from hers, he brought his glass to his mouth, finishing the contents in one swallow.

She lifted her own glass, but could only manage to wet her lips.

"Take off your coat."

A command.

With her coat on, she felt less vulnerable. A little safer.

"Take off your coat."

She slid it from her shoulders. She draped it across the back of a white wrought-iron patio chair.

His eyes flickered over her clothes, her pink nightgown, and she realized her mistake.

"The rest of it."

She couldn't do this. She couldn't let him touch her. Violate her.

Run.

Her face must have given her away—he'd always been able to read her every thought, no matter how well concealed.

The muscles in her legs had barely tightened in order to flee, when his hand lashed out, his fingers wrapping cruelly about her ankle.

He jerked, knocking her off her feet. She fell straight down, her hip striking the side of the tub so hard that her teeth knocked. And then she was in the water, her gown billowing around her, filling with air.

Donovan dug his fingers into her arms. "You bitch," he said through gritted teeth. "You stinking, lying, cheating bitch."

It was coming.

"Don't hurt me," she pleaded, her mouth trembling, tears of terror springing to her eyes. "Don't hurt me," she repeated, hating herself for begging, hating herself for falling apart. Hating herself.

He shoved her under. Bubbles escaped her gown, rising in front of her face. She struggled.

He held her down.

She could see him above the surface of the water, rage contorting his features. He was shouting at her, but she couldn't hear him.

Maybe it's better this way. . . .

He pulled her up.

She inhaled, gulping in air and water.

He shoved her under again.

He pulled her up.

Air.

Blessed air.

She convulsed, gagging up water. Sucking in air.
"Who, Sara? Who?"

She gasped, a rattle in her chest.

"Who were you with?" he demanded. "Tell me and
maybe I'll kill you quickly. Who?"

Under again.

She tried to pull free of his hands, but couldn't. She
struggled, one ferocious last attempt at freedom. Her
knee made contact with his groin.

He released her.

She surfaced, gasping for air. Without pause, she
shoved herself to her feet and lunged for the side of
the tub. She was halfway out when she felt a tug.

Donovan had her by the back of the gown. The
neckline cut into her throat.

Her hands flailed, and her fingers made contact
with the champagne bottle. She grabbed it by the neck.
She turned. She swung, striking him in the face.

He bellowed and let go. She fell against the side of
the tub. Hands braced on the tile, she pushed herself
out. And then she was running, barefoot, her shoes
floating in the whirlpool.

Behind her came a roar.

And then he was coming after her.

Through the kitchen.

Down the hall.

Feet pounding behind her.

Enraged, labored breathing, behind her.

Her hand grabbed the banister.

Fear overriding reason, she ran up the stairs.

An eclipse blocked out the sun . . .

Chapter Twenty

Nash grabbed a handful of clothes and tossed them in the duffel bag. He strode to the filing cabinet, pulled it open, and dug his way through tightly packed papers, magazine articles, and photos.

Nothing he wanted. Nothing that meant anything to—

Sara.

On the beach.

He trailed a finger across the glossy surface—an unconscious gesture.

Forget about her. Don't think about her.

But he couldn't quit staring at the picture. All the elements of earth, sky, and flesh had come together, had somehow bonded in that eighth of a second when the shutter had tripped. The photo was erotic in a pure, spiritual sort of way.

And her face . . . her face . . . Tranquility, and a smile that was sensed rather than seen.

Those eyes. Those huge, soft, sad, eyes . . .

As if it had singed his fingers, he dropped the photo. He was a sap. He should get an award. The Sap Award.

Growling deep in his throat, disgusted with himself, he swung around and picked up a stack of CDs.

Into the duffel bag they went, most of the music alternative rock created by brilliant shooting stars who had either crashed and burned or were on their way.

It wasn't the same in Chicago anymore.

Maybe he'd go someplace warm. Someplace tropical, away from the black dirty snow of the city. Away from the cabs with their crazy drivers. Away from the sky-scrapers that made him feel claustrophobic.

Go south. Get a job flipping burgers at some greasy spoon. Work nights, lie around on the beach during the day. *Live* on the beach. Melanoma or not, the sun had healing power.

Harley.

He'd miss the guy. Miss him like hell.

He'd gotten too close, that's what had happened. He'd tried not to, but with somebody like Harley it was easy. He was in your face, in your blood before you knew it.

Nash picked up a stack of videotapes. He checked the labels. *Godzilla. Godzilla vs. King Kong. Hard Copy. Current Affair. Attack of the Killer Tomatoes. The Ghost and Mr. Chicken.*

Sara Ivy.

He couldn't get away from her. Maybe he was going about this all wrong. Nash laughed in a deprecatory way. Maybe the thing to do was to wallow in Sara Ivy. Get an overload, so he could purge her from his system.

He switched on the TV and VCR, popped in the tape, pushed Play, then plopped down on the couch, crossed legs stretched out in front of him, fingers of both hands linked over his stomach.

Her release from the hospital.

This was good. This would hurt quite nicely.

The camera zoomed in for a close-up. Her face was chalk white, her eyes dark and huge. Bambi eyes. Oh, Christ. What had made him think he could do this?

He'd let himself get too close to her, too.

The voice-over talked about the attacker. About

how he'd never been found, about how attentive Donovan Ivy had been to his wife through her terrible ordeal.

What was Nash's problem? He was slipping. Losing it. How could he have let himself get hung up on another man's wife? Especially a woman with such a devoted husband.

Nash watched as the couple walked down the hospital steps, watched as Donovan opened the limo door for his wife. *His* wife. He said something to her. She looked up—then quickly glanced away.

Glanced away.

What the—?

Nash jumped to his feet and rewound the tape, putting Sara and Donovan Ivy back at the hospital door. Once again he watched them come down the steps. Watched Donovan open the limo door. Watched her look up.

Then away.

Away.

Nash rewound again, finding the spot he was looking for, then pushed the Pause button.

The picture disappeared in a confusion of poor tracking. He couldn't make out anything.

He ejected the tape, caught it, then sprinted down the hall to Harley's office. There, he turned on the TV and VCR, popped in the tape, pushed Play, then Pause.

This time, on the higher quality player, the image was clear, a fragment of a second caught in freeze-frame. An expression, an emotion, exposed before it could be hidden.

Fear.

On Sara's face.

Not only fear, but terror.

Nash's body went limp. His knees buckled and he found himself sprawled in Harley's chair, unable to take his eyes from the screen.

Terror.

She wasn't in love with her husband. *She was terrified of him.*

Little by little, blood began to flow to his brain; his mind began to function. Little by little, he began to put things together.

The attacker.

The reason they'd never found the attacker was *because there wasn't one.*

The attacker was Donovan Ivy.

Memories tumbled.

Sara's medical file. The broken bones.

The bruise on her jaw.

The policeman who'd conveniently moved away. A payoff?

Her hysteria that morning hadn't been due to the fact that she was madly in love with her husband and she was afraid he would find out about her moment of indiscretion. Oh, she was afraid he would find out— that part was true. But not because she loved him. Because he would hurt her.

Oh, Jesus.

Nash ran shaking fingers through his hair, then shoved himself to his feet. He shut off the machine. On weak legs, he moved toward the door, gathering strength as he went.

Without stopping to grab his jacket, he took the steps three and four at a time, airborne most of the way down. He hit the first floor on a dead run. Then he was out of the building, sprinting toward the parking garage and his car.

He fished the keys from the front pocket of his jeans, then took a shaky, unsuccessful stab at the lock.

"Wasting time," he said under his breath. "Wasting time."

He tried again. Key in. Turn. Unlock.

He wrenched open the door, jumped in, and jabbed the key in the ignition. Four seconds later the Fairlane's tires were squealing as he circled out of the four-story garage.

It was late afternoon. Traffic on Michigan Avenue was heavy and insane. Nothing new. He laid on the horn. Nobody moved. He tried to get the lady in front of him to let him in. She flipped him off. Ordinarily, he would have treated her to the same gesture, but he was too preoccupied.

"Come on, come on."

He watched the light turn green, praying he would get through it this time.

Green.

Yellow.

Red.

Shit.

Three cars in front.

Come on.

The light changed. He shot forward, only to stop at the next light.

It seemed hours later when he finally headed up the street to Sara's.

At the gate, he slammed on the brakes, rolled down the window, and hit the intercom buzzer.

No answer.

He hit it again.

He thought about crashing the damn gate with his car, but he was pretty sure the gate would win.

He shut off the engine, jumped out, and punched the button once more, just in case.

Then he wrapped his fingers around the black iron of the front gate and started climbing.

Chapter Twenty-One

Sara sat crumpled on the floor, one cheek pressed to the locked bedroom door.

Donovan had followed her upstairs, demanding that she open the door. When she didn't, he'd left.

How long ago had that been? Minutes? Hours? Was he still in the house?

She had to get up, had to get away, but . . .

Tired.

So tired. Of fighting. Of losing.

Of living.

A sound.

On the stairs.

Donovan. Back.

She pressed trembling fingers to her mouth. She held her breath. Oh, God. Oh, God. *I can't do this anymore, can't handle this anymore.*

And then it came—an explosion, less than a foot from her head. It rocked her, sent her tumbling backward. The area around the doorknob shattered, slivers of wood flying. A cloud of pulverized carpet lifted, then settled.

Before she could fully comprehend what had happened, the door flew open, crashing against the wall, the room shuddering.

Donovan stood in the doorway, a revolver in his hand. Dried blood was caked on his face. Fresh blood from his nose trickled over his lips. His eyes gleamed with rage—and blind hatred.

Deafened by the gun's discharge, Sara scrambled to her feet, spun around, and ran for the bathroom. Inside, she threw her weight against the door.

No good. Not fast enough. Not strong enough. Never strong enough.

The door flew open, tossing her backward, sending her crashing to the floor, between the tub and the toilet.

Donovan walked toward her with slow, measured steps, savoring her fear.

His mouth moved, but she heard nothing, only the tornado roar in her ears.

He said something else.

Mine.

It was like watching a silent movie. She half expected to see a caption under him. A funny thought. Hysterical thought.

She wouldn't cower. She must face him, eyes open, standing.

With one hand braced against the cold porcelain of the tub, the other against the wall, she pushed herself to her feet and stood there, waiting.

His lips moved again.

I love you.

She drew a breath. "I don't love you. I *never* loved you."

It was true. At one time, she'd been in love with the person she thought he was. And even that wasn't really love, but infatuation. A dream.

She watched the impact of her words.

His jaw tensed. He raised the gun, pointing the barrel first at her stomach, then lower . . . His lips twitched. The barrel came up, up, stopping at her head.

Thank God. Make it good. Make it fast.

She waited.

In a second, she told herself, it would all be over. Fear had turned her blood to ice, made her heart beat erratically, made her breathing choppy.

But, beneath her fear, she was ready to die. She had been ready for years and years.

The gun barrel wavered. Donovan's eyes became unfocused, distracted as he seemed to listen to something beyond the small room.

He swung around. *He left.*

Sara sagged against the wall.

Her ears popped, and suddenly she could hear again.

The piercing wail of the alarm system.

Someone had broken in.

Pounding. Someone pounding on the front door.

Shouting.

"Sara!"

Nash.

Oh, God.

What was he doing here? It didn't make sense.

She couldn't think, couldn't move.

Pounding. Pounding.

"Sara!"

His voice. Desperate. Anguished.

The alarm stopped.

Donovan.

Downstairs.

Donovan had a gun.

And now Donovan would know who she'd been with.

That single thought gave her strength. She pushed away from the wall and ran from the bathroom, out of the bedroom and down the stairs.

Donovan stood in the front doorway, gun in hand. Beyond him was Nash.

She hadn't wanted anybody else to get hurt. Hadn't wanted Nash to get hurt.

Why did you come? I was trying to protect you.

Before she could stop it, before she knew it was coming, a sound ripped from her throat. Agony. *Shame.* She hadn't wanted Nash to know her awful secret.

Donovan swung around. "He's the one, isn't he?"

He's the one. The one.

"Isn't he?" Donovan repeated.

She'd never get away with a lie. But she had to try. For Nash, she had to make this good. "H-He's here for an interview," she stammered. "I forgot all about it until now." She forced herself to look at Nash. "This isn't a good time. You'd better leave."

With the back of his hand, Donovan wiped at the blood on his face. "Sara, you are so transparent. What are you saying? This is a *good* time. A perfect time."

Donovan lifted the gun, pointing the barrel at Nash's chest, motioning for him to step inside.

Once Nash was inside, there would be no escape.

She tried to catch his eye. *Look at me. Look at me!*

He looked.

Don't come in. Run. Run.

Nash stepped inside the door.

No! He'll kill you. He'll kill you!

Donovan coolly picked up the hall phone, called security, and told them that the alarm had been set off accidentally. "Forgot it was on," he said, laughing, then hung up. How could he sound so calm? So sane?

Nash took a step toward her. "Are you okay?"

Don't talk to me. Don't look at me.

Her legs gave out. She collapsed on the stairs, both hands gripping the wooden rails for support.

Nash took another step, then stopped, Donovan between them.

"I'm sorry." She spoke through trembling lips, speaking to Nash, focusing totally on Nash. "This wasn't supposed to happen."

That was all it took to send Donovan over the edge.

Veins stood out on his forehead. Spit frothed at the corners of his mouth.

With a roar, he turned and swung, his fist slamming into her face, her cheek. Her head snapped. She fell back against the stairs, eyes squeezed shut against the pain.

Beyond the pain, she heard a shout.

Fighting.

She heard a scuffle, then a crash, followed by silence.

She didn't want to open her eyes, couldn't bear to see—

Fingers wrapped around her arm.

She flinched and pulled away, but the hand held her. Firm, yet gentle.

"Sara."

Nash.

A sob burst from her throat. Relief that he was alive, shame that she must face him.

"Come on. Let's get the hell out of here."

Dazed, she shook her head. "I can't."

How could she possibly go with him? He was the enemy, too.

Again, she shook her head. She tried to pull free of his grasp. "Let me go! Let me go!"

"Sara, listen to me! It wasn't a bet. I lied. Do you hear me? I *lied.*"

What?

"There was no bet!"

He pulled her to her feet. Her legs almost gave out again. From somewhere, she called up reserve strength, enough to descend the remaining steps.

She almost tripped over her husband.

He was lying on the floor, one of his precious antique vases shattered around him.

"I-Is h-he dead?" Heaven help her, she couldn't keep a ring of hope out of her voice.

"No, and he's going to be really pissed when he comes around."

They were almost to the door when Nash stopped and she crashed into him. "The gate," he said. "Can you open it?"

It took a moment for his meaning to sink in, then she spotted his car on the other side of the locked gate.

She punched a sequence of numbers on the control panel and the gate swung open. And then they were running down the drive, Nash half dragging her.

He opened the driver's door and pushed her in, following.

"Here—"

Donovan's gun was suddenly in her hands. Cold. Heavy. She stared at the weapon, her first reaction to drop it, her second to toss it out the window.

Engine running, Nash threw the gearshift into reverse. "Stick the gun under the seat or something."

They backed up, then shot forward, the old car listing to one side, tires squealing, Sara fighting the centrifugal force as she slid the gun under the seat.

She fell back, eyes closed, heart hammering.

They flew down the streets. Somewhere along the way, she entered a state between waking and sleeping. At times she actually thought they *were* flying, that they had lifted off the ground and were circling Chicago.

A blast of lukewarm air hit her, rousing her slightly.

A shiver ran through her. Then another.

Nash's voice came drifting to her from miles and miles away. "We'll stop at *Shoot the Moon* and get you some dry clothes."

Dry clothes? She'd forgotten that her clothes were wet.

Tired.

So tired.

Safe.

"How is it that you're always wet, and I'm always trying to warm you up?"

Nash's voice was light, teasing.

Sara sat on his couch, focusing on a crack in the wall.

He'd helped her into a pair of his jeans and a sweater that fell to her thighs, with sleeves that covered her hands. No panties. No bra. His clothes against her bare skin.

His hands moved over her efficiently, tending to business.

She was grateful for that. Grateful, she told herself, because if he'd shown any tenderness, she just might have fallen completely apart.

Yet, at the same time, she yearned for that tenderness.

An hour ago, she'd been resigned to die. Now she was sitting across from the one man who had made her feel alive.

A man whose betrayal had cut her to the bone.

A bet.

Lie or truth? Either one hurt. Either one had been designed just for the purpose of hurting her.

"Here. Stand up."

He took both her hands and pulled her to her feet.

He lifted the sweater above her waist. "Hold this out of the way."

She held.

He threaded a worn leather belt through the loops, knotted the belt, then pulled the sweater back down.

"Wouldn't want you to come undone."

She sat. "No, we wouldn't want that."

He rolled up her sleeves two turns. "You look like you're wearing a thneed."

"A thneed?"

"You know. Dr. Seuss. *The Lorax*."

Dr. Seuss. As a child, she'd loved Dr. Seuss. *Cat in the Hat. One Fish, Two Fish* . . . She shook her head.

"One of his best, I always thought."

He handed her a pair of socks.

She held them. She stared at them, not quite grasping their function. Wool. Gray. Thick.

Wool.

On your feet. You put them on your feet.

She brought them to her face and sniffed.

"They're clean. I swear."

Wool. She loved the smell of wool. It was a safe smell. A warm and cozy smell. A smell that belonged to another world, another life.

She put the sock to her cheek. Scratchy. Tough.

Nash made a sound. A sort of nervous, clearing of the throat kind of thing. "Yeah, well." He sat down beside her on the couch. He lifted her leg, propping it on his knee. Then he took the socks from her.

"These are socks," he said, dangling them. "They go on your feet."

They were engrossed in a pair of wool socks while more pressing issues were ignored, were tucked away for another time, a time when she would be better able to deal with them.

An enraged madman she must go back to.

Nash's bet, lie or truth.

The mind could take only so much.

He rubbed her feet between his hands, warming them. Then, as if she were no more than a child, he helped her into the socks.

She had wanted tenderness, but she couldn't handle it. Not now. Tears stung her eyes.

So that he wouldn't notice, so that he wouldn't see, she pulled her leg from his lap and got to her feet. She paced to the window and poked her fingers between the blinds.

"I-It's dark." Her voice was tight, trembly. She suddenly realized how much her muscles ached from lack of sleep.

"Dark happens."

"Yes . . . One minute it's light. The next thing you know, it's dark."

"Sun comes up. Sun goes down."

"Yep."

"Yep."

Silence.

Nothing else to say.

Then he asked the question she'd been dreading. "Did you ever tell anybody?"

"Do you like Daylight Savings Time? Some people don't, you know."

"Did you ever tell anybody?"

"I like summer evenings, when it stays light until eight-thirty or nine. And then, right at dusk, the lightning bugs come out. I've always wondered if their lights blink during the day and we just can't see them. Did you ever wonder that?"

"Sara—"

With a pop, she let the blind snap closed. "I *tried*. It didn't work, okay? So let's drop it."

She sensed him behind her, thinking, thinking.

"Me," he said quietly. "You could have told me."

The concern in his voice was almost her undoing. But then she remembered *the bet*.

She moved around the room. A plan. She had to have a plan.

"How is it you're a Dr. Seuss fan?" she asked, not really thinking about her words at all, just wanting to distract him from his question.

"I used to read to—" He stopped. "Never mind."

"No, tell me. You used to read to—" Her voice trailed off. She totally forgot what she was about to say.

Lying on top of the open filing cabinet drawer was an eight-by-ten glossy. Of her. Taken at the beach.

Slowly, as if her hand wasn't her hand, as if her arm wasn't her arm, she picked up the photo.

In it, she was as good as naked. *More* than naked. Her gown was wet and transparent, clinging to her like wet tissue. She turned around, the picture in her hand.

"Tell *you*?" she asked. "Why? So I could read about it in tomorrow's tabloid? Have you been saving this to run with just such a story? Or do you already have plans for it? Are you doing an article on the bet you made? This picture would make a lovely addition."

"No. God, no. And there was no bet. I swear."

If she was one of the worst actors, then he was the best. He looked so sincere, wearing an expression of be-wildered despair.

Even knowing what she knew, he was able to make her want to believe him, want to care about him, trust him. She was such a fool.

"I kept it because . . . I don't know. I couldn't stand the thought of destroying it."

She had no such qualms. While he looked on in guilty horror, she tore the photo into tiny pieces.

He watched as she let the jagged squares fall from her hands to flutter to the floor.

Then she started toward the door. She had to leave. Had to get away.

He jumped up and slammed it closed, a hand braced high on the door above her head, his face hard and unsmiling.

"I saved your goddamn ass. Did you forget that?"

"I never asked you to."

"And what if I hadn't come? What would you be doing right now? Spending a quiet evening at home, listening to hubby read inspirational verse?" he asked sarcastically.

She grabbed the doorknob with both hands. She turned. She pulled. "Let me go! Let me go!"

He made an angry sound deep in his throat and grabbed her by both arms.

She gasped and drew back, flinching.

His face drained of color. His hands sprang from her arms. "Sara—" His voice held the same anguish she thought she'd heard when he pounded on the door of Donovan's house, when he shouted her name.

"I'd never hurt you."

It was true, she realized. Her reaction had been instinct, nothing more.

He may have been bigger than she was, he may have been stronger, but she wasn't afraid of him. From the beginning, she'd argued with him as an equal, somehow knowing he wouldn't hurt her, not physically.

"I'm sorry." He rubbed a hand across his eyes—a

witness to his own execution. "I'm sorry. It's just—Christ, Sara. I don't get it. Any of it."

He had faced Donovan for her. He had foolishly climbed the fence, storming the tower of a madman.

He had made snow angels.

He turned away. He rested an arm and forehead against the door, one leg bent. "Don't leave," he whispered. There was a quality in his voice she'd never heard there before: humility.

She pressed her hands together. "I-I have to go back."

He pushed away from the door, facing her. *"Why?"*

"He's my husband."

"Who just happens to be certifiable."

"I know how to deal with him."

His eyebrows lifted in disbelief.

"Most of the time."

He swallowed. "You love him."

She laughed, but her laugh held no humor. "I hate him."

His shoulders relaxed and he smiled, the subject dropped, at least for the moment. "We're both dead on our feet. Stay here tonight and tomorrow we'll figure out what to do. You sleep on the couch, I'll sleep on the floor. Don't go. Just *don't go.*"

Dear Shoot the Moon:
  Is the Moon really round?
  —Skeptical in Boise

Dear Skeptical:
  No, it's flat, just like the Earth.
  —H.G., President and Founder of Society to Expose
  Really Big Hoaxes

Chapter Twenty-Two

 She stayed.
And Nash's heretic heart sung silent hosannas.
She stood dead on her feet, swaying, eyelids drooping,
while he opened the fold-out couch. Not bothering to
remove her clothes, she dropped into bed fully dressed.
Knees drawn up, hugging a pillow, she immediately fell
asleep.

Nash made sure the building was secure, all the
deadbolts locked. Then, back in his room, he examined
the gun he'd taken from Ivy.

A .357 Magnum.

Five bullets left.

He hadn't felt the weight of a gun in years.

He didn't like it.

Memories came flooding back. Vivid, in a way real
life never was. More vivid than actually being there.
Like watching a videotape of something you'd partici-
pated in, only this time you notice all the things you
missed in the chaos of the moment.

At the time, he'd focused on one thing, and one thing only: killing the man who had killed his daughter. But now, years later, he could see people lined on either side of the courthouse steps. Men. Women. Reporters. Photographers.

He'd done his homework. There was a good chance he'd get but one shot, and that shot had to be lethal. His weapon of choice had been a Beretta. The guy he'd bought it from had assured him it would blow a man's head off at twenty yards. Exaggerated, but it had done the trick, done what Nash had required of it.

In his mind's eye, Nash could see the expressions of the onlookers as blood splattered their clothes, especially one woman's horrified face, her white blouse awash with blood.

The image changed, became the face of his daughter. Pain welled up inside him. He let out a low moan of despair and put the gun down on top of the filing cabinet.

He looked at Sara, half hoping she would be awake, so he could talk to her, hold her. But she was sleeping soundly, one hand curled on the pillow near her face.

He turned off the light and dropped into the only upholstered chair in the room. He sprawled out, feet in front of him and stared into the darkness, the soft rhythm of Sara's breathing a comfort.

Somehow he had to keep her from going back to Ivy. Somehow . . .

A gnat. Buzzing around his ear. Buzzing, buzzing. A smell.
Smoke.
Smoke alarm.
Nash bolted upright, confused to find himself in the chair.

Beneath the nerve-damaging cry of the smoke alarm, he heard a far-off roar. Light from the street cut through the cracks in the closed blinds. Everything was gray and foggy, like an old black-and-white print.

He jumped to his feet and shook the mattress where Sara slept.

She made a faint, sleepy sound and burrowed deeper under the covers.

"Sara!" He shook her. "The building's on fire! Get up!"

Without waiting for her reaction, he hurried to the door and tested the knob. Cool.

He unlocked it and pulled it open. Smoke billowed in, blinding him. Down below, from the vicinity of the first floor, came a crackling and the breaking of glass. When the fire reached the chemicals in the photo lab, the whole building could go.

Half a second after opening the door, Nash slammed it shut, overcome with a paroxysm of coughing.

He felt Sara's hand on his back as he struggled to calm his irritated lungs, struggled to replace smoke with oxygen. While the alarm continued to shriek, he finally got his coughing under control, his chest burning, eyes streaming.

His mind clicked along, remembering the fire escape in Harley's office. Had to get through the smoke to the fire escape.

He peeled off his T-shirt and tore it. He wet the cloth with a half-finished soda, then handed a piece to Sara. "Put this against your face."

Then he found her hand and held on tightly. "Take a deep breath," he instructed. "Then we'll run like hell to Harley's office."

He felt her fingers squeeze his.

"Ready?"

She nodded.

He opened the door.

Heat hit his face like a blast furnace. Smoke stung his eyes.

The building was alive. It roared. It breathed. Through the smoke, in the direction of the stairs, flames shot up the wall, zipped along the floorboards. Below them, something crashed.

Keeping a firm grip on Sara's hand, Nash plunged into the dense black smoke. He closed his eyes, sight now useless, his sense of direction threatened, every step possibly the last, each step one that could send them into infinity.

Sara stumbled and he almost lost her hand. Gripping her tighter, almost dragging her behind him, he moved on, quickly realizing he'd lost his bearings. He dropped the rag that he held to his face. Now, his hand free, he felt along the wall, his fingers traveling over cracks and wooden framework.

Where was the door? Where was the damn door? Had they passed it? Had he misjudged? The building he'd lived in for two years was suddenly alien, no more familiar than a stranger's house.

His fingers brushed molding. His shoulder knocked against something—the crocheted door hanging Tootie had made for her nephew. Tootie. Good ol' Tootie. Tootie and her crocheting. Tootie and her smoke alarms.

Nash shoved at the door and they tumbled inside, lungs about to burst.

He slammed the door, gulping in air that was tainted, but wonderful nonetheless.

Sprinting to the nearest window, he tore down the blinds. Light from the streets poured in.

He turned the metal lock. Hands braced against the

frame, he lifted. It wouldn't budge. Painted. It had been painted shut.

He tried another.

And another.

"Stand back!"

He lifted a chair above his head and slammed it against the window, shattering the glass, the force of the impact jarring him all the way to his shoulder joints.

With a chair leg, he broke out the remaining glass. "Come on!"

Sara took his hand and he helped her through the window, to the metal fire escape.

He quickly followed.

In their stocking feet, they ran down the steps, stopping at the last landing.

Sara stared at the ground ten feet below. In the distance, sirens wailed.

"I'll just wait for the firemen. They'll be here soon. They'll have a ladder."

"No time."

She looked again. "You go first."

Grasping a metal rung, Nash swung down. Dangling above the ground, he let go, falling to the cement sidewalk below.

He motioned for her to do the same.

She crouched on the landing, clinging to the side rails.

He waved his hands. "Come on."

She shook her head and hung on even tighter. "I can't."

"Sure, you can."

"I can't."

"Jump. I'll catch you."

Behind her, the sound of a blast shook the building. Windows shattered.

Instead of lowering herself down, instead of getting as close to the ground as possible before bailing out, she simply screamed and jumped. Like a paratrooper leaving a skydiving plane.

He caught her, the impact knocking him to the ground, knocking out his breath in a loud *whoof*. His ass hit the cement and he rolled back along his spine, Sara cradled in his arms above him. He tried to laugh. It came out a strangled, wheezing cough. He could feel heat from the flaming building on his bare skin.

"You said you'd catch me." Her face was covered with soot.

"I . . . didn't say . . ." He struggled to fill his lungs with sweet, sweet air. "T-To use me . . . for an airbag."

Sara struggled to her feet, grabbed him by the arm, and tugged. "Get up. Hurry!"

He rolled to his knees, then staggered to his feet. Hand in hand, they ran, flying over pavement, tortured lungs feeling like raw meat.

Behind them, a series of explosions shattered windows, sending glass into the street.

They ducked into an alleyway, backs pressed to the brick wall, breathing ragged and painful.

Another explosion filled the air, rocking the night, vibrating in Nash's chest like a sonic boom.

Broadsheet: Prints lies in the guise of truth.
Tabloid: Prints lies in the guise of lies.
—Harley Gillette

Chapter Twenty-Three

C After taking two puffs from his inhaler, Harley jumped in his gray subcompact and headed down the interstate, engine roaring, not bothering with his radar detector.

When he got the call telling him *Shoot the Moon* was burning, the first thing he'd thought about was Nash. But he'd been assured that the two occupants—*two*—were okay.

Blocks before reaching *Shoot the Moon* he smelled smoke. Not nice, cozy campfire smoke, but choking, dirty smoke. Like overheated wiring. Like melting milk jugs. Like cooked rubber.

Up ahead, the road was blocked by fire trucks so he pulled to the curb and sprinted the rest of the way on foot.

When he was little, a house in his neighborhood had burned down, but he'd seen just the aftermath, the charred cold ruins, not the flames. Not the heat. Not the smoke.

But this . . . *this* . . . It was awesome.

With his hands buried in the deep pockets of his thick denim jacket, his shoulders hunched against the winter night, his long hair billowing behind him,

Harley stood and stared in wonder at what was left of his enterprise.

Aunt Tootie's words, as she hacked over a filterless stub held between yellow fingers, came back to him: "This place is a firetrap."

She was the one who'd insisted on putting up the smoke alarms. Who'd insisted on repairing the fire escape.

A hand touched his shoulder, squeezing. "Sorry, man."

Harley pulled his gaze from the smouldering building.

Nash. Standing there, his face blackened by smoke, wearing nothing but jeans and a dark green government-issue wool blanket.

"A pyromaniac's delight, huh?" Harley said, trying to keep his voice light when what he really felt like doing was dropping to his knees and bawling his eyes out.

"You always did want to make a splash."

A splash . . .

A slow-building depression moved like molasses through his veins, working its way to his brain.

"So much for being an entrepreneur," he said. "Guess I should have taken that job with my old man."

"We'll start over," Nash said.

Start over . . .

Harley didn't know. Maybe he just wasn't cut out for this in-your-face, on-the-edge journalism crap. Sure, *Shoot the Moon*'s popularity had steadily increased, but not fast enough. Harley had wanted overnight success. Overnight fame.

A splash . . .

An ugly realization came to him, something he'd been trying to deny and ignore for some time.

It was all wrong.

Somewhere along the way, he'd lost direction.

He'd seen it coming, but he hadn't wanted to face it. *Shoot the Moon* had turned into everything he hated. The politics. The lies.

And to do it, he'd used his friend, he'd used Nash—that was the worst thing. He'd used his bitterness, his fearlessness, his anger.

In the process, Harley had tarnished his own dream.

People were always thinking they had to grab at immortality with both hands, by making a big splash, no matter who they hurt on the way. No matter who was in the fall line.

Harley had never wanted fame, or so he'd always told himself. He'd never wanted *Shoot the Moon* to be *news*. He hadn't wanted it to have an *impact*.

Entertainment. That had been his goal, his statement.

No statement.

A small, ice-cold hand touched his. "I'm sorry, Harley."

Sara Ivy. The other person in the building. Her face was smudged like Nash's. Her lips were blue. She had dark circles under her eyes.

She was beautiful in a soulful way. He could see how Nash had lost his head over her, married or not.

A shiver ran through her small frame. Then another.

"Hey."

He reached into the pocket of his coat, pulled out a set of keys and handed them to Nash. "You two go on to my place. Take my car. It's straight up the block, already warm."

"You sure?" Nash asked, his face showing concern. "You'll be okay?"

"I'll stick around here awhile, then I'll be home."

Nash handed him the keys to his Fairlane. "She's parked in the garage, usual place."

Harley nodded and Nash gave his arm an awkward squeeze. "Later."

After they left, Harley talked to the police and fire fighters. He was interviewed by a television station that had thought *Shoot the Moon* was low-rent housing and had come looking for a tragedy. *There be vultures.*

Two hours later, with the fire under control and no threat to the surrounding buildings, Harley headed in the direction of the parking garage.

He didn't have any trouble finding Nash's car. It was parked in the usual spot, but it wasn't in its usual shape . . .

"Holy—"

Harley slowly circled the car, stepping over debris. Nash's old Fairlane looked worse than something that had been in a demolition derby. All four tires had been slashed. The windows were broken. Upon closer inspection, Harley saw that the seats had been cut with a knife, the stuffing pulled out and tossed on the ground, Nash's belongings scattered across the cement floor of the garage. Nash had always believed he should be ready to travel should the mood take him, so what littered the floor amounted to about two thirds of his possessions.

The fire.

The car.

Sara Ivy.

It all made perfect sense.

Harley moved through the mess, looking to see if there was anything salvageable.

He kicked around. He lifted things. Every article of clothing was ripped to shreds. CDs were smashed.

Books. Science books. High school science books. What the hell had he been doing with them? Torn. Ripped. Spines broken. Walked on.

Paperbacks. Fiction. Nonfiction. Magazines. *Earth and Sky. Night Sky.*

Something cylindrical. Black. Textured. A lens. But not like any Harley had ever seen. Not a telephoto, but more like a telescope. The kind geeky people used to look at the heavens.

Nash's goddamn life was on the floor.

And there was nothing left to salvage.

Harley was learning something he didn't want to learn. The world was an ugly place.

His chest felt tight. He needed his inhaler, but he'd left it at the apartment.

Something rustled. He jumped and swung around.

A pile of pages, torn from a book, moved in the night breeze.

He bent over and picked them up. Tissue-thin pages. Familiar pages.

The Bible.

Tucked deep inside the torn pages was a newspaper clipping, jammed close to the stitching, next to the Twenty-third Psalm. Beside it was a yellowed pamphlet, the kind passed out at funerals.

Haley Michaels.

A kid.

A little girl.

Who was she? What did she have to do with Nash and his painful past?

He slid the pamphlet into the pocket of his jacket and turned toward the exit, ready to hail a cab.

Harley arrived at his apartment to find Sara curled up on the couch, her hair wet. She was wrapped in a white chenile robe that had belonged to his old girlfriend.

Nash came out of the bathroom briskly rubbing his hair with a towel. He was wearing a pair of Harley's baggy shorts and a red flannel shirt. From the pantry came the sound of clothes tumbling in the dryer.

They both looked groggy, and he had to wonder if he'd interrupted anything. He felt a moment of irritation, directed toward Sara Ivy. She was bad news. And she was taking his friend down with her.

"Talked to the fire chief," he said, crossing his arms and leaning against the door jamb.

Nash plopped down on the couch not far from Sara, towel slung around his neck. "Arson?"

"Looks like it."

Sara's eyes widened. Even in the dimly lit room, he saw the fear in them before she looked away.

Harley fished Nash's keys from his pocket and tossed them on the coffee table where they landed with a clink, then slid across the polished surface. "Don't think you'll be needing these. Your car's been trashed. Nothing stolen, just completely destroyed."

It took a moment for his words to sink in. Then Nash swallowed and shook his head in numb disbelief. "God, I loved that car."

"I think you're in trouble."

Harley's eyes went from Nash to Sara. She wasn't looking at either of them. Instead, she sat with her bare feet tucked under her, staring blankly at the wall. Harley looked back at Nash, raising his eyebrows. Chicks were nothing but heartache, this one more than most.

Dump her, he begged with his eyes. *Before she gets you in big trouble, before she gets you killed.*

Nash silently shook his head.

Harley tried to stare him down, send him some brain waves. *She's trouble. Trouble.*

It didn't seem to penetrate his friend's thick skull.

He was about to suggest they call the police when Sara suddenly sprang to her feet, let out a sob, and ran from the room. The bathroom door slammed. The lock clicked into place.

Both men followed her.

Harley cocked his head toward the locked door. Ah, man, she was *crying.* His earlier dislike vanished.

Nash rattled the knob. "Sara. Come on. Let me in."

"I hate it when chicks cry," Harley whispered.

Nash nodded, looking just as miserable as Harley felt.

He heard the sound of toilet paper unrolling. A nose being blown.

"I have to go back," Sara said through the closed door, her voice thick.

"Like hell," was Nash's eloquent reply.

"It's all my fault. The fire. Your car. I have to go back. Before something else happens. Something worse."

Nash rattled the knob again. "Open up."

A minute later, after more toilet paper rolling and nose blowing, the door opened and Nash slipped inside, closing it behind him.

"I have to go back," Sara repeated, sniffling. Her eyes were red. Her nose was red. "He won't stop unless I do."

"He won't stop even *if* you do," Nash said. "Not now. Think about it."

She pulled at the tissue in her hands, turning it, smoothing it. "Maybe I can go back and talk to him, bargain with him."

"Is that how it works? You bargain with him?"

She wiped the back of her hand across her nose. "Sometimes." She stood a little straighter, as if trying to hold up a heavy weight.

"Not this time. You're not going to make some bargain for me, or for Harley."

"That's right."

Harley's voice came through the door and Sara gave a little hiccuping laugh. Then she drew a hand across her eyes and leaned against the wall. "I'm so tired. I can't think."

"Let me think for you right now."

The dryer buzzed. They both jumped, their nerves brittle.

"Our clothes," she said mechanically.

They found Harley unloading the dryer. "Somebody is probably looking for you both right now," Harley said, pushing the bundle of clothes at Nash. "They could be watching this place."

Nash and Sara quickly dressed, the warm clothes feeling nice, making Nash think longingly of sleep, but there was a sudden, unspoken sense of urgency in the air.

Harley dug around in his closet and came up with a pair of black army boots that fit Nash fairly well. For Sara he brought out a pair of practically new Doc Martens. "I bought these for Jolene. She left them when she moved out."

Sara sat down on a kitchen chair and tried them on. Only half a size too big.

"What about calling the police?" Harley suggested.

Sara tugged at the laces, tightening them. "Some of them work for Donovan."

"I was afraid you'd say that." Harley shifted from one foot to the other, his hair swaying. "Listen, I want you two to take my car. Get the hell out of here until things cool off. In the meantime, maybe we can trace this arson business to Ivy and get him put away for awhile."

"He'll be out in an hour," Nash said.

"All I know is you two are hot. Just go. Take a little road trip until things settle down."

"But Harley—your car?" Sara asked. "You just lost everything, and now you want us to take your car?"

"I'm not telling you to *keep* it." He dug out his billfold.

Nash put a hand on his arm, stopping him. "We don't need any money."

"Okay, okay. But at least take this." He thrust a paper bag at them. "Stuff to snack on," he explained.

They were almost to the door when Harley remembered jackets. He pulled a barn jacket out of the closet and handed it to Nash, then he picked up the jacket he'd been wearing earlier and gave it to Sara.

Nash looked at Harley, someone he had tried to hold at arm's length ever since meeting him. But Harley gave unconditionally, and no amount of sidestepping had done any good.

There had been a time when Nash wouldn't have thought twice about grabbing a friend and slapping him on the back. Now, after twelve years of remission, the skill came back to him.

They pulled out of the apartment's private parking complex. As soon as the front tires touched the side street, a spotlight from a parked car hit them full in the face.

Nash flicked on the brights and pointed Harley's nondescript car directly at the blinding glare. Then he floored the accelerator, the back tires burning rubber.

As soon as they flew past the intruder, Nash cut his

lights and took the first corner practically on two wheels.

They sped down residential streets, the car airborne part of the time, the frame scraping pavement when they came down, sparks shooting out behind them. Sara hung on and prayed.

They squealed around corners. Instead of moving in a straight line, Nash kept circling until he whipped into the driveway of a private home, parking alongside a van and directly behind a station wagon. He cut the engine, then put a hand to the back of her head and pushed. "Get down!"

They ducked, their heads almost knocking.

The confined space was filled with the sound of their breathing. Sara could feel her heart thundering, feel the sweat gathering under her armpits.

She became aware of another sound, beyond the safety of the car.

An engine. A car. Moving slowly down the street . . . finally passing them, finally fading into the distance.

Nash let out his breath. "Whoever it was didn't get a good look at Harley's car." His voice was a husky whisper.

Sara started to lift her head, but Nash pushed her back down.

"Here he comes again."

The vehicle made another pass. Ten minutes later, another.

They lay in the darkness, listening.

"You're awfully good at this," Sara finally said.

He let out a breathless laugh. "I was like any other red-blooded American kid. I liked to drive fast to see what a car could do. Good for us, Harley's car can do quite a lot."

Fifteen minutes later, Nash straightened, made a quick scan of the area, then turned the ignition key. The engine rumbled to life, and the car vibrated beneath them.

He quickly backed out of the driveway, then headed toward the nearest on-ramp that would put them on the freeway, get them out of town fast.

"Where to?" he asked.

Where to? Sara thought about it and realized that, more than anything, she wanted to go home. To Wisconsin. To summer storms. To fields of alfalfa.

At the same time, she knew that what she really wanted was to turn back the clock.

"Away," she said. "Just away."

I don't want to own anything that won't fit in my coffin.
—Fred Allen

Chapter Twenty-Four

Nash turned on the radar detector, followed by the radio—couldn't cruise without tunes—and leaned back in the seat.

A road trip.

He hadn't been on a road trip in years. Just driving. Going nowhere in particular. It felt good. It felt young. He especially appreciated the fact that Sara was road-tripping with him.

Wearing his clothes. No underwear.

They headed east along the south side of Lake Michigan, driving straight into the rising sun while pulsing rock flowed around them like a sound track.

"Nice stereo," Nash said. "Harley's really into his tunes." He adjusted the bass. He liked a lot of bass.

"Why are you doing this?" Sara asked.

"I like to feel it vibrate in my chest." His hand moved for the knob again. "But, hey, I'll turn it down if you want."

"Not the music. *This.*" She gestured with both hands. "Helping me."

She cast a nervous glance behind her. The more time that passed, the more her apprehension grew. Traffic was picking up. Cars darted in and out between semis. Were they being followed?

With one hand on the wheel, the other digging into

a bag of pretzels Harley had given them, Nash shrugged. "I don't know."

Why was he putting himself in danger for her? And more than that—*why was she allowing it?*

She passed a hand over her eyes. She couldn't think straight. So tired. Scared.

Maybe Harley would have enough time to get something on Donovan, enough to put him in jail.

No. It wouldn't happen. This was all for nothing. She was simply buying herself some time, selfishly putting Nash in danger.

"Would you see what else Harley tossed in that bag? I need something to drink."

"It's all fruit drinks," she said.

"Figures. Harley's not gonna have anything that's unhealthy."

She pulled out a bottle of brown liquid. It looked like river water after a hard rain had stirred up the sediment. "Here's one called Ginseng Surprise."

"I'll try it."

She unscrewed the cap and passed him the bottle.

He lifted it to his mouth, took a swallow, then gagged, sprayed Ginseng Surprise on the windshield.

"A surprise all right," he gasped, wiping at the glass with one flannel cuff. He held the bottle out to her. "Wanna try it?"

"Think I'll pass. I make it a point never to drink anything natural." She took the bottle, rescrewed the cap, and dropped it back in the bag. "There's some kind of mango stuff—"

"No! Hell no!" He held up a hand, palm out, as if to ward off Harley's health drinks. A moment later, he pointed. "Look—"

An information sign.

"Hardee's comin' up on the right."

They pulled into the drive-through. Nash ordered a couple of breakfast sandwiches and coffee, Sara went for orange juice and a roll.

The stop cost them barely five minutes, but even so, Sara was wary. She couldn't resist the urge to keep looking behind them.

Later, when they pulled off the interstate for gas, Sara got out and went inside the station. She was staring at the refrigerated case full of soda and juice when Nash made an appearance, his hair windblown, Harley's brown barn jacket hitting him at midthigh, his untucked flannel shirt flapping, black army boots and several days' worth of beard giving him a grungy look.

She felt a bittersweet ache—for what might have been. If only . . . If only . . .

Every second he spent with her put his life in more danger.

Let him go. Tell him good-bye. Have him drop you off somewhere. A bus station. Anywhere. Tell him you don't need him. . . .

He shoved some folded bills into her hand. "Pay while I use the little boy's room, will you?"

He had to ask the kid behind the counter for the rest room key, which was attached to a hubcap that clanged against the counter when it was passed from hand to hand.

She paid for the gas and bought a bag of cinnamon candy, some gum and a package of Sweet Tarts, and then they were once again on their way.

They decided to go to Canada.

"Just for the hell of it," Nash said, abandoning the interstate for a less traveled two-lane.

"In the movies, they always head for the nearest border," Sara said.

A few more hours, she told herself. She would give

herself a few more hours. After they reached Canada, she would decide just what to do about Nash.

"Highway hypnosis," Nash said an hour later, pulling to the side of the road. "Care to take a turn behind the wheel?"

Drive? Did she want to drive?

He got out and circled the front of the car while Sara slid over the console.

Once inside, Nash immediately reclined the passenger seat, crossed his arms over his chest, and closed his eyes—while Sara, with both hands white-knuckling the wheel, stared at the dashboard.

She'd driven Nash's car, but that hadn't been real driving, on a real road. And she'd gone only ten yards.

She *used* to drive. All the time. Trucks. Tractors. She'd even had her own car once upon a time. Wasn't driving like riding a bike? Once you knew how, you never forgot. Right? *Right?*

When she didn't immediately put the car in gear and squeal away, Nash asked, "You do drive, don't you?" He was kind enough not to mention the fiasco at the cabin.

"Of course." She didn't want to admit that Donovan hadn't let her.

She'd had an aunt who didn't drive. "Don't allow my womenfolk to drive," her uncle had always bragged. Sara had thought it laughable and pathetic. She'd always considered her aunt weak for permitting herself to be bullied in such a way. Now she didn't think it laughable. Not laughable at all.

She pulled at the gearshift lever, taking it out of park, engaging briefly in reverse, going to neutral, passing the letter D with the circle around it—what did that mean?—to finally stop on drive.

She pressed her foot lightly against the gas pedal, inching the car back onto the road. She watched the red indicator on the speedometer. Twenty-five. Thirty. When she got to fifty, she leveled out.

There was no hood ornament to line up with the edge of the road. When she'd learned to drive, she'd used the hood ornament. Why wasn't there a hood ornament?

They weren't moving in a smooth, straight line. Instead, there was a jerky left-to-right motion to the car as she struggled to keep the vehicle between the white lines.

She knew she should go faster, but now that they were off the interstate, she didn't feel as nervous about being followed.

Fifteen minutes later, she got behind someone in a beat-up truck doing forty. She adjusted her speed. There was no way she'd try to pass.

So she followed. And followed. And followed.

It was the story of her life. The *Reader's Digest* version, enacted in half an hour. Existing. Never taking charge.

She tried to analyze why she didn't want to pass the truck in front of her.

No guts.

No confidence. She didn't trust her judgment, didn't trust herself.

And so she stayed where she was.

A few minutes later, Nash stretched and put his seat back up. "Pull over here and I'll drive."

She was only too glad to comply. Her eyes felt as if she hadn't blinked for hours, her neck and arms were stiff, her fingers numb from gripping the steering wheel so tightly.

She turned toward the side of the road. Earlier she'd

been going too slow, now she was gong too fast. The wheels hit a rut. She and Nash went airborne for a second before she pulled to a stop, tires sliding on the loose gravel, dust flying.

She looked at the digital clock. She'd been driving for exactly an hour. *No way.*

Nash circled the car and took his place behind the wheel while she slid back over the console.

"You're probably just out of practice," he said, seeming to sense her feelings of inadequacy as he pulled back on the two-lane.

"If a person hasn't ridden a bike in say, several years," she ventured, "do you think she'd be able to hop on and pedal away?"

"Is this one of those story problems? I hate story problems."

Sara opened the package of Sweet Tarts and offered some to Nash. "Of course it would depend on her age," she said reflectively. "It would depend on how many years had passed, don't you think?"

He popped a couple of Sweet Tarts in his mouth. "And what kind of bike. One of those skinny jobs with the wedgy seat might be a problem."

Sara popped a round lavender candy into her mouth, and nodded her agreement.

At Port Huron, Michigan, they had to stop at Customs before crossing the bridge into Canada. Sara experienced a brief moment of panic when the attendant leaned out of his booth and examined them with what seemed to her a suspicious eye. They probably didn't look like any honeymoon couple he'd ever seen, that was for sure.

Nash presented his driver's license. There were a few general questions, then they were on their way.

A few more pit stops, a few more hours, and dusk was behind them.

"Toronto," Nash said. "CN Tower. Skydome. Hockey Hall of Fame."

Once out of Toronto, they took Trans Canada north, along Georgian Bay.

For Sara, the day had become nothing more than a blur, a series of stops for gas and restrooms. Food grabbed on the run. Conversation that was about anything and everything but their situation, her situation.

Buying time.

And when you bought time, you didn't fill it with unpleasantness.

The car rolled to a complete stop in the middle of the deserted road. Twin headlight beams illuminated the two-lane in front of them.

Behind the wheel, on the seat beside her, Nash sat with his head back, eyes closed, mouth open, gently snoring.

Asleep at the wheel.

"Nash?"

She gave his arm a small shake.

The pattern of his snoring didn't alter.

She glanced behind them. Nothing but a sky full of stars. She gave his arm another shake, this time harder, this time speaking his name louder.

He came awake with a snort and a jerk of his head, both hands gripping the wheel.

When he realized they weren't going to fly off the road, that they weren't even moving, he let out his breath, his muscles relaxing. "Son of a—" He rested his forehead against the steering wheel, taking a couple of breaths. "Good thing I didn't set the cruise control."

He straightened, rubbing a hand across his face. "Man, I need to crash. Bad."

He stepped on the gas. The car moved forward, slowly picking up speed.

"I'll drive," she offered.

"I'm okay now. How far till the next town? This kilometer thing's got me all screwed up."

She turned on the overhead light and unfolded the map. They were only a few hours from Sault Sainte Marie, only an hour and a half from Wisconsin. "There's a town about twenty miles from here."

"I hope to hell it has a motel."

It did.

The rooms were old but clean, with blond furniture and an orange ceramic lamp that looked like something from *The Jetsons.*

Sara's eyes were gritty, her skin tight, her muscles sore.

She headed straight for the shower. When she was finished, she cleaned her teeth with a washrag. Then, since she had nothing else to wear, she put Nash's sweater back on. She stepped out of the bathroom, glad to get her bare feet off the freezing floor tile.

Nash was sprawled on his back on the bed, boots kicked off, flannel shirt tossed in the nearby chair, wearing jeans and a gray-blue T-shirt. He was asleep again, a lock of dark hair over his forehead, a hand resting on his rising and falling chest.

She slipped back into the borrowed jeans that were too big for her. After belting them, she grabbed Harley's jacket and the motel key, and headed out the door for the bar across the street. She would have a drink. She would decide what to do about Nash.

* * *

He was dead.

It was dark.

Someone was touching him in the dead darkness, coaxing him awake.

Soft skin.

Soft hair.

Smelling of soap.

Smelling of whiskey.

He groaned and shifted his weight, the mattress dipping.

His jeans were being unbuttoned. He heard the sound of a zipper going down. A cool, feminine hand slid under the elastic band of his jockey shorts. Holding him. Stroking him.

Sara.

Hands shoved up his shirt. Hands pushed down his jockey shorts, freeing him. Her soft, warm *naked* body crawled over him, on top of him. He felt the soft globes of her breasts against his chest, felt her long legs straddling his hips.

He reached for her, his palms cupping the smooth satin of her bottom. "Sara," he moaned. He felt the whisper of her breath against his face. Her lips found his. He tasted the warm, erotic flavor of whiskey on her tongue.

He was going to come.

His erection pressed stiffly against the cleavage of her bottom. He lifted her, positioned her. And with her guidance, and with a soul-shaking sigh, she took him deep within her velvety heat.

Hands on his chest, she pushed herself to a sitting position, taking him deeper, grinding herself against him.

He thrust, lifting her from the bed.

Rather than riding him, she braced herself, meeting him stroke for stroke, crashing against him.

He'd always prided himself in his ability to keep a woman hovering at the edge for long, tense minutes. Now, overtaken by sleepless days and sleepless nights, he felt exhaustion wrap around him in an erotic haze, rendering him powerless. In the blackness of the room where there was no conversation, nothing but the sound of their mingled breaths and the feel of damp skin against damp skin, he was unable to hold back.

Sorry.

A thought. A realization.

Could talk, couldn't—

"Sorry." He rasped out the word in a quick expulsion of air.

His body spasmed. His hips lifted. He filled her with his semen.

Two minutes later, they both slept, her damp, nude body sprawled across him.

Nash woke up on his back, his fly open, his jockey shorts shoved down.

From the next room, he heard the sound of water. The shower. Sara was in the shower.

He adjusted his clothes and zipped his pants, leaving the button undone.

He let his head drop back on the pillow. Let his eyes fall closed. Last night . . . God. It seemed like a dream. Like a hot, erotic fantasy.

He drifted.

He fell asleep.

Nash came awake with a start.

The shower was still running.

Unsure of how much time had passed, but sensing

that it had been more than long enough to take ten showers, he jumped to his feet and ran to the bathroom door, rapping his knuckles against the hollow wood.

"Sara?"

Nothing but running water.

He tried the knob. It turned. He opened the door a crack, steam hitting him in the face.

"Sara?"

His heart beat faster. He threw open the door so hard it banged against the wall. He grabbed a handful of plastic and pulled aside the shower curtain.

Empty.

The shower was empty.

He turned off the water.

Not fully awake, he leaned against the wall, brow to forearm. His mind struggled with this new puzzle, pausing briefly on the most obvious possibilities.

Alien abduction.

One of his all-time favorites.

Spontaneous human combustion.

Another favorite.

Stepped out for a pack of cigarettes and never came back . . .

The shower . . .

A cover. Meant to slow him down.

His brain kicked in. His mind began to function.

From nowhere came a new idea, a new possibility he didn't even want to think about.

He pushed himself away from the wall, swung around, and strode from the bathroom, his gaze flying to the television.

His billfold.

He snatched it from the top of the television and dug through it.

Every picture of the Queen Mum, of Washington

and Jackson, every robin, every loonie—all of his money, Canadian and American, was gone.

Cleaned out. She'd cleaned him out.

He straightened, a hand at his waist, another in his hair. Son of a bitch.

Then he had another thought.

He lunged, fumbled with the lock, then jerked open the outer door. Between the two yellow lines where he'd parked Harley's car was nothing but a grease spot.

She looked into his eyes and saw herself, all wrapped in sorrow.

Chapter Twenty-Five

It took a lot to piss him off, and what he was feeling at the moment was very close to rage. Without taking time to shower or shave, Nash threw his flannel shirt on over his T-shirt, shoved his feet into his untied boots, grabbed his billfold and jacket, and headed for the gas station adjacent to the motel.

It took two minutes to locate someone who'd seen Sara.

"Stopped in about a half hour ago," a kid working in the bay area told him. "Asking for directions to Sault Sainte Marie." He pointed.

"Thanks." Nash turned and hurried out the side door, into the cold Canada morning.

His breath coming in quick, visible puffs, he sprinted toward the highway, his untied boots clumping against the cement. He stepped over the self-serve island, passed the diesel pumps, jumped a ditch, and crossed the two-lane highway. Walking in the direction Sara had gone, frost-covered grass crunching under the soles of his boots, he buttoned his jacket and listened for oncoming traffic. When he heard someone approaching, he swung around and walked backward, thumb out.

The car blew past him, wind gusting in its wake. Ten minutes later a semi driver stopped, air brakes hissing as he pulled off what Nash was quickly coming to realize was a sparsely traveled road.

Nash grabbed the handrail and swung up into the passenger seat. He already had a story prepared. As the semi picked up speed he tightened his bootlaces, telling the driver how he and his wife had been staying at a motel, had had an argument, and she'd taken the car, the money, everything. A good lie was always based on truth.

The driver laughed, seeming pleased with the diversion. "Women get bent out of shape about the littlest thing."

"No kidding. No damn kidding."

Five miles out of town they spotted a car alongside the road. Color—dark, maybe gray. Body style, nondescript.

Nash sat up straighter. "This could be her."

The driver slowed until they were close enough for Nash to make out the Illinois plates, close enough to recognize Harley's car, finally close enough to see that the car was empty.

Up ahead, moving into the horizon, was someone on foot.

Someone with shiny black hair. A denim jacket.

Sara.

The driver took off again; he was just beginning to get through most of the gears when he had to slow.

Upon hearing the approaching semi, Sara whirled around and stuck out her thumb. The semi hissed to a stop.

The walk and ride had given Nash a chance to cool off. But now, seeing Sara, thinking about what she'd done, he felt his anger come flooding back.

Careful to keep a lid on it, he opened the door and swung himself to the ground.

"Hi, sweetheart."

A classic Kodak moment.

Her mouth moved, but no sound came out.

Nash waved to the driver, slammed the door, and waited for the noise of the rolling semi to die down before turning back to Sara.

"Surprised to see me? No need to answer. I can tell you are. Hell, you probably expected me to still be back there in Rusty Gables, flashing an empty motel room."

She made a choking sound.

"So, what'd you do to Harley's car?"

"It's out of gas."

Nash let out a loud snort. "Out of gas? You stopped at a station to ask directions, and you didn't get gas?"

She crossed her arms in front of her and tucked her bare hands under her armpits. "Why do you keep following me?"

He wondered himself. Most guys didn't go for a deep analysis of such things, but he supposed other than simply wanting to help her, he'd hoped that when she got away from Ivy, when her life became somewhat normal, whatever normal was, there would be a chance for him.

It didn't look like it. "Don't you give a shit about anything? Anybody?"

She tossed her head, lifted her chin, and turned her back to him.

"You screw a man's brains out, then you dump him, leave him with nothing. To top it off, you take his friend's car. How the hell could you do that to me? I was trying to help you!"

She swung around. Her face was cold, hard. "I don't need your help." The next words came one at a time, so he wouldn't miss anything. *"I'm through with you."* She spun on her heel and marched away, arms swinging.

He watched as she shifted from a fast walk to a jog.

Watched as she went from a jog to a flat-out sprint.

The logical thing to do was let her go. Just *let her go*.

She didn't look back. She just kept going.

He started running. The ground was hard, frozen. Full of bumps. To make it easier, he cut to the side of the road, lumpy ground giving way to smooth blacktop.

He began to gain on her right off.

He was ten yards away when he slacked up in order to keep pace. "Hey! Ms. Ivy!"

She stumbled, caught herself, and kept going.

He was barely out of breath, his heart rate hardly elevated. Sara, on the other hand, was kind of weaving, kind of swaying. He could hear her sucking in air from ten yards away.

He'd had enough.

He poured on the speed and quickly caught up with her. He tackled her, bringing her to the ground.

She didn't waste any time. Her feet dug into the dead grass. She scrambled away.

His hand lashed out, his fingers snagging her belt. He dragged her back.

"Let me go!" She slapped. She kicked. "Let me go!"

He endured her pathetic blows while holding her down and searching her pockets.

"Hold your horses." First her jacket. "I'm looking for keys and cash."

His fingers came in contact with glass. He pulled it out. Pint of whiskey. He gave it a toss, the bottle bouncing on the frozen ground. He jammed a hand into another pocket, this time coming in contact with rough-edged metal.

Keys.

He pulled them out, dropped them on the ground, then went back for the third time.

His fingers touched paper.

Bingo.

"Let . . . me . . . go."

Her breath was ragged, her feet moving in weak circles. She was wearing down.

Keeping the fingers of one hand hooked under her belt, he pulled out what he thought was money.

Not money.

What the——?

A clipping. A newspaper clipping. Familiar . . .

His fingers let go of her belt.

The air left his lungs.

His heart stopped beating.

He forgot about Sara. Forgot about the keys. Forgot about the money.

Sara scrambled away, shoving herself to her feet, her lungs raw, gasping. Hands braced on her knees, she sucked in the frigid air.

She heard the sound of an approaching car. It slowed, then went on by.

A few moments later, she became aware of Nash's stillness.

He was sitting on the ground, elbows on bent knees, one hand pressed to his forehead, the other holding something. A piece of paper.

She took a few steps away, then looked back.

He hadn't moved. He wasn't coming after her.

She retraced her steps, then circled him. His face was hidden by his hand and his hair.

She stepped closer. And closer still.

Until she was close enough to see that he held a

scrap of newspaper. Yellowed with age. Broken along the folds.

Before her eyes, he fell apart.

He let out a low, distressed moan. He shifted his weight, put one knee to the ground, and finally staggered to his feet.

He spun around and came at her. *"Where the hell did this come from?"* He shook the paper in her face and she drew back. "Where did you get *this*?"

"I-I don't know." She watched him in shock, in mesmerized horror.

"My daughter!" It was half sob, half scream. *"My daughter!"*

He wadded up the clipping, tossed it, then fell to the ground, to his knees, and buried his face in his hands.

Sara stared at him, not knowing what to do, what to say. She looked to where the clipping tumbled in the wind, to where it stopped, caught by a clump of dry grass.

She walked over to it. Picked it up. Unfolded it.

An obituary. Of a little girl.

Oh, God. Oh, dear God.

A daughter.

A father.

He, too, had been another person in another life. He too was running away.

Oh, God. She wanted to go to him, wrap her arms around him, hold him. But she wasn't good for him, and he wouldn't want her sympathy. And she couldn't let him know she cared, because then he would be obligated to play the hero.

She folded the paper and stuck it back in her pocket. She began to move away, then remembered the money. She dug into her jeans and pulled out a handful

of folded bills. She separated them, saving a few dollars
for herself. The rest she held out to Nash.

"Here—"

When he wouldn't take them, she tucked them into
the pocket of his shirt. Then she picked up the car keys
from the ground and put them in his hand, folding his
fingers around them.

"Go back to town and get gas," she told him.
When he didn't respond, she repeated her words, slower
this time.

Half expecting him to strike her hand away, she
touched his shoulder, shaking him.

Tough it out, she told herself.

He slowly turned unfocused, tear-washed blue eyes
on her.

Her father had said men didn't cry. Even when her
mother had died, her dad never shed a tear.

The sight of Nash's grief made her love him all the
more, made what she had to do all that much harder.

Tough it out.

"Don't follow me," she said in a clear voice, wishing she could tell him that she loved him too much to
stay. "I don't need you."

Under other circumstances, he may not have fallen
for her pathetic act. But the way he was now, distraught
and preoccupied with the fresh reminder of the loss of
his daughter . . .

The cruelty of her words seemed to hit a nerve. His
eyes became more focused. He looked at her, saw her.
"Don't worry," he said emotionlessly, as if she was no
longer worthy of his time, as if he'd finally had more
than his fill of her.

The pain she felt was worse than any Donovan had
ever dealt her.

He'll be okay, she told herself as she turned and

walked away, unable to face him any longer. He'll be okay.

Nash moved in a fog. Instead of hitching back to the gas station, he walked. When someone stopped and asked if he needed a ride, he waved them on.

Three hours later he was pouring a liter of gas into the empty tank of Harley's car. A half hour after that he was at a pump, filling up the tank.

So numb was he to his surroundings that he hardly noticed the car that pulled up beside him, hardly noticed that it left the station when he did, hardly noticed that it followed him down the road.

Chapter Twenty-Six

After midnight.

Franklin Hart closed the well-thumbed 1985 issue of *National Geographic* and put it on the bedside table along with his bifocals. Then he reached up and turned off the reading light attached to the headboard.

Sleep didn't come easy for him anymore. Didn't seem fair. When you get old and have a lot of time on your hands, sleep should come easy.

When he was younger, he put in fourteen-hour days and slept like a baby. But those days were gone. Days of backbreaking labor. Days when he'd get up long before the sun, and come in long after it had gone down.

Now bed was something he loathed getting into at night, loathed getting out of in the morning. The days lay before him like a road that was too long, a road he was too tired to travel. If it weren't for the daily crossword puzzle in the Sigourney *Herald* . . .

Winter wind howled through the cracks of the two-story farmhouse. Snow mixed with sleet pattered against the paned windows.

Not a night for livestock. Good thing he didn't have any anymore. The only thing he'd kept when he sold out was Sara's old pony. Hadn't been able to sell it. Old, foundered, half-blind thing. But it had lived its years with dignity, taking the kind of abuse children unknowingly bestow upon horses. The animal had put up with having its mouth made sore by inexperience, put up with being ridden double, and triple, feet gouging his flanks. It had put up with being made into a unicorn with a headpiece made from a plastic jug.

By Sara.

The animal deserved to live the rest of its days in relative peace rather than end up dog food and glue.

Yep, he felt empathy for the poor pony. They were a lot alike. Old and worthless. Lonely.

He was a lonely old man. Who would have thought it?

Not that he didn't have company. His grandchildren came to see him occasionally, but he felt it was something they did because they were pressured into it. He didn't speak their language. He didn't know anything about the games kids played on the TV screen, or about movies, or science-fiction, or current fads.

The land.

Hard work.

Those were the things he knew.

Those were the things he no longer had.

He was almost asleep when something woke him with a start, his poor old ticker doing double time. A good strong heart, his doctor had said. Just a might prone to flutter now and then.

He lay in bed, listening, half holding his breath.

Bang, bang, bang.

It came from downstairs. Sounded like the screen door had come unlatched.

With a sigh, he reached up and turned on the light above his head. Then he tossed back the quilt and swung his bare feet to the cold wood floor, finding the slippers his daughter Gloria had given him last Christmas.

Bang, bang, bang. There it was again.

When the kids were little, he was always after them to latch the door.

A big wind'll come up and rip it off its hinges, he used to tell them.

Now *he'd* forgotten to latch it.

Alzheimer's? God, he hoped it wasn't Alzheimer's.

He shoved himself to his feet, then, with the legs of his flannel paisley print pajamas flapping, he shuffled downstairs.

He didn't bother to check the front door. Nobody ever used it. Instead, he went straight through the kitchen to the backdoor, unlocked it, and stepped onto the unheated porch.

Used to be, there were no crimes in Sigourney. Oh, there were the usual toilet-papered trees and tipped-over outhouses. Kids' stuff. But last year they'd had two burglaries.

The craziness was getting closer. It was just a matter of time before people would have to start locking their doors every time they took a little trip into town.

He checked the screen door. The hook was in place.

He flicked on the light and tried to see through the plastic that had been put up for winter. He could make out a shape. A person.

Someone there. Someone—

"Daddy . . . ?"

Gloria?

He slid the cold metal hook from the eye, and slowly opened the door.

A woman. Dark hair.

Not Gloria.

Dark eyes. A stranger.

"It's me. Sara."

His heart did that funny thing it had been doing on

and off lately. It wasn't a pain, but more of a sensation, a change in rhythm.

He looked past her. No car in the driveway.

"S-Sara?"

Her name hadn't passed his lips in ten years. It didn't come easy.

"C-Can I c-come in?"

He opened the door a little wider and stepped to one side. It was the same door that had been there for forty years. When Sara was three, she hadn't been able to reach the handle, so he'd nailed a wooden spool down low on the door, so she could get it open by herself. The spool was still there.

She stepped inside and he closed the door behind her.

Like a dream.

Like a dream he'd had a million times. But he could feel the cold air on his bare ankles, smell the night.

He moved behind her, following her with his eyes, at first just marveling at the fact that she was there.

In the kitchen, she swung around and gave him a self-conscious smile. "I'm sorry. I know it's late."

Late. Yes, late. Ten years late.

She exhaled and looked away, biting her bottom lip in a way he remembered.

Sara had never been like the other women in his family. She had never been bold and talkative. She'd been shy, and when she said something, she gave it careful thought.

He had always wanted to protect her, to shelter her. And he had, until that one summer when she'd pushed him away, when she'd hurt him so badly.

Watching her now, he saw the lines of exhaustion in

her face. He wasn't certain, but he thought he could smell liquor on her.

She was his daughter, and yet she wasn't. When he'd last seen her, she'd been untouched by the world; now she looked as if the world was too heavy for her.

He felt a tight stinging in his throat, a burning in his eyes.

"You're tired."

That was all he said. After ten years, that was all he could think of to say. He wanted to touch her, hug her, but it had never been their way to be affectionate, or show emotion. And he was afraid if he did touch her, he might cry, which would be the most humiliating, shameful thing he could think of for a man to do.

She moved to the doorway that led to the living room.

For the first time in months he noticed the clutter and mess and dirt. There were piles of farm magazines stacked everywhere. There was mud ground into the shag carpet, cobwebs strung from ceiling to floor. Dust covered every surface, the kind that had been smudged and restirred several times.

His wife, Sara's mother, had never allowed them to so much as drink a glass of water in the living room. How had he slipped so much, so easily?

"It looks wonderful," she said.

"Your room is still upstairs."

He didn't want her to refuse his offer, didn't want her to stay because she felt obliged. He'd had too much of that lately.

She smiled again. A slow, sad, fatigued, relieved smile. "I'd like that."

Sara.

His daughter, but not his daughter.

Chapter Twenty-Seven

She shouldn't have come, Sara told herself the next morning as she made coffee. But she'd had an overwhelming urge to see her father, to see the place where she'd grown up. The need to return to her roots had been too strong to fight, like a homing instinct.

She hadn't planned to stay the night, but she'd been so exhausted, and the house had been so inviting, and her father . . . he'd been so glad to see her. *Glad.* Except for the clutter, nothing had changed. The coffee mugs were kept in the same place. So were the plates, the silverware. The same floral paper was still on the walls. The same refrigerator, same stove.

Two days ago, it had seemed as if she'd been gone a lifetime. Now, it seemed but yesterday that she'd last sat at the round oak table.

Her father had insisted upon going to town for groceries. He would be back soon. They would eat breakfast together. Talk a little. Not about her, not about the years in between. She wanted to know about Gloria and her family. She wanted to talk about the farm and the upcoming planting season. The life she'd once had. The life she'd left behind. She wanted to recapture some of what she'd lost, if only for the moment.

Then she would be on her way, reassured that her father was well.

It was a cozy house. She'd never noticed that before. Years ago, it had just seemed old and terribly outdated with its woodwork painted a white enamel, its lace curtains, now dusty and fly-specked, covering windows that looked as if they hadn't been cleaned in a long, long time.

As a child, Sara recalled helping to clean those very windows. She remembered the squeak of the rag against the glass, the smell of vinegar . . .

Footsteps sounded on the porch, startling her out of her reflections. There was a bump, like someone struggling to come in with an armload of groceries.

She smiled, getting to her feet. She'd told her father that toast was all she needed, but he'd insisted upon fixing her a country breakfast.

She opened the door—and the smile on her face froze.

It wasn't her father who stood in the doorway. It was Nash.

His eyes were glazed and bloodshot, slightly unfocused, his jaw dark with several days' growth of beard stubble.

"Hi."

That monosyllabic greeting was followed by a weak smile.

He wasn't wearing a coat. Why wasn't he wearing a coat? she wondered, her mind jumping, trying to make sense of his presence.

His shirt!

His flannel shirt was torn, stained—with something that looked like blood.

And then she noticed a sweet smell about him, not a bad smell, but a strange smell that made her think of an old and creepy hospital, of black dull rubber and a sore throat.

"Nash, what——"

As if shoved from behind, he lunged forward, stumbling over the threshold, almost falling, just managing to regain his footing at the last minute.

Behind him was Donovan.

A gun in his hand, the barrel jammed up against Nash's back.

Her eyes flashed from the gun to Donovan, then back to Nash.

His mouth moved. No sound.

"Sa-ra," he finally croaked. His eyes rolled back and he buckled. Sara was barely able to keep his head from hitting the floor.

His hands.

His wrists.

They were bound.

They were bloody.

On her knees beside him, she pressed a hand to his forehead.

Cold. Clammy. His breathing shallow.

Hovering protectively over him, she glared up at Donovan. He was clean-shaven, but his hair was greasy, his suit wrinkled.

"What have you done to him?" she demanded, feeling no fear, only anger. *Outrage.*

"I think the question is," Donovan said, "what have *you* done to him."

This wasn't happening. This wasn't happening. Not in her father's home, not with the comforting sound of the coffeepot percolating merrily behind them, not with the morning sun spilling in through the lace curtains above the sink. Not with the refrigerator door filled with crayoned pictures created by her niece and nephew, held on with magnetized verses given out by the local feed store. *A broad wife and a big barn never did a man any harm. Bloom where you're planted. Flowers turn toward the sun.*

His lips barely moving, Nash spoke. Slowly, painfully, as if every breath were agony. "I've been telling him—" His eyes clouded over. She could see his train of thought float away, see him struggling to regain it, catch it, bring it back. The haze lifted a little. "I've been telling him . . . what a bitch . . . you are . . . that . . . I don't even *like* you, but the bastard . . . won't listen."

She made a small, hiccupping sound, a half laugh, half sob.

"You have pathetic judgment when it comes to men," Donovan said in the condescending voice he so often used with her. "Do you know that Nash Audubon isn't even his real name? Do you know that he's been in prison? For *murder?*"

She didn't take her eyes off Nash. "You're lying." This was her fault. Her fault!

"It's true."

"True, true," Nash mumbled. His head lolled from side to side, his eyelids fluttered closed.

Murder? Nash? She wouldn't think about it. Not now. It was more than her mind could handle at the moment.

Donovan moved on to more pressing issues— himself. "You hurt me, Sara. Terribly. And now I'm not sure I can live with you anymore, not after what you've done, not after your adulterous affair and betrayal."

Was he talking divorce?

"I've reported you missing. I told the police that Audubon kidnapped you, then he called in with a ransom demand."

Her small flicker of hope was dashed. A familiar feeling of helplessness overcame her. Donovan always had it all figured out, always had the perfect plan, the perfect story. He was a god, controlling his little universe. And he did it so well.

"I could tell the police that he killed you, then killed himself. A double suicide."

This wasn't happening. Why had she come here? Why had she ever had anything to do with Nash?

She put a hand to his cheek, but he didn't respond. *Nash. Oh God, Nash.*

I tried to make you stay away.

Years spent attempting to pacify Donovan made her next action almost second nature. She knew what she had to do. She had to get Donovan out of the house, away from there, away from Nash.

She got to her feet and forced herself to move to Donovan's side.

"Let's just leave," she begged, a hand on his arm. "You and me."

Let's just leave. You and me.

Lying on the floor, Nash heard her words through a long, echoing tunnel.

Let's just leave. You and me.

Words spoken by Sara. To Donovan.

No way could Nash let her leave with that bastard. No way.

He couldn't feel his hands. He hadn't been able to feel them for a long time.

Had to pull himself together. Had to open his eyes. Had to get up. . . .

He shifted his weight. Breath-stealing pain ripped through his side where Donovan's thugs had kicked him.

Where were they now? He tried to remember, tried to focus his thoughts . . . Donovan sent them away . . . Why . . . ?

Suddenly it came to him.

So there wouldn't be any witnesses. . . .

Trying to ignore the pain in his side, he struggled to push himself upright.

He took a couple of shallow breaths, then inched his way to the floral-patterned wall. A wave of nausea washed over him. He took a couple of breaths, then shoved himself upright, his back to the wall.

"Don't . . . go," he bit out through gritted teeth.

He could feel the cold sweat running down his spine and underarms, see flashes of light behind his eyelids, feel the muscles trembling in his legs.

He dragged open weighted eyes, struggling to focus.

Sara's arms were outstretched toward Ivy in an imploring gesture. But her face was turned toward Nash. Eyes that had knocked him out. Eyes full of pain, of fear.

His thoughts slipped away.

He struggled to bring them back under control, struggled to comprehend what was going on. "Don't . . ." He swallowed, his mouth dry. "Don't . . . go . . . with . . . him."

As if from a great distance, he watched as Sara took a step closer to Ivy.

No!

She latched onto Ivy's arm, the arm with the gun, and leaned into him, trying to push him toward the door.

Her face. Her sweet, innocent face. Her eyes. Her huge, soulful, sad eyes.

Leaving with Ivy, but looking back as if she loved him. *Him.* Nash Audubon.

She was trying to save his ass.

That's what she'd been doing all along.

He tried to pay attention to the instructions bouncing around in his head. He tried to concentrate, but his mind drifted. . . . He wished he had time to savor this newfound truth, wished—

Intruding on his dream was Sara urging Ivy to leave.
"Come on!"

Her voice rose, bordering on hysteria. *"Come on!"*

Nash's limbs were heavy, so incredibly heavy, but
his head was light, as if it might just float away . . .
Why was he so fucked up?

Ivy and his goons had beaten him, but there was
more. . . .

Knocked him out with something. Chloroform?
Did people really use chloroform? Didn't know. Or was
it just movie stuff? Didn't know. Didn't know. What he
did know was that he could taste something sweet on
his tongue, smell something sweet when he inhaled.

Ether.

How did he know that? Didn't know. Didn't care.
He just *knew.*

A voice. A man's. Who? Oh, yeah. Ivy. Of the
Asshole Ivys. It penetrated the pea-soup fog in his head.
Donovan was making shushing sounds, placating words,
trying to calm her.

"Okay, darling."

Not that darling crap again.

"But first—"

A scuffling sound.

"No!" Sara shouted, then screamed.

The next two things happened simultaneously.

The kitchen rocked with a deafening blast.

White-hot pain ripped through Nash's side, knocking him hard against the wall.

Shot. The son of a bitch shot him.

His side was wet. Warm. Sticky.

And there was the screaming, the screaming, the
screaming.

He tried to open his eyes . . . tried to move.
Couldn't, couldn't . . .

"No! Donovan! No!"

Another report rang out. A new center of pain ripped through Nash's thigh, canceling out the old. He fought for consciousness, struggled to climb out of the pain-wracked oblivion that was swallowing him.

His ears were ringing. There was a giant reverberation in his head. *Wong, wong, wong.*

Voices. Like ghosts.

Sara's voice.

I love you, Sara.

"Nash!" Her cry was full of anguish.

Dimly, he was aware of a struggle going on in the room. In his mind's eye, he pictured dishes hitting the floor, glass shattering, the sound mixing with the giant tidal wave in his head.

Sara. Screaming again.

There was a shudder, like a body slamming against a wall.

Fading . . .

Fading . . .

Another report rang out, this one louder than the others. It was followed by a heavy thud. Lying on his side, Nash waited to feel another bullet slice into his body, waited for a red-hot poker of pain.

It didn't come. There was a warmth, but no pain, not even in his side. The world was nothing but someone's ragged, uneven breathing.

Eyes.

Had to open his eyes, had to see . . . Sara. Sara.

He dragged his lids open a crack—to look directly into the blank death stare of Donovan Ivy.

And then everything spun away.

Chapter Twenty-Eight

Nash was dreaming an old, old dream.

He stood calmly outside the courthouse, behind the security tape. Reporters bumped him, but he hardly noticed. His eyes were intent upon the closed doors. Doors that would soon open.

How long he'd waited on the marble steps, he couldn't say. Time had no meaning. Life, as he once knew it, no longer existed.

The doors opened.

Nash moved carefully, with slow, deliberate movements that wouldn't draw attention. From his coat, he lifted a revolver. He aimed. He squeezed the trigger. People shouted. A woman screamed. And screamed. And screamed . . .

"Nash! Nash!"

Hands.

Shaking him. Hurting him. Arms holding him. A wailing. A despondent, hysterical wailing.

"He's dead! He's dead!"

Rocking him, crushing him.

Couldn't breathe, couldn't breathe—

"My fault! It's my fault!"

Another voice, one he'd never heard before. A man's voice. The voice of sanity. "Sara, girl, he's not dead, but you're going to kill him if you keep mauling him like that."

The grip slackened. Sweet, sweet air filled his lungs. His eyes opened. Sara's angel face hovered over him. "He walked," Nash explained soberly, his tongue thick, his lips numb. "The man killed my daughter . . . and then he walked. On a technicality."

She smoothed back the hair from his forehead. "Don't talk. Don't talk."

"If the justice system isn't going to stand up for the innocent, somebody has to. Doesn't he?"

"Shhh."

His eyes went past her, to a big man standing over her shoulder. Gray hair, bib overalls, red flannel shirt. A shotgun in his hand.

Nice going. He'd done what Nash hadn't been able to do. Save his daughter.

The past and present mingled, and for a moment, he thought his own little girl was still alive. But it was Sara who was alive, who was safe.

Over. It was over. Time to sleep. Time to rest.

Tired. So damn tired . . .

Before he went to sleep, he wanted to look at Sara again, needed to see her, make sure she was okay, tell her something . . . Something important. . . .

Her eyes were swimming with tears. Beautiful eyes.

His tongue was numb. He couldn't feel his hands, his feet. "Girls with circles under their eyes . . . turn . . . me . . . on."

They wouldn't let her go with him.

The ambulances sped away, one carrying the injured body of the man Sara loved, the other the dead body of a man she once thought she loved.

As the siren faded into the distance, Sara stood on

the porch, her crossed arms pressed to her stomach while the police gently asked questions.

A numbness crept over her. She lost track of time, of reality. At one point, she looked up and realized that the officer had closed his notebook and that he was looking at her with concern. He was young. Maybe twenty-six, twenty-seven. Not all that much younger than she.

Strange. How very strange.

"Looks like an open-and-shut case of self-defense. We'll have to talk to Audubon, get his story. Then there'll be an inquest. If you're lucky, it will all end there."

The policeman left.

Mechanically, she turned and went into the house. She walked up the stairs. In her room, she slipped off her bloodstained shirt and exchanged it for a clean one.

She had to go to the hospital. Had to find her father, ask him to take her . . .

She went back downstairs. Into the kitchen.

Blood. On the floor. On the wall.

The room spun, her stomach lurched. She put out a hand to stop the spinning, latching onto a chair. She lowered herself into the seat.

Better. That was better.

She wiped at the perspiration on her forehead. She stared at the blood on the floor.

Nash's blood. Donovan's blood.

She didn't know how long she'd sat there when she realized her father had spoken. She pulled her gaze away from the floor to look up at him.

". . . talked to the hospital. They said he'll be okay."

Thank God. Oh, thank God.

A shaking started deep inside her, all the way from her soul, slowly radiating outward.

"Did you hear me, honey?"

Puzzled, she stared at her father. He'd killed for her. He'd saved Nash's life. Saved her life.

Thank you, Daddy.

He said something again, but she didn't understand. It was like watching a foreign movie without subtitles. He patted her arm and hurried from the room.

She was shaking outwardly now. Couldn't stop the shaking.

Then her father was back. This time someone was with him. Dr. Hamilton. She remembered him. He'd taken out her tonsils. He'd used ether. The smell. Thinking about the smell made her feel sick, made her . . .

Doctor Hamilton pushed up her sleeve. She felt something cold and wet on her arm, followed by a pinprick, a stinging sensation.

A shot.

Drugs.

Something she understood.

She felt herself go limp. She was melting out of the chair onto the floor. Sliding . . . Sliding . . . Can't touch the blood. Didn't want to touch the blood. . . .

At the last moment, when her body turned boneless, she was lifted from the chair.

Her father? Carrying her? She was too heavy. He would hurt himself. He shouldn't . . . shouldn't . . .

Everything faded. . . .

Sara woke up twenty hours later.

Nash.

She had to find out how Nash was.

Groggy, trying to ignore the throbbing in her head and the cobwebs in her brain, she threw back the covers. Then, still wearing the clothes she'd had on the day before, she made her way downstairs.

The kitchen was back to normal, maybe even a little cleaner than it had been yesterday.

"Daddy?"

No answer.

She wandered into the living room. On one wall was her high school graduation picture. Kind of faded, her hair looking weird, her expression unsure. Beside it was Gloria's picture. Blond-haired, blue-eyed, bold, confident Gloria.

Sara heard a sound outside. She unlocked the front door and tugged. It pulled hard, having been closed all winter.

Sunlight glinted off the snow, blinding her.

Cameras whirred and clicked.

Reporters.

Camped on the doorstep.

Questions were shot at her, rapid-fire.

"Did you kill your husband for the money?"

"If he abused you, why didn't you leave?"

"Did you love him?"

"They're calling you the Black Widow. What do you think of that?"

"Were you involved in a love triangle?"

"If he abused you, why didn't you leave?"

Why didn't you leave? Why didn't you leave?

She wanted to scream at them that she *had* left. Couldn't they see that? She had. And look what happened. Why was it they always asked women that question?

"What's going on out here?"

Her father had come up behind her, dressed in bib

overalls and white waffle-weave underwear, holding a rifle.

The reporters took a step back, then another.

One tenacious young man lifted his camera and pushed the shutter release. "Is that the gun you used on Ivy?"

"No!" her father roared. "But it might be the gun I use on you! This is private property."

He pointed the weapon skyward, pulled the lever that dropped the bullet into the chamber, let off the safety, then squeezed the trigger.

The blast rang in Sara's ears. It echoed off the barn, it bounced up the waterway that cut through the center of the stubbled cornfield.

Reporters scrambled.

Some ducked behind trees. Others ran up the road to where they'd left their cars.

After they cleared out, Sara's father put up a metal livestock gate at the end of the lane, along with a Private Property sign.

Paradise lost.

I'm sorry, Daddy, she wanted to tell him. *I'm so sorry.*

Chapter Twenty-Nine

Nash was in the hospital five days before they said he could go home.

Home.

Home used to be the orange couch at *Shoot the Moon*. Home used to be his car, but he didn't have that anymore either. He didn't have *anything*, not even the clothes he'd bummed from Harley. They'd cut him out of them when he was wheeled into the emergency room.

Having nothing gave him a rather nice, unfettered feeling.

While Nash was in the hospital, Harley had called him every day. So had Tootie. And Sara's father. But not Sara.

"They found my car," Harley announced during one of their phone conversations. "Impounded in some little burg near the border."

"I'll pick it up for you as soon as they let me out of here."

"Tell you what. When you're ready to come home, let me know and I'll pick up my car, then swing by and get you."

The conversation ended with Harley talking about how he was scouting for a new building; the depression he'd experienced after the fire was gone. He was ready to start over, but this time he was going to do it right. No politics. Just the important, fun stuff. And he wanted Nash along for the ride.

Newspapers made their way to Nash's room. One particularly offensive rag had sported a picture of Sara's dad on the front. Standing on a porch, rifle in hand, the caption reading: *Pa Packs a Piece*. The article and photo tried to make Sara and her father sound like a couple of illiterate, inbred yahoos. Nash tossed the paper aside in disgust. No wonder Sara was keeping a low profile. No wonder Harley preferred tabloids to the so-called legitimate press.

Franklin Hart had learned a lot in the last several years. The first time he laid eyes on Donovan Ivy, he'd seen a selfish spoiled brat who wasn't good enough for his daughter. Sara had thought Franklin's protests were because of the land, the farm. Now, he could see that there was some truth to that. The land had a way of seducing people, of making them lose perspective. For a time, the land had been everything to Franklin Hart.

But he'd also been concerned for his daughter. It wasn't right to have favorites, he knew, but Sara had always had a special place in his heart. Maybe because he could relate to her better than anyone else. Maybe because when it came to functioning socially, she'd always been a little like him. Shy, more comfortable by herself than in a crowd. While his wife and daughter had gone off shopping and socializing, he and Sara had gone fishing. He'd taught her how to bait a hook, how to cast, how to paddle a canoe. Later, he'd taught her how to drive a tractor, how to cut and bale hay, how to stack it in the barn just right.

Then Donovan Ivy had come along . . . and Sara had

been totally blinded by the man. And Franklin had been hurt and outraged by his daughter's betrayal.

Now Ivy was dead. Franklin had killed him.

He didn't regret it. In fact, it made him realize that he wasn't so useless after all. He'd saved his daughter's life. What could be more important than that?

And Nash Audubon . . .

He wasn't country, but then Sara wasn't country anymore either. It was easy to see the man was bitter, but he was also human. Deep-down decent. And he was hurting, too. Maybe Sara and Nash could heal each other.

When it came time for Nash to be released from the hospital, Franklin picked him up, offering his hospitality until the inquest. In the hospital room, he presented Nash with a pair of faded bib overalls and a shirt of waffle-weave underwear. "Pant legs might be a little short for you, but it's better than the dress the hospital gave you. The loose waist won't bother your stitches." He dropped Nash's leather boots on the floor near the bed. "These were full of blood, but we got 'em cleaned out. Hope they didn't shrink too much."

Nash was a little taken aback by the bibs— something Franklin found extremely amusing. People around Sigourney started wearing denim overalls before they were out of diapers.

Franklin gave him some pointers. "Turn that flat copper sideways and slide it in the slot. There you go. Now adjust the length right here."

Five minutes later Nash had the clothes mastered. He looked from his new outfit to Franklin's, then back to his. They were almost identical.

Franklin smiled.

Nash further impressed him by smiling back. "These babies are comfortable."

"I haven't worn them for sixty-some years just to torture myself."

At the Hart farm, they put Nash on the couch in the living room where he quickly made himself at home on the white, clean-smelling sheets. He had everything a man needed. Food. Bathroom. Remote control.

The life.

Sara talked to him, but it was surface stuff. What would you like to eat? Are you comfortable? Need another pillow?

Not knowing what else to do, he kept it light, let it slide.

At mealtimes, they ate on rusty metal TV trays in the living room while watching game shows. Franklin Hart, Nash discovered, was addicted to game shows.

At night, Nash would lie awake downstairs in a darkness that was darker than any darkness he'd ever experienced. Above his head, from the vicinity of Sara's room, the floor would creak. And creak. And creak.

The inquest went smoothly, with each of them telling relatively the same story except that Nash's understandably had a few more blanks in it. The death of Donovan Ivy went on record as being an unequivocal case of self-defense.

To Sara's advantage, and what probably saved her from a more thorough investigation, was the fact that she had nothing monetary to gain from Ivy's death. Before their marriage, she had signed a prenuptial agreement—Ivy had wanted proof that she wasn't marrying him for his money. In the event that he preceded her in death, she would get nothing.

Back at Franklin Hart's, inquest over, free to leave, Nash put in a call to Harley.

* * *

Sara stood outside, her hands deep in the pockets of her denim jacket. Even though the temperature wasn't above freezing, the sun was warm on her face. Every time a slight breeze stirred her hair, she felt the promise of spring.

In the distance, sunlight glinted off metal— someone had stopped at the gate. A squeak of hinges was followed by a clink of metal, the sound of a car door, then a revved engine.

A shiny black hearse rounded the corner and headed down the lane toward the farmhouse.

Samuel Grimes.

The man had been trying to reach her on the phone for several days, but she hadn't felt ready to deal with him, so she hadn't returned his calls.

Sara remembered Samuel from years ago. He'd always been an earnest young man, a kind young man. His father had started the Sigourney undertaking business. Before that, when someone died, the body had to be taken all the way to Mayfair.

The one memory that stuck out in Sara's mind was the way Samuel and his family had ridden everywhere in the hearse. To school, out to eat, to the drive-in. Later, when Samuel got old enough to drive, he'd even used it for dates.

The waxed and well-buffed hearse pulled up in the driveway and Samuel got out. He'd put on a dark suit for his visit. In his hand, he carried an urn. Black. Lacquered.

"Your husband's ashes," he announced.

Her stomach knotted. "I don't want them."

His professional demeanor faltered a little. "B-But—" He looked around, as if searching for a clue, for help. "Perhaps you'd like to arrange a small cere- mony . . . I'd be perfectly happy—"

"No."

"The ashes are yours," he said. "To do with as you like—"

He held out the container. When she didn't take it, he moved closer.

She jerked away, knocking the urn with her elbow. It slipped from Samuel's grip and tumbled to the ground, the lid flying off upon impact.

Sara stared in horror at the ashes spilled at her feet.

She was standing downwind. A breeze lifted some of the ashes. They blew on her clothes, on her sneakers.

She screamed and jumped back.

Gray.

Gray.

She slapped at herself, but the ashes clung to her. She looked at her palms.

Black.

She made a choking sound, then turned and ran to the side of the house, to the cistern.

Her breathing ragged, heart knocking in her chest, she pushed the cistern's metal crank. Chains rattled as the slack was taken up. The handle became hard to turn. Water gushed from the spigot.

She shoved her hands under the frigid water, wetting the sleeves of her jacket, turning the fabric dark.

"Sara?"

Nash's voice. Concerned. Puzzled.

Up until that point, she'd done a fairly good job of holding herself together. An excellent job. But now, with Nash a few feet behind her, she felt herself unraveling.

She scrubbed and scrubbed at her hands. She had to get it off, had to, had to . . .

"I have . . . to . . . get him . . . off my hands."

Think about your hands, she told herself. *Think about getting them clean.*

The water was freezing cold, turning her knuckles bright red. It should have hurt, but it didn't. She couldn't feel a thing.

"Sara, they're clean. That's enough."

"No." She was out of breath.

The water slowed, then trickled to a stop.

She quickly turned the crank—around and around. More water gushed out.

"Sara—"

"You don't know, don't *understand.*"

A thoughtful silence, then, "I spotted Grimes out front trying to scrape the spilled ashes back in the urn. I told him to just kick the rest under the bushes and get the hell out of here. Last time I saw him, he was heading for the hearse, a black jar tucked under his arm like a football."

Sara had a quick mental flash of the annoyingly tenacious Samuel Grimes crawling around on his hands and knees, trying to put Donovan Ivy back in his urn.

"Aren't ashes supposed to be good for lilacs?" Nash asked.

"Stop it. That's not funny."

"Don't people get high on ashes?"

"Stop it."

She wanted to laugh.

No, she wanted to cry.

She was angry.

No, she was hurt.

Why hurt? It was funny, when you thought about it. The way his ashes had spilled. The way she had acted. The way Grimes had acted.

Suddenly, she started laughing. And once she started, she couldn't stop. She pressed the back of a cold, wet hand to her lips, trying to hold in the sound. She gasped and stumbled away from the cistern, clutching her stomach, doubled over. Laughing, laughing . . .

And then her laughter changed.

She began to cry. Huge, loud, gulping sobs that overpowered her, that frightened her.

Had to run, had to get away—

Warm hands grasped her shoulders. Warm hands turned her around. Guided her to Nash Audubon's chest.

Arms wrapped around her, encircled her, protected her, comforted her.

"He . . . he's ev . . . ev . . . everywhere," she said in a shuddering voice as she fought to bring her crying under control. "H-He w-won't leave. Even though h-he's dead, h-he w-won't leave."

Nash threaded his fingers through her hair. She felt his fingertips against her scalp. "He will," he said, rocking her against his chest. "He will."

With one arm around her, he led her into the house where he made her sit on an old paint-chipped wooden chair. Moving stiffly, careful of his healing side, he helped her get her shoes off, knowing she didn't want to touch them. Then he made her stand so he could unbutton and unzip her pants. She slid them off, then disappeared around the corner. Seconds later, he heard her feet pounding up the stairs, heard the creak of the floorboards above his head.

He put her jeans and sneakers into the washing machine, poured in some soap, then dropped the lid.

Goodbye, Mr. Ivy.

Later that afternoon, as the sun was setting, as winter crept back for the evening, Harley arrived. Nash left him visiting with Franklin while he searched for Sara. He found her upstairs in her bedroom.

She'd changed into a pair of well-worn black jogging pants. Her feet were bare. She still looked rattled, still looked fragile after her encounter with Grimes.

Not knowing quite what to say, feeling suddenly awkward about telling her good-bye, he stuck his hands in the front pockets of his bib overalls and crossed the room to examine a watercolor hanging on one wall. It was painted in soft hues, a traditional view of a farmhouse at sunset. And then he noticed a name in the lower right-hand corner. Sara Hart.

He pointed. "You did this?"

"Yeah." She came up beside him. "Pretty bad, huh? I remember how good I thought it was. Now it seems . . ." She shrugged. "Pretentious. Too simple."

There was talent there, though. She had an eye for balance, for light and shadow, which was important in any picture, photograph or painting.

He had a sudden inspiration, a desperate man grasping at desperate straws. *Have you ever thought of going into the tabloid business? Altering photos?*

As soon as the idea came to him, he dismissed it for what it was—crazy. As if she'd jump in a car with two guys who had nothing. As if she'd be interested in drawing pictures of bats with human faces. Of aliens having lunch with Timothy Leary.

Nash turned and looked at her. And it was like that time on the beach. Suddenly he couldn't think, couldn't pull his eyes away. Finally he said, "I'm leaving."

She nodded. "I saw Harley's car pull up."

She stared down at her clenched hands, looked back up at him, then away. She pulled in a shuddering breath—and suddenly he was afraid she was going to cry again.

"Tell Harley hi for me, okay?" She bit her bottom lip.

He wanted her to come with him. That was what he wanted, that was what he needed. But he had nothing. *Nothing.* Shit, he didn't even own the clothes he was wearing. After all she'd been through, she deserved better than him.

He nodded. "Sure, I'll tell him."

"Will I ever see you again?"

"Do you want to?" He was putting her on the spot, but he couldn't leave without knowing, without having some inkling of how she felt.

"I don't know."

She didn't know.

"Ouch." Her answer hurt like hell, but he wouldn't let it show. He smiled, and it felt like a fairly good facsimile. "Bye, Sara."

"Nash?"

He stopped. He turned, hoping, hoping . . .

"What's your real name?"

He gave it some thought. "I used to have another name, but that was a long time ago. I'm not that person anymore."

She nodded, as if she understood. "Good. I want to remember you as Nash."

Sara watched from the second-story window as Nash walked to Harley's car. Just before he ducked inside, he looked up, then raised his hand in farewell.

She should have gone downstairs to see them off, to say hello to Harley, but she knew she wouldn't have made it. She would have fallen apart.

Now, watching Nash as he looked up at her, she lifted her hand. She pressed it, open-palmed, against the cold glass.

Bye.

Good-bye.

Do you want to see me again?

I don't know.

Why had she said that?

His question had taken her by surprise. It had been something she hadn't felt able to deal with.

Her breath fogged up the glass. She rubbed it away, she wiped the tears from her eyes, and when she could see again, Nash was gone.

Letter to the Editor of Shoot the Moon:
What can I do about my neighbor? He leaves his Christmas decorations up all year long.
—Pissed in Missouri

Dear Pissed:
In Missouri, it's a law that no *decorations can be taken down until after the Fourth of July. To a Missourian, there's nothing more aesthetic than a pumpkin trash bag at Easter.*
—Ed.

Chapter Thirty

Spring. In the country.

It was everything Sara had always hated.

The bone-chilling dampness. The knee-deep, boot-sucking mud. Roads that had to be closed because they couldn't support a car. Roads left soft by the thaw. Roads that, when walked on, bounced like a trampoline.

The rain.

Endless. Running through the tilled fields, filling the streams and ponds, falling gently on the roof, gurgling in the downspouts, trickling down windows of poured glass.

After the rain, there was the soft morning sun, glistening on a green as green as the Emerald City. And there were robins. Singing before dawn. And flowers. Tulips. Daffodils. Hyacinths, waving in the breeze, dispersing their sweet scent on the rain-washed air.

Spring.

It was everything she'd always loved. Everything she'd missed.

One day, when the lilac leaves were no bigger than squirrel's ears, her sister Gloria drove in from the city. Sara and Gloria had never been close, and now, with the gulf of the last ten years between them, the ugliness of Sara's life, their reunion was awkward. It would have been easier to talk to a total stranger. They would have been able to start from square one.

Gloria was still chatty and petite, with her smooth blond hair and whirlwind energy. "Daddy looks five years younger," she said, putting coffee cups on the table.

The porch door slammed; followed by the sound of running footsteps and laughter. Then Gloria's children, a boy and a girl, appeared in the doorway, breathless, red-cheeked. "Grandpa says he'll saddle up Pepper!" They spoke in unison.

"Say hi to your Aunt Sara," Gloria said, pushing at the back of each child.

Their smiles vanished. They kept their knees locked, hands at their sides as they struggled to remain rooted to the spot while Gloria continued to urge them forward.

Sara had no experience with children, but the incident took her back to the days of her own childhood when her mother had forced her into uncomfortable situations. First it had been Santa Claus with his bad breath and body odor. Later, Great Uncle Jesup and his wooden arm.

"That's okay," Sara said, trying to smile at the balking children, feeling her lips stick to her teeth.

"They'll come around," Gloria said.

Sara kept smiling. "Of course they will. Of course they will."

A couple of weeks later, Sara decided she needed a job, and jobs weren't plentiful in Sigourney.

Lucky for her, the local café was hiring.

The Coffee House. An original name for an original place, she thought wryly.

"A waitress?" her father said when she told him about her new position. "What about those pretty pictures you used to paint? Do you ever do anything like that anymore?"

Pretty pictures.

She smiled, recalling a time when he'd ridiculed her for those very pictures, when he'd called them a waste of time, something for dreamers with their heads in the clouds.

Pretty pictures. She doubted she had any pretty pictures left in her.

"No," she told him.

"Your watercolors are still upstairs. You should get them out."

She smiled and nodded. "Maybe I will." But she knew she wouldn't.

One day Nash called, but their conversation was awkward. Sara told him about her job at the café. He told her that it was hot in Chicago.

There was all the usual city background noise. Cars honking. Sirens going off. So different from the country, reminding her of the transience of their relationship, reminding her that their paths had once intersected for one brief moment, then moved on.

"I can hear the traffic," she said.

"I can hear the birds," he said.

"And the corn growing."

"Can you really hear corn grow?"

"It's just an expression."

"Oh."

Silence.

More silence.

"Gotta go," Nash said.

"Okay."

"Take care."

"You, too."

After hanging up, a dark depression washed over her, and she almost wished he hadn't called. Almost.

Sara had been home a month when her father talked her into going to church with him.

As soon as Sara and her father stepped inside the church, with its stained glass windows and oak pews, heads swiveled.

Rubbernecking, her father called it.

The back pews always filled first, the front ones remaining empty, even for Easter service. She and her father were forced to walk down the aisle and take a seat four rows in.

Not looking to the left or right, Sara picked up the cardboard fan that was tucked behind the Bible. On one side was an old-fashioned, practically colorless picture of Jesus looking toward the heavens, a beam of sunshine enveloping him. On the other side was the address and phone number of the Sigourney Funeral Home. It could have been the very same fan Sara had held in her hand at age six.

Nothing changed in Sigourney. . . .

After the wave of whispers ran its course, the church-goers settled down to reading their bulletins and finding the correct hymn in the hymnals. Sara took the

opportunity to do a little gaping of her own. She lifted
her head, her gaze running across the backs of the family that had taken a seat a couple of pews ahead and to
her left.

Josh Hastings, the boy her father had hoped she'd
marry, his father's land bordering theirs. A perfect
match. Josh was a man now, with a wife and three tidy-
headed children.

*It could have been me. I could have had a nice, nor-
mal life.*

But then she thought about a man with dark,
unruly hair, a man who had entered her life and turned
it upside-down. A man who had named his little girl
after a comet.

Sara's vision blurred. She pulled in a trembling
breath and sat up straighter, her fingers wrapped tightly
around the handle of the fan.

Her father leaned close. "You okay?" he whispered.

"Fine, Daddy. I'm fine."

At the café, Sara worked the eleven A.M. to seven
P.M. shift. Lunch and supper, or as the locals called, it,
dinner and supper. They served up specials like salty
baked ham, grainy mashed potatoes with grease gravy,
plus canned green beans. Their one claim to fame was
their peanut butter pie—the only edible thing on the
menu as far as Sara was concerned.

At the café, Sara wore a pink striped shirtwaist
dress with a white apron and white sneakers.

She'd taken the job to get her mind off what had
happened, but she ended up loving it. It was so normal,
so Midwest, so far from the life she'd been leading. She
felt like another person when she was at the café.

But one day as spring turned to summer, when
Queen Anne's lace and black-eyed Susans danced in the

roadside ditches and red-winged blackbirds sang from bowed electrical wires, she realized she'd never be a part of it, not deep in her heart. She could slip into her old clothes—her cut-offs, her jeans—she could sleep in the bed she'd slept in as a child, but nothing could change the fact that she wasn't the person she used to be.

You can't go back and expect life to be the same.

The weather turned hot and humid. Her father didn't believe in air-conditioning. He thought of it as a sign of weakness.

At night, Sara would toss and turn as a fan hummed on the floor, stirring the hot, sticky air. Finally, toward morning, when the temperature dropped a few degrees, she would fall asleep, only to wake up with the sheets damp from perspiration, her skin clammy.

The humid morning brought no relief, and when she arrived at work for her shift, it was hotter inside the café than out. Ceiling fans couldn't compete with body heat, grills, and hot dishwater.

Not many people showed up for the luncheon special, not even the diehards. By one o'clock the place was empty.

The short-order cook shuffled out of the kitchen, her thin white T-shirt clinging to her sweaty body, a cigarette dangling from one corner of her mouth. Her face reflected a hard life, with deep lines under the eyes and around the mouth. Sara had been shocked to find she was only thirty-five.

"We should close up and go home," Maxine said, leaning a hip against the counter and wiping a strand of hair from her face with the back of her hand.

"I'd like to go for a nice cool swim," Sara said.

"At the quarry."

The quarry . . . Sara had forgotten about the quarry with its crystal-clear, ice-cold water.

The screen door squeaked, then slammed shut.

"Crap."

Maxine pulled the cigarette from her mouth and flicked ashes into her palm. She glanced toward the door and her tired eyes perked up. "Don't look now, honey, but a real hunk just walked in."

Sara automatically started to turn.

"Don't look!" Maxine whispered in her husky voice.

With Sara's back to the door, Maxine gave her a play by play. "He's checking things out . . . Picking up a menu . . . Now he's sitting down in the booth by the door."

Maxine rubbed the handful of ashes against her pant leg, then took a long drag from her cigarette, eyes squinted against the smoke. "Good thing we didn't close up."

"That swim still sounds good to me."

Maxine pointed her chin in the direction of the booth. "Go take a gander at that and see if you still think so."

Sara laughed and pulled out her order pad and pen, then headed for the hunk behind the menu.

Pen poised on the green tablet, she asked, "May I take your order?"

The menu was lowered.

Nash.

Suntanned. Sleeves cut out of a gray-blue T-shirt. Arms bare and muscled. Hair wild, as if he'd been in a tornado. He could look good in anything. Harley's baggy grunge, her father's overalls.

He raked his hair back from his forehead, giving her a quick glimpse of armpit. Then he tossed the plastic-covered menu on the table, crossed his arms at his chest, leaned back in the booth, and looked up at her with a smile in his eyes. "What's good?"

While Sara dug in the ice machine with the metal scoop, Nash checked out the jukebox. He put in some money. Pushed some buttons.

Music.

There hadn't been any new songs on the jukebox in years. What came out was old, slow, lazy rock.

"It's like that commercial."

Maxine had appeared beside her, lipstick fresh and red-orange.

"Commercial?" Sara asked blankly. Her TV viewing had been almost nonexistent over the last several years.

"You know, the one where the guy walks into the hot café where everybody's sweating and it starts to snow, right inside the building."

Sara shrugged and shook her head. "Sorry." She lifted a slice of peanut butter pie from the case, grabbed the iced tea, and headed for Nash.

Pie in front of him. Tea to the side. Napkin. Fork.

She stood there a moment, then, hands splayed on the tabletop, she lowered herself into the seat across from him.

"Pink-and-white stripe," he said, eyeing her uniform, talking around a mouthful of peanut butter pie. "Very . . . becoming."

She fiddled with the polyester white cuff on the short sleeve, then her fingers fluttered to the collar. "It's what everybody wears here."

He took a long swallow of iced tea, and looked at her with an intensity that made her insides feel funny.

"Somehow I imagined you in something more . . . well, I don't know anything about fabric, but something a little more . . . bohemian."

She didn't know if she should be flattered or insulted.

"What time do you get off?"

"Not for five hours."

"I'll wait."

"You can't wait here all afternoon." She thought about having him sit there, watching her every move. His gaze shifted as he focused on something just past her shoulder. Maxine.

"You go on," Maxine said. "Nobody's coming in when it's this hot. I was fixing to send you home anyway."

Nash smiled a smile that probably sent Maxine's blood pressure up a couple of notches.

"Thanks," Sara said.

"Thanks," Nash said.

Outside, Sara quickly discovered why Nash's hair had looked so wild. He was driving a convertible. An absolute boat of a car.

"Do you have a thing about ugly cars?" She circled the monstrosity, a hand trailing over one chromed fin. "I can't imagine how much gas this guzzles."

Arms crossed, biceps in relief, he leaned a hip against the grill. Behind him, on a power pole, tinsel from last year's Christmas decorations drooped in the heat.

"It's not as bad as you might think. Only thing is, I can't toss my trash in the backseat 'cause it blows out. And it's not handy when it rains."

"How's that?"

"No top. That's why I got it so cheap."

"No top?" She looked at the gaping hole behind the backseat where the top should have been.

"I've learned to drive fast and keep my head down."

She laughed.

He smiled at her.

And she realized what a relief it was to see him. Even though she loved her father, even though she enjoyed her job at the café, she hadn't realized how alien, how alone she'd felt until that moment. Here was someone who spoke her language, someone who was, in a strange, scary way, a part of her.

Unfortunately, he'd seen the movie *Children of the Corn*.

—Nash, contemplating the life of a farmer

Chapter Thirty-One

Nash opened the passenger door. The front seat was covered with a clear, yellowed plastic made up of millions of raised diamond shapes.

"Here—" He reached in back and dropped a blanket on the seat. "Sit on this"—he spread out the blanket—"or you'll burn yourself."

Sara slid onto the passenger side while Nash closed the door.

The plastic was scalding through the thin fabric of her dress where her shoulder blades met the seat back. She sat up a little straighter.

Nash vaulted into the driver's seat. "The door works," he explained. "It's just a little hard to close once you open it."

The dashboard used to be red, but was now pink, faded from the sun, covered with a fine layer of dust. Where the radio should have been was nothing but a gaping hole and colored wires. On the seat between them was a stereo, plus a stack of tapes and CDs.

"Gotta have tunes," Nash said, popping in a CD. He turned the ignition. The engine rumbled to life, sounding deep and powerful, the floorboards shuddering under her feet.

With one-handed precision, Nash backed out of the

parking space, turned, and headed down the nearest dirt road.

"Where to?" he shouted, the wind whipping their hair about their heads, music blaring.

Where to?

"Anywhere."

They cruised the backroads, hitting the high spots. "Old Mr. Newton's house," Sara said, pointing. "His wife died when she was twenty-two. For the last fifty years, he's kept that lighted picture of her in the window."

A few minutes later: "Those two houses belong to the Lewis brothers. They married sisters, divorced them, then traded mates."

"That was handy."

"This is Carla Day's house. I went to school with her. She's married and has four kids."

Married, married, married. Sara was approaching middle age, and what did she have to show for her life? She was afraid the best years had been wasted. There was only so much time. On one hand, she felt the urge to hurry; on the other, she wanted everything to stop.

Fifteen minutes later, she suggested they go by her house. "We could have something cool to drink."

"Point the way."

Within ten minutes, they were driving down the dirt lane that led to Sara's home.

All the years she'd lived with Donovan, she'd never thought of the house they'd shared as her home. But this place, wherever she was, wherever she went, would always be home.

The two-story farmhouse looked good, with a field of corn on one side, beans on the other. It was like something from a Beatrix Potter book, with its fresh coat of white paint and purple clematis vines trailing along the trelliswork that bordered the back door. Hollyhocks lined the road.

She and Gloria used to make dolls from the blooms. A full blossom was used for the doll's skirt, a bud for its head.

Looking at the house, she felt a soul-deep ache for something that was no more, for a time of her life she hadn't appreciated enough while she'd lived it.

Her father was gone for the day, to an auction "out Sycamore way," he'd said. He went for socializing more than anything else, but Sara knew he would come home with a small something for her, an antique hat pin or an old photograph.

"We don't have air-conditioning," she told Nash, suddenly feeling shy and awkward about being alone with him.

He took the hint and waited outside in the shade while she hurried upstairs, trying to ignore the nervous excitment building in her. She threw off her uniform and pulled on shorts she'd made out of a pair of old jeans. She cuffed them just above the knee, slid her sneakers back on, plus a white sleeveless blouse, then hurried downstairs for two glasses of iced tea.

At first, when she stepped outside, the screen door banging against her heels, she couldn't find Nash. But then she spotted him, sitting in one of the metal chairs under the big maple.

The chairs had been around ever since she could remember, painted with layer after layer of green paint. As a child, she hadn't liked them because of their color and the way they were so cold against her bare skin. Now, in a world where nothing seemed to last, she admired them for their longevity.

She handed Nash his tea, then sat down beside him, the curved metal slats bouncing gently with her weight.

They sipped their tea.

"I'm moving," he suddenly stated. "Away from Chicago."

The excitement she'd been feeling vanished. "Where?"

"Corpus Christi."

"Corpus Christi?"

So far away. He may as well have said he was moving to another country.

"Harley's moving the paper there. He got a good deal on some property."

"Oh."

She'd never been to Corpus Christi, but she knew it was in Texas, knew it was on the gulf, knew it was far, far away. How would she be able to picture him there, someplace she'd never seen?

He came to say good-bye, she told herself, suddenly understanding the purpose of his visit.

There were a lot of places she'd never been. A lot of things she'd never done. Her life was slipping away and she felt both helpless and angry with herself for allowing it.

He came to say good-bye.

They sat facing the road, a field of corn and a mailbox their entire view. And the sun was going down behind the field, getting lower in the sky, looking blurry as it struggled to cut through the haze.

Like an old married couple, they sat sipping tea in the shade, watching the day go by.

There were so many things she wanted to say to him, but she didn't know how to go about it. Her family had never talked about how they felt.

She wanted to tell him she was sorry for deserting him that day in the motel. She wanted to explain that she'd done it out of concern for his safety. She wanted to tell him she was sorry he'd gotten mixed up in her messy life. She wanted to thank him for getting mixed up in it.

She wanted to tell him she'd missed him, that she would miss him.

There was more, much more, but the rest was better left unsaid, especially if he was leaving for Texas, especially if this was good-bye.

"Would you like to go for a walk?" she asked. He was used to things moving fast. The country had to be boring for him.

"Good idea."

They got to their feet, put their empty glasses on the chairs, then moved off down the grassy lane that ran the length of the pasture ground that Sara's dad still owned. On the left was row after row of corn, the stalks towering over their heads, the leaves curling from the heat, the high humidity keeping the heavy, almost tropical smell of green, green leaves from drifting away. It was a smell Sara had always loved, a smell she thought should be bottled.

She searched her mind for something to say, for the right words to thank him. "Knee-high by the Fourth of July." Where had that come from?

He slowed and looked at her. "Huh?"

"Farmers used to say the corn should be knee-high by the Fourth of July."

He eyed the towering stalks. "That right? What does head-high by the end of June mean?"

She smiled, feeling a little less nervous. "It's been a good year."

Nash's gaze moved from the corn to the adjacent field. "A pond," he said, spotting shimmering blue water. "Can we look at it?" He sounded eager.

"The pasture and pond are the only parts of the

farm Daddy didn't sell. He's made them into kind of a wildlife sanctuary, and he just couldn't let them go."

Rather than walk half a mile to the gate, they climbed the stile next to the road. Then, side by side, they waded through the waist-high grass to the pond.

Instead of mowing the grass near the water or letting cattle graze it, Franklin Hart had left it in its natural state. Above the water were duck houses; near the shore, bluebird houses. In the middle of the pond, he'd made an island, a haven where geese could nest and lay eggs in relative safety.

"A canoe!"

Nash spotted the upside-down craft left near the water's edge.

Sara raised both eyebrows, wondering how on earth a canoe could excite anybody. "Want to take it out?" she asked, fulling expecting him to turn down the offer.

The words had hardly left her mouth when he was moving toward the metal craft, arms high to avoid the tall grass, his body cutting a path to the pond.

He turned over the canoe, wooden paddles rattling against the bottom. Then he began shoving it into he water, nose first.

When it was almost completely waterborne, Sara said, "You get in first and I'll push off."

Without hesitation, he stepped aboard. Bent at the waist, hands out for balance, he moved to the opposite end, the canoe wobbling, her side lifting free of the ground.

Feeling his stability weakening, Nash dropped to the seat while Sara stepped in. She grabbed a paddle, pushed off, then sat down, the craft gliding silently across the water.

"Oh, wow," Nash said, as if he couldn't quite take

it all in, like a kid who was seeing Disneyland for the first time. "This is great."

She smiled and thought, *Yes, it's nice.*

After a couple of minutes, he picked up the other oar, stuck it in the water, and began paddling like crazy.

The canoe immediately veered into a tight circle. Sara laughed, dropped her oar in the boat, and clung to both sides.

With a look of determination, Nash lifted his oar and stuck it in the water on the other side. Slowly, the canoe came to a stop, water splashing the hull. He paddled. Like a dog digging up a bone, he dug the paddle deep and pushed the water away. They shot forward. He dug again, and again—and they began to circle once more.

Sara laughed out loud. "There's a technique where you don't have to switch sides, but I never mastered it."

"Ah."

He nodded, understanding, eager to perfect his craft. He stroked once on the left, lifted the oar, splashing her with water—"Sorry"—and stroked once on the right. Left, right, left, right. Now they were moving in a jerky motion.

"You're trying too hard," she told him.

"That's a first."

She laughed again, for the third time in a matter of minutes. "You're oversteering. Canoeing is supposed to be *relaxing*," she said, careful to maintain her grip.

He quit putting so much muscle into it. The boat began to move more smoothly. "Here we go. Now I'm getting it."

They glided through lily pads. A few feet away, startled frogs jumped off logs to splash in the water.

"Now we're cooking." Nash's face was a study in concentration.

Out of the corner of her eye, Sara saw something flash across the bottom of the canoe. Something small. Something gray. A field mouse.

They liked to build nests under the banked canoe. Tipped over, it made a cozy little roof. She'd forgotten about pounding on the canoe bottom before tipping it over—to make sure all the mice were out.

She lost track of the mouse, but suddenly she heard a skittering sound—tiny claws raking metal.

"What the hell was that?"

"A mouse."

"A *what*?"

He quit paddling and stared at her in disbelief, as if she'd just informed him that they were trapped in a canoe with a rattlesnake.

"Mouse."

A tiny gray form zigzagged, then darted under Nash's seat.

He let out a shout and jumped to his feet.

The canoe rocked.

Then capsized.

Chapter Thirty-Two

Nash hit the water with a huge splash.

Ice-cold.

Took his breath away.

He gave a strong scissor kick and his head broke the surface. He sucked in air. Sunlight, reflecting off the metal bottom of the capsized canoe, blinded him.

Sara.

Treading water, hands and feet and legs and arms in constant motion, he searched for her. His gaze shot across the rippling surface of the pond, his heart racing. "Sara!" Panic blossomed in his chest, echoed in his voice.

"Sara!"

"Here! I'm here!"

Her voice came from the other side of the canoe.

He swam around to find her clinging to the hull, wet but calm. Even smiling. Suddenly feeling stupid, he said, "Oh, yeah, I forgot you can swim."

A stricken look wiped out her smile. That was quickly replaced by a total lack of expression.

He hadn't meant to say it, hadn't meant to bring it up.

There had been a space of time in the last hour when he'd sensed that she was relaxing, that he hoped they might have something going, that there might be some chance for him.

He'd screwed up.

She gave all of her attention to the canoe. "Help me turn this over."

He grabbed one end of the craft, she the other. They counted, then turned, righting it in one motion. Not bad, he thought, for a city boy. They retrieved the floating paddles and tossed them inside. Then they sidestroked to shore, the canoe between them.

When they reached shallow water, his thigh and side, where he'd taken the bullets, were aching with a dull throb he'd become accustomed to whenever he put too much strain on the still healing muscles.

His wet and dripping clothes a dead weight, he grabbed the bow of the canoe and tugged. The craft slid through the grass with a shushing sound. That taken care of, his leg and side still screaming, he collapsed at the pond's edge.

"Have you ever been in a canoe?"

He looked up to see Sara standing over him, feet braced, hands on hips. Not mad, but irritated. And irritated was better than ambivalent, better than afraid.

"As a matter of fact—no."

"You're not supposed to stand up in one."

"Now you tell me," he said, rolling to a sitting position, staring at the water seeping from his shoes. He didn't think it would have mattered even if he had known. He didn't like mice.

He pulled off his sneakers and dumped out the water. As he peeled off his wet socks, he cast a surreptitious glance Sara's way.

She was still very fragile looking—that was the first thing he'd noticed when he stepped into the café. She had a dusting of a tan, giving her skin a deceptively healthy glow. She was still as graceful as ever, still as lean—maybe a little too lean. And there were still smudges under her eyes. In some ways, she seemed better than when he'd last seen her, in some ways worse. It was impossible to miss the way her hands sometimes shook, the way she closed them into tight fists, her knuckles bloodless.

He twisted pond water from his socks—socks that had been white but were now gray. "I'm sorry about that crack I made back there—the swimming thing."

She'd taken off her shoes and was sitting in the grass, arms around her bent knees, staring off across the pond.

He raised his arms and reached behind him, grabbing the back of his shirt, tugging it over his head. He squeezed out the excess water, shook out the shirt, then spread it across the grass.

A gasp sounded beside him. He looked up to see Sara staring at his side where the bullet had ripped through his flesh. Damn.

It had left a scar, still raised and red, with dots along the raised section where they'd stitched him up. Not a pretty sight. He should have left his shirt on.

"Your side." Her face was a combination of fascination and repulsion.

Self-consciousness was something entirely new to him.

He didn't like it.

He experienced the overwhelming urge to cover up. Instead, he lay back on the ground, hands behind his head.

The grass was surprisingly soft. He could see the seeded ends of the stalks bobbing gently against a hazy sky. A breeze moved across his damp skin. His thoughts went back to her earlier observation. There were worse scars than physical ones.

"It's the kind of scar I can live with," he finally said.

He closed his eyes, hoping that would be the end of it.

He felt the sun's heat on his bare chest, saw red behind his eyelids. And the sounds . . . All sorts of sounds he hadn't been aware of before. Amazingly loud but tranquil sounds, so different from what he was used to in the city. Insects buzzing, some far away, some close. And birds. Lots of birds, calling high and sweet.

"Sometimes," Sara said, her voice distant, as if her face was turned away, "I think I see him. I feel like he's watching me."

His heart constricted. He waited, wondering if there was more, afraid there was more.

"I-ah——" She stopped, then started again. "I try not to think about that day, in the kitchen, but I have this . . . this *image* stamped in my brain. It pops into my head when I least expect it. I can be taking someone's order at the café, and suddenly there he is——"

She let out a sob.

Nash opened his eyes and sat up.

Her back was to him, her arms hugging her knees. She was breaking his heart.

He went to her, scar be damned. He sat down next to her. "Sara, don't cry." He couldn't stand it when she cried. He pulled her to him, holding her tightly, her wet blouse cold against his chest.

"I want it to go away," she said in a muffled voice.

He just held her, stroking her dripping hair.

"I used to have a daughter," he found himself saying. He'd never told anybody what he was about to tell Sara. "Two-car garage. I used to be a teacher. Yeah, hard to believe, I know. One day my daughter was . . . killed. It was one of those random acts of violence that make no sense to rational humans. The kind of thing that leaves you numb, that leaves you asking why, over and over."

"You killed him." It was a statement. "The man who killed your daughter."

A pause. Then, "Yes, but I couldn't save Haley. I couldn't save my little girl."

"But you may have saved other children, other little girls. . . ."

"Yes." She had hit on the one thing that had kept him going all those years between losing Haley and finding Sara.

She lifted her head and looked up at him. Her lashes were wet and spiked, her eyes swimming with tears. "Sometimes," she whispered, "I dream Donovan killed you." She swallowed. "And it seems so real that I wake up thinking you're dead." She looked down. With trembling fingers, she gently touched his scar. "When I think about what almost happened . . ."

He cupped her chin, lifted her face to his. "But it didn't. Think about that."

Tenderly, so as not to scare her, he lowered his head. His lips brushed hers . . . and he thought her heard her sigh.

Slowly, slowly. Carefully, carefully. He kissed her, a lazy, nonthreatening, open-mouthed kiss, wet lips brushing wet lips, soft breath meeting soft breath.

This was the woman who had sent him over the edge. This was the woman who had come to him in the middle of the night with a passion that had left him wrung out and mindless.

But today he sensed that she was different, far more fragile. When Donovan was alive, she'd had to be tough. But now her defenses were down . . . and he wasn't sure if he knew how to keep from breaking her.

The kiss deepened until it was tongue meeting tongue, until he knew they were going to make love. Before things reached a point of total mindlessness, he forced himself to stop long enough to pull her deeper into the grass—the tallest damn grass he'd ever seen—so no one would be able to see them. He leaned back on his elbows, hands on her arms, gently drawing her closer.

She put a trembling hand to his chest. "I-I don't think I can do this."

Sara was suddenly afraid. More than afraid. She was *terrified.*

She'd never made love like this, in the bright light of day, with total clarity of mind. With Donovan, sex had never been more than something to endure, and she had quickly learned to drink a lot beforehand. She had quickly learned that oblivion could be a very good thing.

Nash didn't push it. Thank God he didn't push it. Instead, he let her go. Instead, he shrugged his shoulders as if to say it was nothing. Instead, he gave her a little smile, squinted up at the bright sky, and said, "Why don't we just get naked?"

"Naked?"

"Yeah. Just lie here in the sun while our clothes dry."

To demonstrate, he unbuttoned, unzipped, and peeled off his jeans, cussing most of the time as he struggled with the clinging, damp fabric. Once off, he turned them right side out, shook them, then spread them over the top of the grass, where they lay suspended, a foot from the ground. He was going for his jockey shorts when she looked away.

* * *

Everything was quiet except for the birds and insects.

And Sara's pounding heart. Her shallow breathing. She sat in the grass for quite some time, not looking in Nash's direction. She'd heard him finish taking off his clothes, heard him lie back with a contented sigh. . . .

Slowly, ever so slowly, she turned her head. His eyes were closed. His hands were behind his head. She could see the dark armpit hair surrounded by muscles.

Her gaze moved down. . . .

Flat brown nipples amid lots of chest hair.

Down, down, down.

Muscled ribcage. Flat stomach, flat navel, narrow hips . . . dark thatch of hair.

Her gaze darted away, flew back to his face.

His eyes were still closed, his chest rising and falling.

Asleep?

Slowly, she worked at the buttons of her blouse.

Finally everything was off.

Naked, she lay down beside him, tightly closing her eyes, waiting for her heart to stop its rampaging.

Slowly, ever so slowly, she began to relax. New sensations crept into her consciousness. The sun, warm against her skin, against her breasts, her abdomen . . . It felt good. Incredibly good . . .

She may have fallen asleep, she wasn't sure. Sometime later something soft fell on her. Then another soft something. On her breasts, her stomach, her legs. She opened her eyes to see Nash leaning over her, sprinkling her body with clover.

"I looked for ones with four leaves, but couldn't find any," he said.

She stared at him, couldn't pull her eyes from his. "I can't do this sober," she said tightly, breathlessly, her heart hammering again, knowing her fear showed in her eyes, hating herself for it.

"I'll help you," he whispered. And then he smiled at her, a smile that was at once sweet and tender, a smile that took her breath away. "I'll talk you through it."

The fact that he understood the panic that beat so frantically beneath her taut skin made her love him all the more, this man who would soon leave, this man who would soon tell her good-bye.

She kept her eyes on his face, watched him as he looked down at her body, as he dropped another clover on her, this one brushing her nipple, falling against her ribcage.

"Close your eyes," he instructed.

She closed them.

"Keep them closed."

Time ticked away.

"God, you're beautiful." There was a catch in his voice that made her feel a little coil of heat deep inside.

With the soft leaves of the clover, he stroked her. Lightly. Everywhere.

And then he used his hand, his fingers.

Touching.

Stroking.

Slow.

Fast.

Wet.

Deep.

Her body stiffened. She felt herself spasm around his fingers, her ecstasy blooming, drifting . . .

Slowly, slowly, she floated back to earth.

Her heart racing, her body covered with a sheen of perspiration, she lifted heavy lids to see Nash lying on his side, head supported by one hand, elbow on the ground, watching her.

"You're too good," she said, feeling sated and weak and hungry all at the same time.

He rolled to his back, an arm flung over his eyes, his breathing ragged.

Her gaze traveled down from his half-closed eyes, past the pulse beating in his neck, down his damp chest, his flat stomach. Lower . . .

She was braver now, bolder now that he was no longer watching her. She touched him. Tentative. Cautious.

"*You* are so beautiful," she said huskily. "Soft. Like a flower."

She heard his indrawn breath, knew that all of his senses were riveted on her hand. But he didn't move to touch her. It was her call.

And then she said what she knew he was waiting to hear. "I want you."

In a heartbeat, he was on top of her, whispering her name, his hard heat filling her, stretching her. "Sara, Sara," he said, raggedly, looking down at her, his hands braced on either side of her head.

He wrapped his arms around her, pulling her to his chest. They rolled, the sweet scent of clover enveloping them. They tumbled. He cupped her bottom, holding her, his ragged out-of-control breathing thrilling her. Broken words, sexy words, words of need, of pleasure. Her name, over and over.

"Sara, sweet, sweet Sara . . ." he rasped.

They rolled. They tumbled.

She was overwhelmed. Their coming together was something so pure, so blindingly brilliant, so right, that she felt like laughing and crying at the same time.

He took her higher than any drug had ever done. Her name, a cry of pain and torment, of anguish and ecstasy. His hands on her breasts, his fingers threaded through her hair, his mouth against hers, the weight of his body . . .

She let go of his waist and dug her fingers into the grass, the earth, her back arching to meet his deep, shuddering release as he took her out beyond the stars, beyond the moon.

Little by little, she became aware of the heaviness of his body between her thighs, the pounding of his heart against hers, the harsh breathing against her ear, the sun, the sun, bright and brilliant and blinding.

He lifted himself slightly, so he wasn't lying so heavily upon her, then he pressed his lips to her hair. "Come away with me."

"I think I just did."

He laughed. The rich, deep reverberation vibrated against her chest.

"No," he gasped, still out of breath. "To Corpus Christi. Come away with me to Corpus Christi."

What doesn't kill you makes you stronger. . . .

Chapter Thirty-Three

Eight months later

Sea air drifted in the window of the upstairs apartment, lifting the white gauze curtain. Evening sunlight spilled softly on the wooden paste-waxed floor, and prismed in the water glass on the corner of the drafting desk where Sara sat perched on a stool, pencil in hand. In the glass was the white gardenia Nash had tucked in her hair last night when they'd gone for a walk, its sweet, heady scent filling the spacious room.

Corpus Christi was different from any place Sara had ever lived. The weather. The ocean. The casual life-style.

The difference was good. It helped her to forget.

Harley had been lucky enough to find an old Victorian-style warehouse in which to set up the new and improved *Shoot the Moon*. It was just a block from the bay, with enough space to convert the upstairs into huge apartments.

Sara had worried about leaving her father, abandoning him after such a short reacquaintance, but he had been adamant that she leave, that she take another chance on life.

A few months ago, when she'd tactfully suggested that he move to Corpus Christi, he'd told her he could never leave the farm. He said he would be there whenever she wanted to come and visit. A place of refuge. Of peace. Security.

She and Nash wouldn't stay in Texas forever. Someday they would probably go back to the Midwest, maybe to Chicago . . . maybe even Sigourney.

The two times they'd driven to see her father, Nash had expressed more than a passing interest in farming. And Sara realized that she, too, like her father, had ties to the land.

But for now . . . for now they were in Corpus Christi, where the air smelled like ocean and the sun was always warm. Where gardenias bloomed. Where life was perfect. . . . So perfect, that sometimes, when she wasn't thinking about it, when her attention was focused on something else, a sense of panic would overtake her, coming out of nowhere. She was afraid of losing it. Afraid of waking up one day to find that she was still with Donovan, and that her shattered mind had only concocted Nash and their life together.

Whenever that feeling came over her, she would pace the floor until Nash came home, until he took her in his arms and talked her out of her fear, until he comforted her with his touch, with the strong beat of his heart beneath her ear.

Downstairs, a door slammed. Feet pounded on the stairs.

Nash . . .

He had endured. He had survived. He was brave. He was her hero.

Breathless from his dash up the stairs, Nash found Sara bent over the easel, her delicate, fine-boned wrist poised above the drawing board. Her hand moved; he heard the soft scrape of pencil on paper.

She was barefoot, bare-legged, wearing a sundress,

its cotton skirt flowing around her. Her head was bent as she concentrated on the paper in front of her. Her dark, shining hair was parted at the nape, revealing porcelain whiteness. He stepped closer . . . and pressed his lips to that exposed skin. He inhaled, breathing in the scent of gardenia that clung to her hair.

He heard her soft indrawn breath, her quiet sigh.

She put down her pencil and straightened while he wrapped his arms around her, pulling her close, her back to his chest. He rested his chin on her shoulder so he could look at her drawing.

Every picture she did amazed him, each one better than the one before. "That's great."

"Think Harley will like it?" There was a satisfied smile in her voice as she admired her creation: a female alien sharing a recipe with the First Lady.

He brought his hands to cup her slightly rounded stomach. "Harley will love it."

Last week she'd awakened him in the middle of the night so he could feel the baby move for the first time. It had humbled him. And he'd cried.

Nash kissed her again, this time just below the ear.

She slid her palms over his forearms and leaned back against his chest.

She was healthier than he'd ever seen her. She'd put on weight, and her skin glowed. She hadn't had a drink in months, and the only pills she took were the vitamins prescribed by her obstetrician.

It hadn't been easy to get to this point. There had been rough times. Times when he was afraid he couldn't be what she needed. Times when she'd sobbed as he held her, rocked her in his arms.

But his love for her was strong, so strong it scared the hell out of him.

"I need to talk to you about something." He'd

hoped to sound casual. Instead his voice came out strained. He immediately felt her stiffen, sensed her wariness.

His heart beat faster. Perspiration broke out on his forehead.

This was it, something he'd been thinking about for a long, long time, not knowing how to bring it up, not knowing how she would react.

"Let's get married."

Marriage.

He'd never mentioned it before, hadn't wanted to back her into a corner, hadn't wanted to risk scaring her off. But now, with a baby on the way, he'd been thinking about it a lot.

When he was living on the streets of Chicago, if some guy had come up and told him that in four years, he'd be expecting a baby, that he'd be *happy*, Nash would have told him he was crazy.

He hadn't come to terms with his daughter's death, he never would—no more than Sara could forget what she'd been through with Ivy. But they were both living with it, and every day became easier. And now he found he was ready to embrace tradition once more.

Marriage.

For her, it would mean marrying an ex-con. Their baby would have an ex-con as a father. Not a warm thought.

He'd put everything at stake. If she said no . . . what would he do?

He looked across the room, at the small, framed picture of his daughter, Haley. Life was so hard.

Sara slid off the stool, then slowly turned. Tears glistened in her eyes, and his heart thudded painfully. He'd never wanted to see that look of sorrow on her face again. Ever. He'd wanted to make her happy, not make her sad.

She was crying.

He'd risked it all—and lost.

Wishing he could erase the marriage proposal, he spoke in a flustered rush. "Forget what I just said. I'll go back out and come in again. You don't want to marry me—"

He tried to get away, but she stopped him, a hand on his arm. She made him turn to her, taking his face in her hands. She looked up at him. "You didn't let me answer."

"Do you?" He swallowed. "Want to marry me?"

She smiled through her tears. "Does the sun come up? Does the sun go down?"

"Actually, the earth revolves around the sun."

"It does? When the world is so flat?" Her voice held a light, teasing quality that had just recently emerged. "And here I always thought the sun sank into the ocean."

"You mean with the Viking ships and sea serpents?" he asked, playing along.

Then he realized what she'd said. What she was saying. His heart beat solidly, not in panic, but with joy. She *wanted* to marry him.

"When I was in prison, I didn't think it mattered if I lived or died. What did I have to look forward to when I got out? But at night, if I stood in a corner of my cell, I could look out the window and see a little bit of sky. A few stars. It always made me feel better, made me feel a flicker of life."

"It was me. I was out there waiting for you."

"Yes," he said, recognizing truth when he saw it. "It was you."

He pressed his lips to hers, tasting tears—tears that

put a bittersweet ache in his chest. But pain was good. There had been a time when he hadn't felt pain, or sorrow, or happiness. When he had existed, nothing more.

Yes, pain was good.

Four months later

The latest copy of *Shoot the Moon* hit the stands. On the front page, in letters two inches high, was the headline:

HUMAN COUPLE GIVES BIRTH TO BABY BOY

And inside, the story:

Mother is fine, father is exhausted, and the baby . . . Doctors say, "He's cute as a button and smart as a whip."

About the Author

THERESA WEIR lives with her husband and two children on a working apple farm in Illinois, not far from the Mississippi River.

Her book *Amazon Lily* was selected by the *Romance Reader's Handbook* as an All-Time Recommended Read, and won her the *Romantic Times* Best New Adventure Writer award. Theresa has loved to write ever since high school, when she entertained her friends (if not the administration) with stories generated from the typing class IBM.